RACING AGAINST TIME

RACING
AGAINST TIME

J. McVay

Palmetto Publishing Group
Charleston, SC

Racing Against Time
Copyright © 2019 by J. McVay
All rights reserved

First Edition

Printed in the United States

ISBN-13: 978-1-64111-383-0
ISBN-10: 1-64111-383-9

PROLOGUE

WELL, HERE I AM, TRAPPED, BEATEN, AND WILL MOSTLY likely I will die here. I am being held captive in a cell in the middle of who knows where. My home is very small and dark with a cold dirt floor. Wooden would have been slightly better. It's damp and keeps everything in the cell chilled. It must be some sort of root cellar or storage room underground. Let's just say if a tornado struck, I'd be safe. There is only one way in or out and that is through a large and extremely heavy wooden door with a massive number of locks. Only on the outside. Night or day, I have no f***in' clue. I live in darkness.

I never would have thought I'd end up being held and tortured by my former employer. All I know is I'm Jessy Connors and I will die here.

OVER A YEAR AGO, I WORKED FOR A COMPANY THAT WAS, well, not completely honest about their transactions. The Federation, run by a man called the Emissary. It's an organization that is between corporation like and military. Employees move up in rank and the right of succession implies to a person or persons killed or missing in action. The Federation is very well oiled and takes no shit from anyone.

After my initial origination, my assignments for the Federation were complex, and my very own sister assisted me to complete them with very little revealed.

The last assignment was given to me well, *reassigned* to me after my sister's employment were suspended. Yes, she was removed and disciplined because of her deception to the Federation.

Susan, my twin sister, attempted to steal vital information, a data chip code named Aries. She had been working to collect the data to integrate with our system to make the Federation unstoppable. What her true intentions were, have not been revealed but she either wanted to sell it to the highest bidder, who would either dismantle Aries or use its information for power. Or return it to people who could use its knowledge to better the world. Realizing the power she had, she'd thought it was her way out. She was discovered smuggling it and was captured trying to disappear. Afterward, her failed assignment was handed over to yours truly, after some persuasion.

Soon, I will be joining my twin because of my own deception and betrayal to the Federation. I too will soon suffer the same consequence as Susan.And no one else will ever know the real truth about me...

PART I

CHAPTER 1

Over a Year Ago

"JESSY, I HAVE A NEW ASSIGNMENT FOR YOU," MY Federation boss said to me as he swiveled around from his view of the park. The Emissary, a military-looking man who commanded the Federation demanded complete attention from anything or anyone. Our company was a middle ground between military and civilian, so it suited him.

"Yes, sir. I am prepared for whatever you have for me," I said as I took my eyes off the impressive view and redirected them at him. The city outside the window was bustling with busy traffic on a beautiful sun-filled day.

As we met eyes, he spoke. "I want you to head up the team to collect Aries." He rose from his desk, so I knew this wasn't going to be just any assignment. My boss means business when he gets up.

"Aries, sir? I'm confused. Isn't that my sister's assignment?" I asked, puzzled.

"Yes, but circumstances have arisen, and she's no longer able to complete it. I need you to take over."

I was very surprised with this statement. I felt my twin-sense kick in and further information was needed. "Yes sir, of course, whatever you need. But may I ask what has become of her? It is unlike Susan not to complete any assignment." I was trying my best to sound curious instead of concerned.

"She is to be disposed of after we have compiled all the information. Once everything is back to its proper place, this matter will never be spoken of again," the Emissary stated as he turned and walked back to the window.

Shit, she must have fucked up good this time, if she is being disposed of. I knew my sister, so she must have had her own reasons why she botched her assignment. Knowing how my twin operated, I knew I needed to talk to her face to face and figure out a way to complete the assignment. "If I may ask, sir..." I looked at his back, knowing he would turn to face me. Slowly he did, and I stared at his deep blue eyes, eyes that have been a part of my life for many months, maybe a year. His handsome features outweighed the pale skin and lack of hair. Yes, the Emissary was older, but wasn't bad looking.

"I would like to speak to her before you *dispose* of her," I insisted. "She might open up to me about the whereabouts of Aries. Or where she has placed it."

"We won't dispose of your sister until Aries is recovered. I will consider allowing you a visit with her. I will inform you of my decision shortly. But I don't want any anomalies getting out around this situation. Susan will pay for her duplicity, and I will not change my mind. Is that clear?" The Emissary wasn't fooling around.

"Yes, sir, crystal," I answered just as sternly.

"Good." He turned back to the window, holding his hands behind his back. "I am authorizing the use of funds to retrieve Aries. I don't care how you get it back, just get it back."

That was the end of our conversation and I knew it.

"Yes, sir. I will not let you down."

"Good. Dismissed." That was it, we were done, and I was heading out the door.

Later that afternoon, I returned to my apartment on the outskirts of San Diego. I tried to stay close to the city but far enough away to keep the Federation at a distance. My mind has been buzzing all day after hearing of my twin's betrayal of the Federation. We had a good life with these people, despite what we're really doing but for her to just turn like this, it baffled me. My gut tells me there is more to her story than the Emissary is revealing. Also, more than he knows.

I was just getting settled when my cell rang. My caller ID stated it was the Emissary himself. Code name: Crème Brûlée. Corny I know, but if I was captured or my phone lost, anything regarding the Federation wouldn't be revealed to the wrong parties.

"Yes, sir," I answered.

"Jessy, I give you authorization to speak to your sister. You will report to our facility on the south side tomorrow morning at oh-eight-thirty. You will have ten minutes with Susan. After that, you will be escorted out and proceed with your assignment." He was direct and to the point.

"Yes, sir," It was more than I'd hoped for.

"And Jessy?" The Emissary paused.

"Yes, sir?"

"Don't disappoint me. I would not want to you to suffer the same fate as your sister," he said with a little more heart than normal. Like I meant something to him.

As I was about to respond, the line cut off and all I had was dead air. But I wasn't going to pass up the opportunity to speak to Susan. Even though it would be brief, I had to make the most of our conversation. Luckily, as twins we can say a lot without saying anything.

Entering the facility, the following morning, where my sister was being held captive and most likely tortured, my brain went into overdrive. The energy of this place was so disturbing, it raised the hairs on the back of my neck. It looked like an old storage warehouse with its many units up and down the halls. A guard directed me toward the left hallway and led the way to my sister. The closer we got to my twin's cell; my anxiety level started creeping up on me. A million questions whizzed through my brain. I couldn't sleep last night with scenarios of how my visit was going to go. I had keywords outlined in my mind for our upcoming conversation. I just hoped she did too. With her guidance and clues, it should point me in the direction I need to go.

I proceeded down a dimly lit corridor with the guard. The Federation had many facilities, and every place had its own personnel. We exchanged no words. The only sounds were the echoes of our steps as we walked. Breathing slowly, I tried to calm myself and hold it together.

We rounded a corner, approaching a series of doors that looked like the doors you'd see in a grocery store or restaurant—walk-in freezer doors. *Oh Jesus Christ, please don't let Susan be in a freezer*, I thought. I counted silently. One, two, three, four, five, six coolers with sealed steel door and locks. Susan was in one of them.

We slowed in front of number four. My escort went over to the door lock, starting the sequence of unlocking it. It wasn't a normal lock, and the time it took him seemed like eternity. Holding back, I composed myself to face whatever condition my sister was in, both mentally and physically. Susan was tougher than people give her credit for. So am I, but I didn't know how I'd take the condition of my own flesh and blood.

Focus, Jess, focus! I sternly said in my mind. *You must hold it together.*

As if time were standing still, the door to Susan's cell glided open, and what sat on the other side took my breath away.

CHAPTER 2

SUSAN, MY TWIN, SEATED ON THE FLOOR WITH NOT A SIN-gle mark, scratch, bruise or blemish on her. I was in disbelief and was totally expecting her to be bloody and beaten, but she looked like she did the last time I saw her. Were the powers that be trying to send me a message that I wasn't getting? I was so confused. I swear my mouth was wide open. I had to compose myself.

I took a step forward. "Susan," I said, almost pleading. Trying to communicate with her without words. Telling her it was me and not her captives.

She slowly raised her head, and her eyes told a different story. They were dark and cold, not the bright hazel they used to be, but now a steely gray with puffy rings around them. Susan had been tortured, just the kind that shows no marks. The emotional and mental abuse was taking its toll on her. My guess was they were slowly either poisoning her through food and/or other methods, sleep deprivation perhaps. The Federation in my experience isn't cruel unless it must be. In this instance, they were in full force. I was complete awe. Susan was a high-ranking person in the Federation and had worked her way up there through the years. And with her help, no less, I had the inside track and it had helped me work my way up. We had good lives, now that changed, and I was damn sure going to find out why.

I stepped forward, confronting the prisoner. "Hello Susan, it me, your much prettier sister!" I always put tease in when I wanted to get her attention.

Susan glared at me and tilted her head down to show me her hands where bound and her body was not allowed any give in her restraints. I saw her wrists, and knew she knew why I was here. We were now ready to talk.

I looked over to the guard at the door, "Leave us!" I commanded. I had more authority over him, and I damn well was going to use it.

"Ma'am, I am not permitted to leave this prisoner unattended while you are here. My orders come from the Emissary himself. No harm is to come to you." The guard had his orders, but I was going to make sure mine were followed.

"I understand you have your orders, but I need to speak to my sister, and I don't believe she is going anywhere. You have her tired down better than gold at Fort Knox. I don't think she will escape. Besides, she is my twin sister. Unless she has completely taken a One Hundred and Eighty degree personality turn, I'll be just fine." I looked at him and back at Susan.

"Ma'am I have my orders."

Wow, this guard was not budging.

"Fine, then you can wait on the other side of the hall," I said. "That way you can still see me and watch her. I have my orders and you have yours. You will not be breaking them this way, and if the Emissary has a problem with it, then he can speak to me. Is that clear?" I was pulling out the big guns now. I was getting tired of this shit.

"I will comply ma'am, but I must be able to hear both of you," the guard insisted.

"Really?" Now I was getting pissed. "So, if we decided to discuss our breasts hurting when our periods are approaching or how well our flow is during our time of menstruation, that's the information you want to hear?"

The guard was starting to look uneasy. No man likes to hear anything about women's problems. It was my best shot not to be totally overheard.

Behind me I could feel the energy level from Susan rise from my words. It was like heat came from her dark and dreary cell.

"I'll just wait over here." The guard, now looking uncomfortable, took a few steps back toward the other wall and allowed me to have a private conversation with my sister. Sometimes you must use the bitch card.

Now was the time to collect my thoughts and prepare to get answers. I took a deep breath and proceeded in toward my sister.

Susan and I met eyes as I approached her. Our thoughts were becoming one, and now we could have a conversation.

"Hello Susan," I said to her.

"Hey Jess, looks like I have gotten myself into a little mess," Susan said as she held up her restraints to me and looked around her cell.

"Yes, yes, I think you have, and I think you know why I am here." It was time to get to business.

"Jess, you were always the one to get right to the point," Susan snapped out and grinned at me. Her wiseass comments were never that funny to me.

"Yes. I only have a brief time with you, in hopes you will give me the location of Aries. If there is a chance to get it back in its entirety, they might go easy on you." I was trying not to sound desperate.

"You and I both know my fate for my defection." Her gaze locked on mine. She knew the consequences of betrayal. "This cell, it reminds me of our old ice fishing days. Cold, confined, dark. We would be in that shack for hours on the pond. Huh! I hated every minute of it. But now, what I wouldn't give to be there."

"Ice fishing? We have only a brief time together and all you remember is ice fishing?" I was starting to get flustered.

"Yes, Jessy! I have a shit ton of time to think in here, and that is the closest I could relate to this horrible prison of mine. All I do is think, dammit!" Susan was not happy with me. What was I not sensing?

"I'm sorry. I have a lot of pressure right now. I want to retrieve Aries and my sister. You have got to help me. Or—" I was trying to reason with her.

"Understand what I'm saying to you, *I cannot help you*. I will not see Aries given to the Federation. It will put the Federation in a very powerful position, and that cannot happen. My fate is sealed but yours is not. One of us must prevail and overcome. That's you. My serious other half." Susan's words were very true and hit me very close to home.

"Susan, they will kill us both if we don't return Aries. If I can prevent that, I will. I can't go on without you. You are my soul mate, my thoughts, and you're the reasonable one." I was tearing up as I got my words out.

Susan being the strong-willed sister said, "You will go on and keep both of us alive. All I ask—"

"Anything, I will do anything." Now I sounded desperate.

"All I ask is that you find Lincoln. Take care of him. He will be lost without one of us. Make sure he gets loves. I don't have much, but Lincoln is all there is. Promise me." Tears were swelling up in Susan eyes. She knew.

"I promise, I'll find him." My gut hurts; this conversation is twisting my soul. A moment passed, and I finally had to push on and trying to retrieve what the Federation needed to know. The location of Aries.

"Susan." I took another deep breath. "Please give me the location of Aries. If you don't give me something, the Emissary will make your suffering much greater than either of us can imagine. I can't bear that." I took another breath. "I made him promise he would make it quick. But I need to give them, give me something. Anything." My words were pleading now.

"After all the history the Emissary and I have had, if he wants to make my last moments painful, then so be it. I will not break. Fuck them all, Jess. Fuck all of them. I am done being one of the pawns in their power game. I'm *done!*" she blurted out without a care in the world. Her words were deep and there was no point in moving forward. My goal now was to hold it together until this was over.

I loved my sister very much, and this conversation was one of the hardest things of my life. She was standing her ground, and I had to honor her for it. I don't know if I could be in her position and not break. Susan was by far the stronger twin.

"I understand." My emotions were taking over my heart, body and mind. Tears streamed down my cheeks as my heart was breaking. This was the end, and my world was falling apart.

"Good, and you make god damn sure that the Emissary knows—" She paused, looking above my head to a camera over the door frame. She looked directly to it. A smug look only Susan could give. "—that he knows he will never break me. No matter what he or anyone does. The Aries information with go with me to my grave."

If my sister could have, she would have flipped off the camera. As delightful as that would be, her hands were restrained. But the evil look she gave it, she would win queen bitch.

I LEFT MY SISTER WITH MY HEAD HELD HIGH AND MY IN-sides rolling like a roller coaster. Susan had said a lot but also very little. But it was enough for me to work with.

After my escort showed me to the door, I hurried back to my office. I knew I was being watched at my apartment and my car, so I had set up a place where I could go off radar when I needed to. Luckily, my boss trusted me enough not to put a tracker on my phone. Okay, well, that's a big fat lie. I found out very early on I was being tracked and bought one of those pay as you go phones. Every time I needed to head toward my office, the Federation phone tracker would show I was stationary at my apartment. To the Federation, I was still at home and, I was. Well my phone was.

My office was in a rundown building in a poor part of town. The slums. The Emissary wouldn't think to look out here. The outside wasn't much but inside was far nicer. Someone put some money into these and rented them for cheap. In my pocket were my keys to the deadbolt of my bright red door, on which a sign read, CAUTION, EMPLOYEES ONLY. But I was the only employee. I feel as though someone had guided me to this place where I could have peace and analyze intel. It isn't much, but as the deadbolt turned and the brilliant steel door swung open, my shoulders felt relief.

As I scampered in, Susan's words echoing in my mind.

Closing the door behind me as quietly as I can, reached into my pocket and extracted a small digital recorder. To my surprise the guard didn't pat me down, or I would have been busted. I found myself behind the desk, got my fingers to work and listened to my conversation with Susan.

In one corner is a six-foot table with stacks of papers and pens floating around. The walls have multiple photos notes scampered everywhere. Some have words, circles, anything to give me an advantage. My desk was mostly clean, compared to the rest of my space. I listened to Susan, I noted down key words with more emphasis to them, such as the word *shack*. It was slow and drawn out. To the average person, it would seem Susan was exhausted but to me, my twin was giving me a clue. My hint to where she stashed Aries. At least I hoped it was a clue.

Listening on, Susan gave me more key words and phrases to help. The power reference to the Federation translated into the time was close. Aries was the last piece of the puzzle. We both knew the Federation would do anything to get Aries, no matter the cost. Susan had betrayed them to help the greater good, and now it was my job to complete it.

My only confusion regarding Susan's conversation was Lincoln. My sister was trying to tell me Lincoln was important. Why now? Lincoln hasn't been in the picture for quite some time. She was telling me to find and take care of Lincoln, which in her language meant, "Get your ass moving and go see him." Let's just say, we have history, and Susan is pushing me to find him. Lincoln was the one I guess you could say that got away.

I looked up from my notes, closed my eyes, and took a moment to collect my thoughts. As I breathed, my emotions began to take over and I felt my eyes well up. The situation with Susan, the Federation, and now with Lincoln, was becoming unbearable. I try and shake my head to rid myself of this feeling. Hanging my head, I allowed myself thirty seconds of quiet, and then I was done. Most of the time, it cleared my brain enough so I can refocus. I have work to do.

I guess my first step is to get my ass up and go home. Soon, I'll have to go see the Emissary and explain my conversation with Susan. Of course, the information I extracted and what was heard are two completely different things. I need time. Time to figure out where I must start, and if I have taken enough time finding Aries to keep Susan alive.

The clock is ticking.

CHAPTER 3

STROLLING DOWN THE UGLY OLIVE-GREEN CARPETED hallway of the Federation's headquarters, I was on way to meet with the Emissary again. This wasn't going to be the highlight of my day. His office was on the fifteenth floor of the twenty-story building, and his office had, of course, the best view.

Brenda, the Emissary's secretary, knew I was coming and glanced up at me with a smile as I approached. "Morning Jessy," she said in her southern accent. I liked Brenda; she was very down to earth and had a sweet side to her. I only wish she knew what kind of place she was working for. I had a feeling she knew of some of our dealings, but the whole truth is only revealed to the higher-ups. Yes, that includes me.

"Morning Brenda, beautiful day outside isn't it?" I replied with our usual topic of conversation.

"Oh, Yes, it is. I am thankful every day for it. God is truly with us today!" Brenda said sweetly. She's also very religious, if you didn't catch that. It drives the ever-loving piss out of me. I can't stand it, but that is Brenda and I won't hold it against her. She is from the south and that is how many families are raised. Me, not so much.

I am not from the south but from the depths of New England. Susan and I came from a much more difficult life. My mother left when Susan and I were around seven or eight. She had fallen for another man with more money and had to decide between her family or money. The selfish bitch chose money. To this day, some twenty-five years later, I have never seen or heard from her, and I could care less if I ever did. I had the means of finding her with the help of the Federation and my skillset, but I don't care. She could be dead, and it wouldn't bother me.

My father, he was a hard ass. Not being blessed with boys to do all the work, he put Susan and me to work. We learned how to chop and stack wood, shoot guns and bows, hunt, and other activities that boys would do. Susan would complain all the time, but I rather enjoyed it. I worked hard at home and school. Look where I have gotten, I am a rung on the ladder of this powerful corporation, and I owe it all or some of it to him. My asshole father molded me into what I am. I am a hard, sarcastic, and passionate person. He taught me I could do anything a man could do. There are no limits. I am grateful for that.

Anyway, I smiled at Brenda, grasping the door handle. "Yes, we have lots to be thankful for today."

She beamed back at me, knocking and I proceeded in.

I closed the door behind me and the found the Emissary was leaning on his desk waiting for me with his arms and feet crossed. *Oh shit, this doesn't look good. Hold it together.*

"Good morning sir." I tried breaking the silence and tension.

"Jessy, good morning. If I recall you had your visit with Susan yesterday. I am anxious to hear your results from it." The Emissary knew very well how my conversation went. He saw and heard every detail. To his knowledge, she gave me nothing but bullshit.

"Of course, sir." I didn't move a muscle until he summoned me over to the chairs in front of his desk.

Slowly, I proceeded over and parked my ass in one of the chairs. I crossed my legs and placed my hands-on top of them. This conversation could go a few different ways—the good, the bad, or the oh-shit way. I was hoping for good.

"I have reviewed the tape from Susan's cell, and she is determined to make life difficult," he said to me. "Her words were so unorganized that it was difficult to comprehend. I have ordered her guards to encourage her to give more information or she will not have a pleasant ending to her life." He was trying to be casual and pushy at the same time. He was all business and never joked about situations like this. I knew he meant every word.

"Sir, Susan wasn't helpful at all, but I would still like this assignment for the recovery of Aries. I can use our resources to retrace her steps, and hopefully retrieve Aries before its fallen in the wrong hands." I was trying my best not to beg or plead, but I needed this.

"Jess, I know how difficult it was seeing your sister like that. But it is a necessary consequence for her actions. I am quite fond of your sister and regret what will happen to her. She was a great asset to this organization." The Emissary moved closer to me and placed his hand on my shoulder, just a few fingers, then he slid his body around to my back. His fingers lingered so his hand was fully on my shoulder.

I did my best not to move a muscle or wince. *Calm is my goal. I cannot let him use his power over me; I am in control.*

"No sir, it wasn't pleasant seeing her like that, but I will complete what she failed to do. I just ask for a chance." Confident now, I needed to convince him.

"I will give you that chance, as I told you before you met with your sister. I have the utmost confidence in you, and I know you will not let me down." The Emissary's fingers started drifting south toward the top of my collar bone.

I knew where he was going with this action. It has happened before, and I am not proud of it. I did have to give away a part of my soul to make it this high up in the ranks in such a brief time. The Emissary has taken a fond liking to me, and I must put my repulsive feelings aside. When I realized what the little Emissary in his pants was thinking, I took full advantage of it. I made sure I was indispensable. As I said, I am not proud to be treated like a whore, but I needed to get here. He was never rough beyond what I could handle and was even gentle at times. But it wasn't my world. I had my orders and I would obey them.

Unwillingly, I placed my hand on top of his very gently, giving him what he wanted. Permission. "Thank you, sir, I appreciate your confidence in me." I turned my head to look up at him. His eyes glowed with passion, the passion that I had to give in to one more time.

I locked eyes with him as his slipped his hand further down my V-neck shirt and onto my breast. I stole my gaze away and could see the bulge in his pants. *Fuck, that didn't take long. Let's get this over with.*

I slid my hand off his hand that was now foundling me and placed it on his bulging erection. I started messaging it and caressing him in my hand as he squeezed my breast harder. It wasn't a turn-on to me, but the Emissary got what he wanted. Right now, that was to fuck. I had to pleasure him in anyway and everyway if I wanted this assignment. That was the deal. Sex for advancement. Typical in a lot of companies.

Unzipping his fly, I glided further into his pants and really got a grasp on him. His breathing grew faster, and he started to moan as he hardened. Before I knew what was going on, I was hoisted from my chair and turned with my back to him. He reached around my waist and began to unzip my jeans. A hand made of leather plummeted into my panties, slid them and my jeans down to my ankles. He parted my legs and thrust into me from behind. I cried out for show, and because it was so sudden. I dreaded these minutes every time they happened. I don't have any feelings for him and having sex with someone you hate is so... Disgusting! Ugh! I hate what I have become.

As a sign of power, he likes taking me from behind. No face to face; total control. The Emissary pushed and thrust into me for what seen eternity, and I just acted. I went along with the motion. Playing a part was all it was. I moaned when it felt like I should and moved the way he liked it. You learn tricks after doing this a while. I know just how to please him. I added some fake panting to our movement, and that was always a trigger to him climaxing. Sure enough, that was all it took. Old men are so easy.

He pulled out, slapped my ass hard to make me jump, and zipped his ego back in his pants. I could get whatever I wanted now. A powerful rush moved through me. He had used his power; it was now my turn.

I had to take a second and collect myself, breathing more than normal, keeping the drama going. I glanced at my watch. Three minutes, thirty-eight seconds; three minutes and thirty-eight seconds of degrading work. How do hookers and prostitutes do it? I mean, having men control you. Good thing my father made sure self-esteem wasn't an issue. Or I would have been gone long ago.

As I reached down to redress myself, the Emissary went to his side table and poured himself a drink from a glass carafe. Clear liquid, my guess was pure moonshine with only one ice cube. "Can't ruin it with rocks," I'd heard from say too many times.

I zipped up my jeans and repositioned myself back in my chair. He approached me and lowered handed me a glass. My ice clattered in the crystal glass as I let it rest on my stomach. I needed to stay level-headed, and this shit would put your ass on the ground. A few tiny sips were all I allotted myself.

"So, what's your plan for Aries?" the Emissary asked, business as usual.

"I need to go to Susan's place and conduct my own search. Our people I am sure have searched her place, but I just have my gut to direct me. Susan and I could never keep secrets from each other, no matter the distance. I would like permission to start there," I insisted so I could get into her place.

"Permission is granted, and whatever you need is at your disposal."

I always get what I want after he does. We both took a sip of our clear liquid. It burned all the way down. Moonshine or vodka. Not my drink of choice. I'm a tequila girl. *Olé*!

"Thank you, sir, I won't take any more of your time. I will commence as soon as possible."

I placed my glass on a granite coaster on his desk and stood up to leave. He did the same on his side of the desk.

"Good luck to you, and please keep me informed of your situation. I don't need to tell you the seriousness of this assignment." He walked around his desk to meet me. "Once we have Aries, there will be nothing in the world that can stop us. Power will be redefined in our favor. And you, Jessy, are a part of that. You should feel proud. I am."

Proud was not the word I was thinking of. The Emissary was just beaming because he got laid. *Fuck off pal. I won't be proud until this situation is over.*

I want my life back.

CHAPTER 4

TIME TO GET DOWN TO BUSINESS. I HEADED OVER TO Susan's condo to gather what I needed to proceed. First order of business, I was going to take advantage of her shower. I needed to wash off the Emissary filth. Gross! Water always cleanses my body and clears my soul.

Luckily, I had my own key to Susan's place, so I just let myself in and made myself at home anytime I wanted or needed to. The place was beautiful before the Federations goons searched. If Susan could see her place now, she'd be pissed. They turned the place completely upside down. I couldn't believe how trashed it was. Pictures shattered, clothes strewed all over the place, and every piece of furniture was destroyed, either sliced or broken. Knowing far in advance the was the state I was going to find, I continued my way to the bedroom, collected some clothes, and went to shower.

Oh, my fucking word, a shower made me feel like a new person. 20 minutes of pure heat and water, ah! I'm a person with purpose and new will. I dressed in Susan's clothes— Well actually, they were my clothes that Susan never returned. Does that surprise anyone? Not Really.

Once I'd dressed, I went in search of Lincoln. Susan had made a point to mention Lincoln, so she wanted me to find him. When the search team came looking for Aries, they did more than trash her place. They demolished it. Some people are very dense when they have one thing on the brain. I only had to look in her closet and there it was. Lincoln's a stuffed teddy bear. He was soft and cuddly. But Lincoln wasn't just any old bear. He was a symbol of our or my former life.

In the back of our teddy bear was a strip of Velcro and inside him was a momma bear device. It made heartbeat sounds like you'd hear in the womb. Okay, it's for babies, but what it held inside was what meant the most to me. I'd had Susan hold onto Lincoln bear when I moved out here and began progressing up in the ranks. The memory of the real Lincoln still broke my heart. The bear reminded me of the past I'd sacrificed for this job.

Behind the battery-operated device was a photograph. A photograph of me and the real Lincoln. We were much younger back then. He had dark brown hair, a very muscular build, and a baby face with the scruff of a beard. His bright blue eyes sparkled in our happy photo. He had a tough boy look to him; he was big lovable teddy bear. Hence the teddy bear he'd given to me with a heartbeat inside. It was the most emotional gift I'd ever gotten. But when I took this job, I'd left it behind; my past and him all behind.

It wasn't my direct choice to leave Lincoln, that's for sure, but with this opportunity, my life wasn't always up for discussion. Susan offered to assist me when the job with the Federation came up and blatantly gave her opinion. She said, "Jess, I am your sister. You and I have not had the best life. Lincoln can change your life. Don't let a job ruin that. He is the real deal." She added. "But if you choose to join the Federation, I will guide you in ways that will make your advancement smoother."

I knew what my sister was implying, and I contemplated her words. There was so many variables to either decision. If I don't choose the

Federation, I jeopardized my career. On the flip side, life with Lincoln would be more than I have ever experienced. Proceeding with the Federation, I would advance my career greatly and be well off for whatever life threw at me. The money alone was more than I'd ever make.

On the eve of my decision, Lincoln and I fought about what the consequences the job was going to do whether if I took it, or not. For hours we argued with and at each other, and when it was over, I left. My heart was broken, and mind was selfish, I left. I'd worked too hard in my life to get to where I was. After a childhood where I was never good enough to an opportunity like this. Or for someone who loved me more than I have ever known. I was supposed to give all of it up for him. Just Lincoln. No! Hell, no. I wanted both. At that time, it just wasn't an option. I had to choose, and it chewed me up inside. And after our argument, I left. I went to see Susan and haven't seen Lincoln since that night.

After seeing the teddy bear, my entire body knew I wasn't over him. I'd never be over him. Susan miraculously went on a long detour and spoke to Lincoln after my departure. The next time I saw her, she was holding the bear. My heart broke into pieces when I held that bear. How could a bear break my heart? We'd made our decision, or I made my decision, and that was that.

But it wasn't. Our actions have a reaction and my actions were gut wrenching. The bear symbolized Lincoln and my life. So painful, I had Susan keep the bear for me. At that point in time, I needed to focus in the here and now.

I'm pretty sure the real Lincoln has moved on by now. But deep down, I was hoping he hadn't. By her this having the bear, pushing me to find it, it was her way of kicking me in the ass to get out while I still could. Susan had given me the opportunity with Aries. My way out. The one she doesn't have.

I have my starting point, and that was to find Lincoln.

The real one.

CHAPTER 5

I DEPARTED FROM SUSAN'S CONDO TAKING LINCOLN BEAR in tow and headed for my car. I knew I would have to ditch this car for my other one, to keep off the Federation's radar. So, off I went to the CEO (Caution, Employees Only) home and swapped out cars. I left my Federation vehicle in a shopping center parking lot and walked the three blocks to CEO. Yes, I still had my bear with me. He was the key to all the chaos Susan had started. I'd also grabbed my backpack and purse, things you never leave home without.

In the other space was my early '90s red Mustang convertible. She may be dirty and old, but holy shit, can she move. My toy always solved my problems and was going to solve this one. Hopefully, eventually fixing my fucked-up life. Turning the key, after the first try she purred like a kitten, and my face lit up with pleasure. She never purred like that, but I needed all the good luck I could get.

I let her idle while I put my stuff in the back and my purse in the front. It had been far too long since I had driven her, and I was anxious to get moving. Of course, with the beautiful sunshine and warm air, the top should go down. Unfortunately, I had to wait to get on the road and out of the Federation's in-town cameras. They are everywhere and anywhere you could possibly think of throughout the country, not just the city. For this reason, I had to keep my phone on and have a secondary phone to use. The Emissary will trace me without question, but I was prepared.

Sliding behind the seat, she hugged me like an old friend, and we headed out and into the city. If I was a guy, I would be hard right now from the roar of the engine and her smooth ride. She was my baby. I have had her for years and it was amazing to be riding in her once again. We cruised through the city getting strange looks as the engine roared. Who gives a fuck! I certainly don't, and some looks were because a woman was driving. I wanted to flip off every one of them. People suck! Did I mention how much I don't like people? Well, if I did or did not, I don't like people. End of story.

The edge of the city approached, and I had only a few miles to go until freedom. Ten miles to keep safe should do it. I know of a gas station outside the outer city limit would be an adequate place to stop and put the ol' ragtop down. The radio blared old '90s pop tunes and it was as if the world of the Federation and my former life never existed. I was just me and I cherished ever second. Before I knew it, my stop arrived, and I hauled ass in. I filled up my Mustang and let her hair down.

We were going to enjoy the day in style.

I paid for gas, a couple bottles of water, and a few snacks—mostly chips and candy bars, but who am I trying to impress now? The clerk gave me a look of "Ah, hel-loo, you are mighty fine," as he eyed me from head to toe. *What? Have you never seen a woman driving an old convertible wearing a shirt and jeans? Get a life, pal.* Sometimes, I would love to say what I think and be a bitch. It always sounds better. There are times I do let my mouth just vomit out whatever it wanted, but the results are never the best.I just swallowed my thoughts and said, "Thanks."

"Have a nice day, ma'am," he replied as I went out the door with a bag of junk food. My car was pointed east, heading toward answers... toward Lincoln.

The last time Susan said anything about Lincoln, he lived in Albuquerque, New Mexico. Not our last place of residence, but one he found on his own. That was where I needed to go. It wasn't a huge city, and I hoped to find him without a lot of difficulty. Lincoln wasn't a face people forgot, and I knew he wouldn't be able to stay off the radar.

Hell, for all I know, he may have a new life. It had been a sometime since we departed. I could be making a fool of myself even trying to find him. Well, I will soon find out. Susan knows something I don't, and when I see her next time—if there is a next time—she is going to get ol' holy hell from me.

It was about a twelve/thirteen-hour drive to Albuquerque, but I had plenty of daylight and warmth left in the day, I'd be there well before midnight. Fingers crossed, of course. I just drifted away to my music and let my hair flow in the breeze, just a cruising.

But now the hours seemed to take an eternity. Driving through desert isn't the most glamorous, and it gets boring after the first six hours. If I didn't see more signs of life soon, I'd need to stop. My trip was getting somewhat...okay, it fucking sucked ass. This was my freedom, but it was not what I'd expected. I just needed to keep going and make it to New Mexico. I was stubborn enough; I would make it and would find where my first clue was hidden.

I just wish Susan hadn't meant Lincoln.

AFTER TWO MORE LONG ASS HOURS OF DRIVING, I MADE IT to New Mexico. The towns hadn't changed much from years past when I traveled through here. Another four hours brought me to Albuquerque. Albuquerque has many sights to explore but isn't a huge city. It's a nice place to visit, in October especially. The hot-air balloon gathering starts around then, and it's incredible. I have witnessed it once, and it's amazing to see. At the time I was only passing though, and only spent two days here, but if I'd been able, I'd have come back for more. This place is just alive and full of energy.

I headed to the outskirts of Albuquerque. No big box businesses here, just your average Joes, and mom and pop diners. My kind of place. I parked my Mustang in front of a quaint little diner that was still open and proceed in for a bite to eat. The place looked like an expanded airstream that sat on a slap and had a feel of kindness. Hopefully someone would know where I could find Lincoln. The door even had a little bell on it as you opened it, how cool was that? I know I'm lame. The diner was all outfitted in the old fifties-style retro décor, and even had old soda machine behind the counter. I parked myself on a red bar stool and grabbed a menu.

An older waitress came over. "What can I get you, dear?" By her voice I swear she had smoked everyday of her life and was eighty years old. She was great! Not fake all.

"Can I get a cup of coffee?" Pause. I glanced back at the menu, my eyes ablur and asked, "What's good here?"

"Depends," the waitress answered not glancing my direction as she poured my coffee.

"I've been traveling all day and had nothing but junk food. Got any ideas?" Exhaustion was kicking in now that I stopped.

"Salad, hun?" She sat down my coffee. "I'm partial to our Chef or Greek salad. But that's just me."

With a quick glance at the menu, "I guess I'll have chef salad with ranch dressing, please?" I tried not to sound unsure of my selection.

"Coming up." She worked her pad and headed off toward the kitchen.

Gazing around the room, I saw many empty booths just waiting for customers to warm the cushions and I smiled. This was the life, simple and ordinary. I liked it, but it would never be my life; I was far from simple and ordinary. That was wiped clean from my vocabulary when my mom took off. As much as I dreamed of this, I knew it wouldn't come true.

Minutes passed and my food arrived. I looked at the waitress and thanked her. I was still staring at her when she asked, "Is there something else I can get you?" Her Southwestern accent was very foreign to me, but I enjoyed it.

"Actually, I am looking for someone." I paused, trying to play out my story. "I'm looking for my brother in-law. He moved here a few months ago. He isn't in the directory so I'm asking around."

"Maybe he doesn't want to be found," she bluntly said. Wow! Wasn't expecting that response.

"No, maybe your right." I hung my head and picked at my fingers. "I just wanted to let him know that my sister has died." I produced a tear almost on queue. It was a lie, but I could work with it. The information was almost correct. Susan wasn't dead quite yet, and Lincoln was the wrong in-law. But the waitress didn't know that.

"Oh, I'm sorry my dear. How did she die?"

Here we go, story time.

"She had cancer, ovarian. She came out to see me and tried to get treatment. She just separated from my brother-in-law, and now I have no way to tell him." I let out a small sob.

"Oh, my. Well..." The waitress felt guilty now. "I see a lot of people throughout the day. What's his name?"

"Lincoln. Lincoln Matthews." I stiffed another sob and wiped my tears with a napkin.

"Oh, I know that name. Nice man, but he never said anything about a wife." The word wife was drawn out, making her accent stand out. She wasn't from New Mexico but somewhere in the southwest.

"Yeah, it was messy, from what my sister told me. They had a huge fight and she just left. I can only imagine what he felt." I was completely lying now; the fight was my past, not Susan's.

Just then, another customer interjected into our conversation. "Ah yeah, I know Lincoln and the girl you're talking about. You even look a little like the one from his picture." This heavyset man was a hick from the wrong side of life.

"Sir, you know Lincoln Matthews?"

"Yeah, we play poker together every couple of weeks." He explained

"Lincoln still has pictures?" I almost stuttered looking over at him. Lincoln still has pictures of me. Me!

"Yes, ma'am, he does. I have seen them. Pretty gal. He will be devastated when he hears your news. He loves that gal, or he did. I am sorry for the loss of your sister." Each word he spoke was drawn out very slowly.

I scooted over to sit closer to him, preparing to get as much information as I could.

"Would you happen to know...where I can find him?" My nose began to run as I pretend sobbed. All part of the show, even though I was very unprepared for what he'd said about Lincoln's feelings toward me.

"Why yes, ma'am!" The patron said with much enthusiasm.

"Ah Hank, maybe Lincoln doesn't want to bring up ol' memories," The waitress added.

"Louanne, Lincoln would want to know what happened to the love of his life. Every time I see him, I swear that all he talks about. You should see his house. There is nothing but pictures of her everywhere you look."

My heart skipped a beat at his words. I wanted to let my eyes cry a river. But I needed to hold it together for just a little longer.

"Can you tell me where he lives? I wouldn't want to explain to him on the phone. It would seem improper. And disrespectful of my sister..." I poured it on thick.

"Yeah sure, he lives about three blocks from here on, ah...Maple Street. It's toward the end of the street, a little ranch house. Blue, I think. You won't be able to miss it. There are big bush flowers out front. Light purple."

Oh fuck, I scored big here. What were the odds I would find Lincoln on my first stop? Not good, but clearly not impossible. I don't think this man was devilish enough to send me on a wild goose chase. I didn't get that vibe, and I am good at distinguishing people.

I got off my stool, pulled a twenty out of my pocket, and asked for a to-go box for the salad. It would have been rude to not take it. I know it didn't cost twenty bucks, but it was worth the information.

"Thank you, sir, for your help. I don't know how to thank you." I truly was grateful to him.

"No problem just promise you'll make sure Lincoln is all right before you head home. It broke his heart when she left. I don't know what will happen when he finds out she's dead." Hank was saddened by his words. I feel he was truly Lincoln's friend. Bar buddy maybe, but a friend.

"I will, I promise." This time my words were sincere.

I grabbed my takeout and headed out the door to my Mustang.

It was too late tonight, so I found a cheap motel nearby for the night. The clerk gave me a key to number fifteen on the first floor. Good, I was too tired mentally and physically to think about stairs. I pulled the car around the corner, in front of my rundown room, grabbed my shit and unlocked the door with an actual key.

The room was small with a single queen bed, nightstand, small table and dresser with a puny flat screen tv perched on top. Bathroom was almost claustrophobic. Any one any bigger than I wouldn't be able to turn around. At this point, I didn't care. The room was clean, and the shower water was hot. I'll take it after this long day.

The next morning, after an interesting night sleep and coffee, I did as Hank directed me, and went in search for Lincoln. I retraced my steps back to the dinner and from there continued three blocks down to Maple Street. It wasn't a half bad neighborhood. Pretty quiet, and the houses look decent. I slowed the Mustang so I could find Lincoln's house, and boy, Hank was on the money. About eight houses down was a blue house with a big purple rhododendron. Rhododendron. They were one of my favorites. I have never been to this house, but by the looks, it was made for me. What the hell is going on?

The driveway had enough room for two vehicles to park, so I pulled up behind a small dark pewter gray pickup, left the car in first gear, e-brake on, and took a couple deep breaths. I was about to see my past in the flesh. Someone I missed with every fiber of my being. I was anxious. So anxious and nervous that my hands trembled. Squeezing them helped, but it wasn't enough. It was time to face this problem head-on as I always do.

Taking a deep breath, I opened my door and got out of the car. *God damn you, Susan!* I wanted to scream. This wasn't how it was supposed to be. *You just had to go and get yourself in deep shit, and now I must clean up the mess. Fucking sister!* I took another breath and turned toward the front door.

I stepped up into the covered entry and rang the doorbell. With my luck, Lincoln would be out. Boy, was I ever wrong. Footsteps came closer to the door, and with a click and turn of the knob, there stood Lincoln.

My Lincoln.

He looked like he had seen a ghost when I said, "Hello Lincoln."

CHAPTER 6

"WHAT THE HELL ARE YOU DOING HERE?"

Not quite the greeting I was expecting, but what more could I ask? I'd left him, and feelings were damaged. His eyes were surprised by my presence, and there seem to be a slight twinkle.

"It nice to see you as well. You look good." Keeping this civil was going to be more difficult than I'd thought, especially after what Hank said.

"What the hell do you want, Jessy?" Lincoln was direct, all right, that hadn't changed.

"I um, I, well need your help." I am not sure how I am going to do this. *Thanks, dear sister!* "Can I come in, or should I tell the whole neighborhood why I need your help?"

Lincoln wasn't pleased, he looked pissed. Or tried to look pissed. He blew out a disgusted breath and turned, leading the way in. *Why thank you, you are a great host. Oh, don't worry about the door, I'll shut it.*

I shut the door proceeding after him. In his living room, he turned around, looking at me with his arms crossed. Yeah, this was not a good sign. I went into the living room and saw multiple photos spread

31

throughout the room. There were many of him and his brother and family. Then it was like someone punched my hard in the stomach. Many of the pictures were of me. And many were of the two of us.

That took the wind out of me and put me in a mesmerized state. If I could have cried, I would have. Lincoln's eyes were piercing through me, and that helped me keep it together.

When I turned to look at him, my eyes were watering with emotion and there was no way to prevent it.

"All right Jess, what do you want? This better be good." Lincoln tone shifted when he saw my eyes and was keeping his cool but for how long? I'm a mystery to him.

I took a quick breath and began to explain. "I need your help getting a piece of information that my sister stole."

"Susan? What does my involvement have to do with your sister? She is the only one of the two of you that I've seen and was here not long ago," Lincoln added, frustrated.

"Susan was here not long ago?" This new information surprised me.

"Yeah, about a month ago. She just stopped by to see me and said things would be back to normal soon."

"Holy shit!" Realization came over me. She had been planning this much longer than I had anticipated.

"What do you mean, holy shit? She was here asking how I was doing and made sure I was coping. More than I can say for you."

It took me a minute to process this information. Susan knew what she was doing, and for some reason had brought Lincoln into the picture. But why? Not for me. Or was it? I regretted leaving him as soon as I walked out the door that night. I am stubborn as we all know and had too much pride to go back.

I needed to sit down.

I slowly backed my way back and perched myself on an arm of a love seat. I lowered my head and tried to explain. "Susan stole a crucial piece of information. Information that would give whoever had it all the power they need to do anything. Power that could make weapons, destroy countries, or do good. Banish hunger and make medicine for the sick. It all depends on who has it. We call it Aries. And she has sent me on a wild goose chase to find it."

I looked back up at him, hoping this made sense.

He started to look more confused, "She has hidden an information chip that could take over the world, and somehow I'm involved...?" Not sure if that was a question or statement.

"When I spoke with her, Susan made a point for me to come see you. She is being beaten and tortured over this chip. I need to retrieve Aries before she is executed." *Wow, this just keeps getting harder.* "I need your help to find it and give it to your brother. But I'm being watched and tracked. You have always protected me, even when I could protect myself. I think that was why Susan directed me to you."

"Let me get this straight. I am to help you find this Aries chip and take you to my brother? My brother is on the eastern seaboard. How in the hell are we going to do that?"

More questions. Well at least we were not yelling, but it was getting close. Tension was rising rapidly.

"Yes, I need to deliver Aries to your brother, my boss. Before it gets in the wrong hands. If Aries gets out and the highest bidder wins it, all-out war could blossom. That can't happen. I need to get this chip to Mitchell before they, the Federation kill Susan."

I was getting in deeper than I wanted.

"Wait, Mitchell? You have to get this to Mitch. He is..." The realization was kicking in, and Lincoln was adding everything up. "Mitchell is Division. You are still on a fucking assignment for him." Lincoln was angry now.

"Yes, I have been undercover since I left. The assignment we fought about that night was from Mitch. With my training in psychology and profiling, I wasn't given a choice. I was ordered to take the assignment, reassigned or fired. Since, I loved my job and what I do, I didn't approve of the alternatives."

I was having trouble talking now. The truth was growing more painful than I expected. I had broken my lover's heart and my own that night.

"You should have been fired. You could have prevented all of this and your sister wouldn't be on the verge of dying right now." Yup, Lincoln was angry. "We had a great life together and Mitch knew it. There were other people who could have done your job, but he chose you."

"Yes, I am one of his most trusted agents and I had a job to do. I am doing my job. My personal life was..." I paused. "My personal life was to be put aside." I couldn't restrain them anymore, a tear stream down my cheeks.

"So, what you are telling me is, you're still undercover, and are still Division?"

"Yes," I admitted as I dropped my face.

I SAT IN LINCOLN'S LIVING ROOM SILENTLY AS HE PRO-cessed all this. I let my head hang, so he wouldn't see the emotions coming through. No sobs came out, only sniffles.

Lincoln turned away from me and ran his fingers over his shaven head, frustrated. These were not wording he wanted to hear from me. After what seemed hours, he turned back to look at me. I peered up at him and his whole face changed instantly when he looked in my eyes.

"I didn't want this assignment from Mitch," I explained. "I had turned it down once. Then you and I had our massive blow out. I was too heartbroken to come back to you. As you know, I am a little stubborn." I waited for a reaction.

"No kidding," Lincoln said sarcastically, as I knew he would.

"I was so angry that I called Mitch and told him I'd do it. By the time I realized what I had done, I'd already been transported to the interview with the Federation. I got the job and moved up fast in the ranks. I'm close to the top but hollow out. The things I've had to do eat my soul away, and that is the worst feeling."

I don't know why I was explaining my actions, but I felt like he'd earned it.

"You could have come back. We could have found a way to leave or to make us work." Now the Lincoln I knew was coming back, not the angry person who was just here.

"By that time, it was too late. I didn't want to endanger you. It was bad enough Susan was involved with the Federation. She took me under her wing until I was able to move up in rank. Now, she will suffer the consequences for her protection of me and the theft of Aries."

The words struggled coming out, reflecting my pain.

"I would have been there if I'd known," Lincoln said. "I went to Mitch, and he said he had no clue where you were. Asshole! I knew he was lying." Lincoln's angry words were projected onto his brother, my real boss and best friend, Mitchell Johnson. Oh yeah, I should mention, Lincoln and Mitchell are brothers, but only half-brothers. They are both great people, but very different. Lincoln is a cop and has been a great detective for many years. He knows how to protect and how to roll with the punches until the right moment surfaces. He's also a great shot. Between Mitchell and Lincoln, I'd choose Lincoln any day for my backup.

Probably why Susan chose him to help me.

"I know you would have been there, but I couldn't risk you, either. If something happened to you because of my activities, I would never forgive myself."

I took another deep breath and stood up, wanting very much for Lincoln to hold me like he used to, but that wasn't going to happen. There was too much anger and resentment between us right now.

"I am going to leave," I said. "Let me know what you decide. Um, I will stay in town today and probably head out tomorrow." I walked over to the table and wrote my cell—not the Federation cell—number down. So, Lincoln could decide what he would do.

"Thank you for seeing me." I was trying to sound polite and hide my emotions. I was failing miserably.

He didn't comment.

I walked to his front door, grasped the handle, and turned. "I am sorry. And I wish I could go back and change everything, but I can't. It eats at me every day and I have to live with it. I just want you to know how sorry I am."

I turned back to the door and walked out as the tears collapsed into crying. This was not how I saw this going, but with months of pent-up emotions, my flowing eyes said it all. It would have happened eventually, but Susan pushed for it earlier, and I am afraid she will pay the price.

CHAPTER 7

I DROVE THE MUSTANG AROUND IN A COMPLETE BLUR UNtil I got back to the motel. My emotional days were having their toll on me and I needed some rest. Swinging by the office, I went in and rented the room for another night. I figured that would be long enough for Lincoln to make his decision. With or without him, I would leave tomorrow and be on my way.

The Mustang took me around the corner, and I parked in front of my room. On auto pilot, I opened the door. Immediately, I threw myself onto the bed, knocking off my backpack. Who care, right now I really didn't.

I thought about my conversation with Lincoln. Being brothers, I was sure Mitch would have told Lincoln that I was on assignment. There is only so much information he could disclose Not even to his brother. Then again, he probably played stupid and just pretended to have no idea why I left

Mitch is the smartest and closest of my friends. We met in college, took similar courses, becoming instant friends. Others in our classes thought we were more than friends, but not so. Because of the courses

I was taking in profiling, I knew I wasn't Mitch's type. It wasn't until a party that my instincts were confirmed. Mitch was no doubt into men. I wasn't surprised when I walked around the corner to see him making out with another man. I was far from bothered; I was actually relieved that my suspicions were correct.

So, Mitch and I grew closer, and were inseparable most of our college careers. After graduation, we both were recruited for the Division. Division, an organization that deals with issues concerning threats and information that could harm this country. We are not exactly part of the federal government but do help them occasional. The fields we'd studied advanced us to the top of our class, making selections a no-brainer. We were beyond excited. Mitch decided to throw a congratulations party for us. This was when I was introduced to Lincoln. My best friend had been scheming to get us together. "You'd make a perfect pair," he said. And he was right on the money. Lincoln and I became inseparable while Mitch and I were at the eight weeks of orientation. We started building a life. I knew he was my person and best half of me. I wasn't going to fuck that up.

Once in Division, Mitch advanced in the ranks and became my boss rather quickly. I didn't care, our paths were very different, and our fields were too. I had no interest in being a supervisory special agent. All I wanted was to go to work and come home. Years went by, and I was selected to work under Mitch directly in a top-secret mission. Can you guess? Yes, it was the infiltration and take down of the organization known as the Federation and the custody of the Ares chip.

Lucky me. At the time I was honored, it was a huge opportunity for me. Lincoln showed concern about it, with what little I could tell him. I reassure him, we'd be okay. I wasn't a field agent, just an analyst.

You see how that worked out.

Lincoln and I grew closer than ever, and so was my ranking for undercover. My whole body would ache with the knowledge I possessed, but I couldn't share it with him. I hoped someday he'd be my husband, we'd have a family, and life would be perfect. Mitch's boss had other thoughts. Mitch had pretty much become my brother and was still my best friend, but he had a job to do. I was the best candidate for this undercover mission. He insisted he had tried to find another more suitable, but I was the best. I could read people and interact without any issues, almost like an actor.

I advised Mitch I would have to explain to his brother about this assignment and what it would do to our lives, including Mitch's. It was his brother, his best friend and sister he was assigning. Our conversations were long and heartfelt.

"You are my sister, Jess," he said to me "I would not be the same if something happened to you. We are not blood but we're family." I was very touched by Mitchell's words, but I knew there was a "but" coming to this conversation.

"But—" *Nailed it.* "But being your boss, I have orders from above to encourage you to take this assignment. Or—" *Great I had more coming.* "Or I'll have to recommend you for a transfer or worse. How about Nome, Alaska?"

My mouth dropped at Mitch's threat. I was shocked. They would send me to some fleabag armpit field office if I refused this assignment. I loved my job, right where it was. I suspected Mitch felt horrible about this ultimatum, but he had his orders. At that moment, the brother in Mitch came out. "Talk to Lincoln, explain to him what will happen if you do or don't take this assignment. I love you both, and I hate being put in this position."

That was it. Mitch let me go, and I went home to try and figure out what to do.

And you know the rest—about our fight, and where I am now. Lying on this bed in a motel room in New Mexico. Reliving the last few months and years, I wish I had taken the other road and not taken the assignment. Alaska was better than joining the Federation. Life would have been hard, but I would have been happy and complete.

Tonight, I lay here wondering what could have been, and preparing for what was to come after tomorrow.

CHAPTER 8

WHAT THE HELL?

Who is pounding on my door?

What time was it?

I looked at my phone. Ah shit, it was 8:00am. Damn, I must have slept twelve hours. I'd wanted to be out of here by now. Rolling myself out of bed, I teetered over to the door, unlatch the lock, and opened it.

Lincoln stood in the doorway holding a tray of what smelled like coffee. Thank the gods! Coffee! And a very determined Lincoln.

"Hey," I said still sleepy and leaning on my door. "How did you find me?" It had only just occurred that he found me. I didn't tell him where I was staying.

"You don't have the most— Well, your car gave you away. Not many in these parts drive a '90s Mustang with ragtop. And I happen to know that car very well."

Good point; score one for him. I perked up a little with the hope one of those coffees was for me.

"Can I come in?" Lincoln asked.

"Only if one of those coffees is for me." Coffee was one of my weaknesses and he knew it.

A small grin came across Lincoln's face and he handed me one of the cups. *Cha-ching. It was going to be a good day.* I stepped aside and let Lincoln enter my so-called room. I could sense he was taking in my surroundings and wasn't impressed.

"You picked a great motel." Being facetious, Lincoln placed the tray on my very small table.

"It's where I ended up," I responded, closing the door and turning. I halted, bringing my coffee up to my nose, and inhaled the aroma. It was intoxicating, almost to the point of coffee-gasm. It was one of my favorite things on this planet.

"Ah, I see you still smell your coffee, that hasn't changed. Are you still on the edge of a coffee-gasm?" Lincoln certainly hadn't forgotten how I was with coffee. He was still watching me as I enjoyed one of the few things I had left.

"You know it!" I beamed.

"I guess some things never change," Lincoln added, but I didn't care. I had coffee.

I slowly pulled my coffee away from my nose and held it to my chest. "Thank you for the coffee, it was just what I needed." Without hesitation, I took my first savory sip. It was as good as ever. You have your good coffee, and then you have your shitty coffee, and this was about average. Still... Yum!

Okay, now that my coffee-gasm had dissipated, I wondered what Lincoln was doing here. I was positive when I left his place yesterday, I had his answer. No, of course.

So, this was just a little odd to me.

"Lincoln, I appreciate the coffee, but why are you here? And if you tell me it was to bring me coffee, I call bullshit." As much as I wanted to hold tight to my coffee, I set it down to prove a point. I knew, and he knew, I could figure him out. I wanted to hear it from him.

"I wanted to bring you coffee," Lincoln said innocently.

All I had to do was give him the "Yeah, right" look.

"All right, fine. After you left yesterday, I pondered on your situation. I'm willing to help but I have a price."

"A price." I was a little shocked. I folded my arms and asked, "What is your price? All I need help with is to get away from here, grab the Aries device, and deliver it to Mitchell. You have the training, and I was encouraged to contact you. But now you have a price?" The more I thought about it, the more frustrated I got.

"Yes. Susan knew you needed my help for this to work, and now I have a price."

"Okay, what is it?" I shifted from one foot to the other.

"The Mustang!" Lincoln said with full confidence.

"*What!?!*" I couldn't believe my ears. He wanted my car.

"Yes, your heard me. You want my help; I want the car. I have just as much interest in it as you. And when you go back to Mitchell, you won't need it." His voice started to creep up.

I let out a prissy chuckle and turned away. Turning back, I looked in his eyes. He was for real. I knew his eyes and they were not joking.

"You realize I need to get my ass to the east coast, which means driving. You would have to come with me in that little car for many, many long hours. And first we'll have to stop in Vermont, and then drive down to headquarters. That is a hell of lot of time together."

"For the car, I think I can handle it." Lincoln was so smug right now; it was making me angry.

I was at a loss for words. He was going to help me only if I gave him my baby. But I needed backup, and if Susan had pointed me to him, then he was the one I wanted. She most likely had ulterior motives for this arrangement. Possibly getting us back together; making us speak and get along. Sounded about right for my pain-in-the-ass sister.

"All right, I'll agree. Once you have delivered the Aries device and me to your brother safely, the Mustang is yours." God damn, that really hurt to say out loud.

"We have a deal," Lincoln smugly said and took a sip of his coffee. He was fucking with me and I didn't like it.

"Deal," I agreed, and grabbed my coffee by reaching around him. Holy fuck, he smelled good. And so, did my coffee. I think this is going to be harder than I thought. If his smell puts my libido into high gear already, what else could happen? Then again, I'm on his shit list, and bad emotions will no doubt reach the surface. Hell will let loose. He must, or this will never work.

"I need to shower and dress. If you need to grab stuff from your place, feel free. We can meet back here in a bit," I suggested.

"No, I'm good. I already have a bag packed. I'll be waiting outside beside my new car."

Damn this was going to be a long ride if he kept rubbing it in. *Put salt in my wounds why don't cha?*

"It's still mine for now," I insisted, gritting my teeth. I wasn't giving in yet.

Lincoln just smiled back at me with his shit-eating grin and cocky attitude. He took another swig from his coffee and waved at me to go get ready. "If we have all this ground to cover, I suggest you go shower. We haven't got all day."

Wow, I wasn't used to being told what to do, unless it was the Emissary.

"I'm going. Don't get your panties in a twist. Is that your polite cop way of saying get your ass moving?"

"Yeah, something like that."

I turned on my heels, walked into the bathroom, and shut the door behind me. For a moment, I leaned up against the door and took a breather. Why did I ever get into this mess? My father would be so infuriated at me. He didn't teach us to have a no-win scenario, always have options and be able to get yourself out of anything. And yes, he would have been pissed to high heaven knowing I had been dating a cop. Dad did not like cops. Dad didn't like anything or anyone, now that I think about it. Not even Susan or me.

I flew through the shower, dressed, and was ready to hit the road. I would need food, and with the Federation thinking I was on their payroll—which I still was—I had everything I needed at any time. I just had to prove my progress. I knew a call would be coming through any time now. Maybe not today, but soon. The Emissary didn't like waiting.

Before the hour was up, Lincoln and I were out the door, and on the road. Lincoln tried to head for the driver's seat but was quickly detoured to the passenger side. This was still my baby. I backed out of the parking lot and we were off. Our journey across the country began, and depending on the variables, we might have this mission completed in about a week. Fingers crossed.

CHAPTER 9

WE WERE TWO DAYS INTO OUR ROAD TRIP, AND WE'D mostly remained civil to each other. We'd stop for a stretch and food and gas every so often and made small talk about absolutely nothing. I wasn't ready to get into anything personal just yet, whether it was our past or the possible near future. And neither was Lincoln. Most of the time we spent quiet or listening to music or finding music we could both agree on. There were many bickering matches over that one. I even let him drive; it was nice for a change not to be in control, and it wasn't like I didn't trust him, because I do and always have. I once gave him my heart and soul, and if anyone shouldn't trust the other, it should be him. I broke him, and I know deep down I could never mend that betrayal.

It was getting close to sundown and we had driven a little past St. Louis and decided we both need a break. As we drove, we both kept a look out for a motel or hotel, somewhere we could sleep in a real bed and have a hot shower. The last couple of days it had been minor stops and quick meals. I needed getting the hell out of this car. Stretch. And I had a slight pinch in my stomach. That feeling comes when it's time

for an update for the Emissary. This was going to be a shit show if I couldn't convince him that I was on the right track.

On one of the outer highways, Lincoln pulled into a small-looking motel with a little takeout stand in it parking area. Oh, hot damn, food and a shower. It was like I had been given a gift and could feel myself glowing from it. Yeah, I know, not the best gift, but I was willing to take anything right now over McDonald's. I never wanted to see fried junk food again. Okay, too harsh—make that at least for a while.

We pulled the car up to the office and I went in to rent a room for the night. The clerk was very sorry all the rooms were booked, but he was willing to let us have a cottage for the price of a room. That was sweet of him, and then he beamed out at Lincoln. "After all, we wouldn't want to turn away newlyweds," he remarked, bouncing looks from Lincoln to me. I choked a little, returning his comment with a smile. Only in my dreams...and by the looks of the clerk, I wasn't his type. The clerk eyed Lincoln from stem to stern. I wanted to say something rude like, "Sorry he's mine," but I didn't. I just took the key and went back out to my fake husband.

"Hey," I called to Lincoln who was leaning on the hood of the Mustang. "We have the cottage over there, number three, and if I were you, I'd make sure you are madly in love with me. Or our friendly clerk in there might have you for dinner."

Boy this was going to be comical.

"What?" Lincoln asked, confused.

"Yeah." I walked over closer to him, holding my hand over my eyes to block the sun. "Let's just say our friendly clerk doesn't like women. He's into dick."

Lincoln wasn't expecting that. His eyes grew twice the size and he inched closer to me.

I chuckled at his reaction.

"Ah shit, why the hell do I have to be so fucking sexy?" Lincoln muttered, rolling with the punches.

That, I wasn't expecting.

A big ol' smile came across his face and I beamed back at him. We still made a good team.

We moved the car around to the front of the cottage and I went in to scope the place out. For the size it was, it was a quaint little place with two beds, a bathroom, and mini kitchen area with a microwave. Underneath, hidden was a mini fridge. I was finally living in style. Bullshit, I was. This was nothing like the place the Federation had assigned to me. That place was deck out to the nines. You wanted something, you got it.

Lincoln came in a moment after me. "You want something to eat? I think the small takeout place might have some sandwiches."

"That would be great. Thank you." This polite stuff was starting to get easier.

I'd just placed my sore and tired body on the side of one of the beds when my cell rang. Ah shit, I knew who it was. My gut has been telling me all day. I grabbed it out of my pocket and, sure enough, the name Crème Brûlée buzzed across my screen. I took deep breaths, and after two, I answered.

"Good afternoon, sir," I greeted the Emissary, and it hit me I was on Facetime. We would be looking at each other. Fuck, this could be bad.

"Good afternoon, my dear. Progress report." The Emissary was direct to the point.

"Sir, I have started across the country in hopes my hunch will pan out," I started to explain.

"Excuse me? You are making your way across the country? You aren't driving, are you?" There was irritation in his tone.

"Yes, sir, I am. Susan gave me things to think about and driving help me process the pieces. I believe she has hidden our buried treasure along Route I-95, somewhere along the eastern seaboard. I have found clues that she has been through there very recently." I was rolling with what I had to work with. And that would be nothing.

"I see, I would have expected more progress from you, Jessy. But I trust your instincts." The Emissary put emphasis in his words.

"Thank you, sir." I was a little proud and trying not to drop the phone from all my shaking.

"And Jessy, I have a little incentive for you, to feel the reality of this situation," he added.

"Sir? I understand how important this assignment is to the Federation. I will complete it." I knew what this meant to him.

"I know you do, but to make sure you are not feeling a little slack..." He paused and held a picture up to the screen. It was a snapshot of Susan, beaten, bloody and in poor shape. She wouldn't be able to hold out much longer. "I will give you a few more days, and after that, your sister will pay a deeper price. Do I make myself clear?"

I worked my hardest to show no emotion after seeing Susan's image. I was breaking, but I couldn't let the Emissary see it.

"Crystal, sir. I will not disappoint you," I answered and was suddenly shut off. We disconnected and I gave a huge sigh. I didn't move a muscle. The conversation and image of Susan had disturbed me. I felt as if my world were coming apart, and panic was starting to set in. I just stared at nothing and my brain went blank.

"Hey, I got us some sandwiches and beer," Lincoln said, coming through the door. It startled me and I gazed over at him. "What's going on? You look terrified."

"Are your cop senses telling you that?" I said in a low mumble, feeling very uneasy.

"Yes and no," he answered, setting out food and beer on the small table by the door. Something was terribly wrong, and it must have shown on my face. "There are three people in this world who know you better than you do. Your sister, my brother, and me. We know your look, body language, and tone of voice. And right now, I know you are terrified about something." He started moving toward me. "I have seen you scared, shocked, surprised, in despair, and many other sides, but this... You're terrified." He stopped about a foot from me.

"You think, I'm terrified?" I tried to make my voice sound confident, but I was failing miserably.

"Yes, I do."

"Of course, I'm terrified. I just got my extra push to complete this assignment. The Emissary showed me an image of my sister, beaten and bloody. My own blood, and I am the only one who can save her. But I also must keep Aries away from the Federation or this country will be in some extreme difficulties in the near future. How to I chose between my own flesh and blood, and my country?" The level in my voice rose and was very shaky.

"You know the answer to that," Lincoln assured me.

Yes, I did...at the cost of my twin sister's life. Susan knew the consequences of her betrayal, but the reality was hitting me like a ton of bricks. My anxiety had started to set in.

"I know, that but how do I choose?" Tears welled up in my eyes. "I know what I have to do, and I know what he is capable of doing. What he will do to her before he executes her."

My voice cracked, and so did I. I was started to tremble as the words flooded out.

"You have no idea what he can do, but I do. I have been there and lived through all of it for months. Everything I have done or was punished for has taken a piece of my soul every day, every minute. I hate myself b-because I-I—" I was stuttering now with the pain and hurt flowing out. "I let it happen. I have had the bruises and lacerations. I've had pain inflicted by him. And I couldn't stop it. I had to play the part. And now, now I am hollow." My voice was sinking lower.

My eyes flowed, with tears running down my face. Reality was crushing me like a bug.

"I gave up my life for this misery. I'm all alone." Hysteria now enveloped me, and I couldn't stop it.

Lincoln took a step toward me, grabbed my face with both his hands, and kissed me, hard. Not a peck, it was a hard, passionate kiss that only comes from someone who deeply cares for you. His lips did the talking, and I talked back. Just as he was pulling away, my body eased, not all the way, but enough for me to breathe. I had been on the verge of a panic attack, and Lincoln had eliminated it. Just with one kiss. He could always calm me down.

He released me and put his forehead to mine and said to me softly "You are not alone."

Pondering his words, I fell into his arms. Strong arms wrapped around me as I silently sobbed and shook within them. This was the first positive emotional connection we had made since we reunited, and I was not ready to let it go.

AFTER MY EMOTIONAL BREAKDOWN EASED, I WAS ABLE TO eat a few bites, then Lincoln took me over to the bed and cradled me until I fell asleep. I felt so secure and safe within his arms that I didn't want him to let go. It was as if we'd never parted and the outside world wasn't there.

I awoke with Lincoln still holding me, and for a moment I felt a faint smile twitch on my face. Sneaking out of the bed, I went to the very cheap and old coffee pot and got the baby brewing. Enough for two, it was only fair. Once the brew cycle was complete, I took my cup and slipped out the door, allowing quiet for Lincoln to sleep. I glanced back toward the bed I just vacated and smiled. He was there for me, and I am so grateful.

I held my coffee in both hands as I parked myself on the bottom step of our cottage. The sun shone on me as I sipped my coffee. And I didn't forget to take a moment to smell it either. That is probably my favorite part. Sitting there, time just seem to stand still. The sunshine beamed in my direction and reenergized me. It was a pleasant experience. I wanted to slip into it and out of my current predicament. What the hell was I going to do? But at this moment, in this time, I wasn't going to do a damn thing but sit on my ass and drink my coffee in the golden sunshine.

I wasn't sure how much time had passed when the door creaked open from the inside. Lincoln had awakened from his slumber and had his coffee in hand. He came over and sat down on the bottom step. "Good morning," he said to me with a sweet smile.

"Good morning to you. As you can see, I left you some coffee." I was joking with him threw squinted eye because he knew damn well, I would have taken all of it.

"I appreciate that." He sipped the hot liquid.

Turning slightly to look at him, for a moment I was lost in him. The glisten in his eyes was captivating, and I could get lost in them all over again.

"I want to apologize for my meltdown last night," I said. "I should have handled the situation better than I did. I guess the pressure finally built up enough that I couldn't contain it."

Lincoln turned to me giving me his attention. "It okay. It's not like we haven't been through stressful times before. I know what pressure you are under." Lincoln stated.

"You do?"

"Yeah, I could see it in your eyes the day you came to see me. And I knew what I needed to do. I protect you, like I always have. Last night...

Well, you needed to release, and I handled it how I saw fit. We've been through hard times, stressful times, and painful times, but we made it through. We always will." If people didn't know Lincoln like I did, no one would ever believe he could be this sweet, thoughtful person. He gave me a pat on the back and got up, going back into the cottage.

And he was right; we have been through many rough times. There was only one other time I had a breakdown in front of him, except last night. A couple years ago, Lincoln and I were having the best year together. Jobs were going in the right direction. Life couldn't have been better for us. Then I found out I was pregnant. My emotions were very mixed about my new state, excitement, and more fear than ever before. I was terrified all day about my pregnancy. What was Lincoln going to say or do? Will he be excited or pissed? We had talked about kids, but it was meant for way down the road, not now.

All day my anxiety took over body until that night when he came home. Shaking and pacing, I almost worn a path in the floor. My eyes were red and bloodshot when he walked in the door, and immediately he knew something was wrong. After more pacing and trembling hands, Lincoln stopped me and I finally got the words out, "You're going to be a dad."

As he gazed at me, I saw his eyes go into shocked. Holy shit, this wasn't what I was hoping for. I mean we had talked about our future, but it wasn't meant to be right now. He just stared at me. His eyes sparked and turn to a sparkle with excitement. I lost it. Completely lost it. Laughing and crying at the same time. He grabbed me by the waist, hugging and twirling me. I'd worried for no reason.

I was horribly sick from the day I found out to the end of my first trimester. My body protested every day. Eight weeks later, morning sickness had finally subsided, and Lincoln was excited every day for this new life. He would put his hands on my belly and talk to it every chance he could. But the day came when my body finally couldn't carry it anymore. I had a miscarriage, and it was the most painful, emotional thing I have ever experienced. It was days after that I'd had my meltdown. I blamed myself for the miscarriage and there was no forgiveness. I cried for hours and one night I just started screaming at the world. Lincoln came home to me curled up in a corner. He reassured me it wasn't my fault, that it wasn't our time for a baby, and he never let go of me. My Lincoln held me and caressed me as he'd done last night.

LINCOLN WAS INSIDE THE COTTAGE MOVING ABOUT. THE memory of my miscarriage still burdened me. How did I get here? I keep asking myself that...and until I figure it out, I will still be lost.

CHAPTER 10

LINCOLN AND I CONTINUED OUR TRIP TOWARD NORTHEAST in search of the Aries device. We had causal conversation, but never brought up the kiss or the hugs from my emotional night. It was if it had never happened, and I wasn't going to bring it up. When we left, I let Lincoln drive for a while, after the night I'd had. All I wanted was to let the wind whip through my hair and erase my anxiety, even if it was temporary. With him driving, I could enjoy the sun and forget.

After we passed over the Mississippi River, the weather decided not to be in our favor. After making good time and headway, we were stopped just outside of Ohio. Severe thunderstorms slowed out progress until we encountered hail. The Mustang's ragtop was very pissed at us, enough so that we had to stop and find a place to stay with a covered parking lot. Not long after we got off the highway, a two-story hotel building can into view. It wasn't a five- star place but it had some coverage for cars to park. It would make do for the time we needed, and the roads were passable. We checked in and found our room in the second level accessed via a covered porch that ran the whole length of the hotel. Awesome, we were out of the rain. Not just rain, down-pour-ing soaking rain.

Lincoln grabbed our bags and we both raced for cover. Our room was up the stairs and not too far down. I opened our door quickly so we both could escape splashing the rain. He went through the door first and tossed our bags on the bed. My bag was practically unzipped, and the only thing that fell out was the one thing I didn't want Lincoln to see. The Bear. The one he had given to me before we found out I had miscarried.

I was still shaking off the rain when Lincoln spied the bear on the bed. He went over to the bed and pulled the bear out of my bag. Grabbing my bear, he held it up to analyze, then turned to me. "I see he hasn't left your side." Then he looked back down at the bear and smiled.

Realizing what he was doing, I walked over and touched my bear. Lincoln pivoted to let me see it. "Susan actually had him for a while. When I left, I did take the bear, but it was too painful having him around and not you. So, I had Susan hold on to him. It wasn't until the other day, after I had my conversation with her, that I retrieved him." Shame was filling my body as I explained.

"Susan had him. I sure that was a treat to listen to you explain to her what he really meant." Lincoln commented, still grinning.

"No, not really. It was one of the things she said to me last time I saw her. She actually made me promise I had to take care of Lincoln." I paused for a reaction but got nothing. Not even at glance at me. "Luckily, the powers at be probably thought she meant an animal of some type. After I went to her place and found the bear; I knew what she was implying. It was meant to you, and not a stuffed bear."

Lincoln finally looked at me with puzzled eyes.

"She wanted me to find you. I had to promise I would." I shrugged my shoulders and went on. "So here we are."

"Smart lady that sister of yours." Handing over my bear, Lincoln added, "As I mentioned, she came to see me a while ago, telling me I might have visitor from my past on my doorstep soon. I never dreamed it would've been you."

Returning his smile, I said no more. I just took the bear, hugged him, and put him back into my bag. I wasn't ready for more emotions to spill out yet.

A day passed, and there was no end to the rain in sight. Weather forecasters were advising motorists to drive only if they had to. Didn't look like Lincoln and I were going anywhere for a few more days. Knowing my next step, I had to inform the Emissary of my progress. Not my favorite idea, but I knew he would be chomping at the bit for lack of information. He isn't a patient man, if you haven't guessed. The cell service was low where we were, in a small town and a rainstorm. There was a chance my message might not get out. So, I resorted to a very improper alternative form of communicating with the Emissary. Email. He absolutely hated email or any sort of written communications. He would always say *People can be more deceptive in written form. I prefer verbal.* But I could explain why I had to use it and give my progress report. Simple. There may be enough service to connect.

I sat down on the bed with my phone in hand and started to compose my email with hope the message would be sent when there was a slight break in the weather.

> *Emissary,*
>
> *I apologize for my improper communication with you through email. My options have become limited and my urgency to give you a progress report warranted this. I have deciphered some of Susan notes I found in her apartment, and I have recruited an associate she used for the Aries theft.*

I have taken him under my employment to help me retrace her last whereabouts. The price was high for him to betray my sister, but it was worth the payment. We are making our way to the Northeast which is the location he last took her. With hope Aries will be at this location. But luck hasn't been in our favor. We crossed the Mississippi River and drove right into a severe storm. The highways are too dangerous to drive on at this in time. We will commence our journey when we are able to. I apologize for this setback. I will be in contact.

It was short, sweet, and to the point. I wasn't going to give him any more information than he needed. I just hoped it was enough. Though my gut was telling me differently.

Another day passed with no letup in the rain. The threat of tornados increased, and people were strongly urged to stay put. Of course, the Emissary wasn't going to like this. But the end of the day, Lincoln was going stir crazy. There was only so much pacing a person could do.

Finally, throughout the night, the weather started to ease, and the tornado warning was lifted. The chances we would be able to leave in the morning were looking up. Lincoln decided to go out for provisions for our continued journey. He left once the coffee was gone and he was dressed. We really didn't need much of anything, I knew he just needed to get out.

I sat on the bed writing notes and reliving Susan's last conversation with me. Hard to believe it had been over a week ago. I was finally able to focus without Lincoln around; his pacing was starting to get on my nerves. Always had, and most likely always will. That was him, and I learned a long time ago to deal with it. Patience and wine.

Just kidding.

No, I'm not.

I was deep in my thoughts when my cell rang. It was the first time since the storm it has had any service. I glance over and noticed Crème Brûlée was on Facetime.

Ah shit, this can't be good.

I took a deep breath and answered. "Good morning, Emissary. I am glad your call came through." I was being civil.

"Yes, my dear, I was *finally* able to reach you. I wasn't pleased when I received your email." The Emissary was pissed. This conversation was going to be bad, and I was doomed for punishment.

"I apologize for the improper communication. Our position was dead center in these storms moving across the U.S. I was very surprised when this call actually got through."

Keep your cool. You have done nothing wrong, I thought to myself.

"I see. Well, now I have you, there is something I want to show you." The Emissary took the focus off himself and turned the lens toward a dark room. The lights were so dim I moved closer to my screen, squinting.

The camera held for a moment before the light came up. As the room illuminated, a figure was being held by chains on each arm and positioned in the Christ crucifix. The lights were finally on high, and the prisoner was... I couldn't tell. The head was hanging down. The Emissary perched the phone on something and stepped over to the body. He jerked the head up to reveal—

Fuck! It was Susan, beaten to a pulp. Her eyes were almost completely swollen shut and dried blood caked her face. A rag gag was tried around her mouth.

"Susan," I silently breathed.

The Emissary held her chin tight and forced it to move to each side, showing me her profile. She was in hard shape; she would be lucky to live much longer.

"Yes, here we have our defector. She has been unwilling to give us any information pertaining to the recovery of Aries. I wanted to give you one last opportunity to speak to her before she is executed." The Emissary was being very brutal.

"What? But I need more time!" Panic was squeaking out of my voice. This wasn't supposed to happen; it was too soon.

"Think of this as an incentive for you to complete your assignment sooner rather than later." The Emissary didn't move a muscle. "Your allotted time has expired, and there are consequences for the delay. Susan has become uncooperative and her presence isn't needed any longer."

I was speechless, and my body was frozen in place. I didn't know what to say or do. The Emissary ripped off my sister's gag with force, tossing it to the floor.

"Is there anything you would like to say to your sister before we remove you from this pathetic life of yours?" he taunted Susan. There was so much evil in his voice, it was awful that a person could even think like that. It was frightening.

"Susan!" Tears filled my eyes and her name was the only thing I could say. There were so many words I wanted to say, but I was paralyzed.

Susan took a swallow and began to croak. "Be still my heart!" was all she could get out, and with her eyes shut, she blinked out a tear.

My own tears flowed down my cheeks; I was unable to be strong. Weakness was never an option, not with the Emissary. Now, it didn't matter.

"Well that was titillating and heartfelt," he mocked her. "But the time has come, Susan, for you to leave this world." The Emissary grabbed her hair from behind and brought a large angled blade to her throat.

A gasp escaped my lips as I watched, helpless. The Emissary looked at me with devilish eyes and a smile of devious enjoyment. In a slow, agonizing cut, he slit her throat. Not with a quick swipe, but slow and deep, making sure he completed the work with as much pain as he could. Blood rapidly flowed from her neck and the arterial spray coated the room. Susan's eyes grew wide and she choked as her life force drained from her wound.

The Emissary grinned with pleasure. His face becoming splattered with Susan's blood, along with the rest of his crew. Her head was still being restrained by the Emissary, and he had a death grip on her, making the blood splatter decorate the room even more.

It seems like an forever for the suffering end to my twin's life. The pain of her dying tore our connection apart, and pieces of my heart and soul converted to dust. I was in complete disarray witnessing her murder. My body and mind began to fog over, and it was as if I was floating underwater.

When the light dimmed and faded from Susan's eyes and her spirit was emptied from her body, the Emissary let her go. Her head went limp. She was dead, and a part of me died along with her.

A split second went by, and the Emissary was back with his face saturated in blood, stared into the camera looking directly at me. "Now, I will make this clear, my love. I want Aries in my possession within three days or this will become your fate," He paused for me to react, but I was silent and motionless. "If I do not have it, I will seek you out and the matter of your delightful death will be far less pleasant then the speediness of your sister's."

"Yes sir," I squeaked out, my face wet with tears.

"Good." The Emissary ended the call. He was gone.

I was frozen and stunned by what I just witnessed. The phone fell from my hands and I didn't move to grab it. Fuck it. I just sat and stared into nothingness. Tears rolled down my face and floods of emotion rose up like bile. Bile indeed rose up, enough that I was going to vomit. My paralyzed muscles released enough for me to round the corner and rush into the bathroom. The toilet was within reach, and I retched my brains out. I vomited and vomited some more.

When I thought I was done, the sobs and screams came, then I vomited again. There was nothing left in my stomach to throw up, but more came. I dry heaved until my stomach muscles had nothing left. Sitting back between the toilet and wall, I curled up into a ball and cried, sobbed, heaved, and shook.

Shock was setting in, and I didn't resist.

CHAPTER 11

I COULDN'T MOVE; NOISES AROUND ME WERE MUFFLED and not coherent. My body curled in a ball, arms wrapped around my knees, shivered with cold sweat and my eyes bugged open with no moisture left in them. Things, movement, going on around me, but I couldn't move or make a sound. My brain kept replaying my sister's brutal end, and now I was next. The Emissary called me his love. I vomited that up too. Revolting! Every moment of that call played and rewound, played and rewound. A broken record in my brain.

Out in the room, a loud sound was amplified, until the sounds came closer to me. I had been discovered. Lincoln saw my collapsed form on the bathroom floor and rushed over to me, worry and fear taking over. He was speaking to me, but I couldn't hear him; the buzz of his voice was like a language I couldn't understand. Sobs still filled my lungs, but they were soft sobs, for my throat was so sore there was nothing left of my voice.

Suddenly, hands cupped my face and moved my gaze to look up. Lincoln's face showed so much emotion, it cleared the fog from my eyes enough to see him. His lips moved, and now his words were clearing and contacting my brain. I could start to decipher what he was saying.

"Jess, Jess." His words were penetrating.

"Lincoln." I was able to get out his name, and then I squeezed my face, sniffling more sobs. My body was shaking more and Lincoln's hands on my face helped me stay in control.

"Jess, babe, what's going on?" He was trying so hard to help me. "What happened?"

I looked at him through strained eyes and saw him. His grip loosened as I was coming out of my trance.

"Lincoln, the the—" I stopped, heaving. "The Emissary." More heaving and rapid breathing.

"What did he do?" Lincoln with his background as a cop pushed.

"He. He killed Susan." I paused to get my words to come out. I tried to look away from him, but Lincoln held me firm. "He slit her throat and made me watch. He just—" I blurted out between my screams.

"Susan is dead?" Lincoln's words echoed shock.

"Yes, he killed her," I bellowed, and my tears began again, along with my shivering.

Lincoln never said another word. He scooped me into his arms and cradled me on the floor. I laid my head back into his embrace and continued to cry. We just sat there for who knows how long, and no words were exchanged, just consoling. How did I ever give this man up? Because I wouldn't be here in this position if I hadn't run.

I HAVE NO IDEA WHAT TIME OR DAY IT EVEN WAS. LINCOLN sat with me in his arms until I stopped shaking and crying. He then lifted me up and set me gently in the bathtub, clothes and all. The water came on with warmth, and I was showered in its power. Lincoln, clothes and all too, climbed in behind me and wrapped his arms around me. He stayed there until the water began to turn cold, and as if I was an infant, he took me out the tub, stripped me of my wet clothes to my undergarments, and wrapped me in a towel.

I have never been so helpless, but he didn't care. At least I don't think he did. Leading me to the bed, the covers were drawn back and I rolled in. My shivering had stopped, and exhaustion took over my fragile body. Watching Lincoln walk off to remove his clothes, my eyes blinked shut and sleep overtook me.

NOT SURE OF THE TIME, I WOKE UP WITH MUCH CONFU-sion. Did I just dream the previous day's events, or where they real? My brain was so jumbled, frustrated and ached, I just wanted to fall back asleep.

I let my eyes ease open and adjust. Blinking for clarity, I stretched my arm out to the other side of the bed to see if Lincoln was beside me. There was nothing but bedding and a pillow; I could feel no sign of warmth. He'd been absent for a while. So, I laid my head back on my pillow and tried to sort out the chaos in my mind.

The one thing I couldn't shake was the dream of my sister's murder. Real or not real? Moments more, I lay with confusion. Flashes of her demise bounced through my head, and I concluded, real. My sister had been murdered by the Emissary, and I was going to be next on the kill list if I didn't follow his orders. Guess I better keep a gun under my bed, because I wasn't going down without a fight.

Susan didn't, and neither will I.

The longer I lay in bed reliving her death, the more I realized my back had shooting pains rolling around to my hips. I had been lying down for longer that I thought. With a push to get up, I got out of bed and went over to the window, pulled the shades back, and— *Holy shit*! What the hell was that? Damn, that thing is bright. The sun had made her appearance after days of storms. And it was bright!

My phone lay on the table beside the window and I checked it to see just how long I had been out. Shit, two days. I had been unconscious for two whole days. No wonder Lincoln was gone. We had been in this room for almost a week. Luckily, he wasn't nuts yet.

Still in my underclothes, I made my choice. I needed some fresh air to evaluate my situation. I'd go for a walk.

After dressing and searching for my sunglasses, I headed out into the bright sun. The air smelled so fresh and crisp after an intense storm; it was almost cleansing. I made sure I locked our room and proceeded to leave down the front stairs. My Mustang was gone, so walking was the only choice. Better for me anyway. More air and exercise do the body good. I wasn't going far, but I did need some food. The rumble in my stomach reminded me it had been a while. I went to the sidewalk, looked both ways, and decided to go left. More life was evident in that direction.

I walked for a bit, taking in all the surroundings. Being to so weak from the lack of movement, my speed was that of a tortoise. It was helping me forget the horrible thing I had witnessed and cope with truth of it all. I needed to sort things out in my brain before I could proceed with my mission. Aries was going to Mitchell and Division. There was nothing holding me to the Federation accept my life, and a price. Only if I was willing to participate. Looking over my shoulder would become a fulltime job from this point on. But I would not be a pawn to the Federation any longer. This undercover operation needs to find conclusion.

Rounding a corner, off the street a bit sat a small grocery store, and my feet were taking me to it. My brain wasn't in control any longer, my stomach was. Good thing I had some cash in my pocket. I strolled through the doors, staring at everything and watching. My stomach protested, so I grabbed a food basket and grabbed simple things that would be snackable for our journey, wherever then hell we were going. Tortilla chips, fruit, and a small Caesar salad with chicken for now. It would do. More things looked better, but I stuck with healthy. Yogurt and granola were added, and then off to get water. My head still hurt from all the crying, I needed water.

I came upon the beverage section and ran into an old friend. The water was on one side and other held a girl's best friend, or mine at least. Jose Cuervo. He never disappoints, and with all the memories and pain, I just wanted it all to go away. I want peace for one night and no responsibility for a change. I have work to do. I turned from the tequila and walked away from it, hesitated, then went back and grabbed a bottle. A couple sips wouldn't hurt, and I could be free of emotion and guilt.

After paying for my stuff, I proceeded outside and sat on the picnic tables out front, forcing myself to eat. The salad wasn't great, and the yogurt wasn't ice cream, but they filled the void and my body thanked me with a burp. Not ladylike, but it felt good. And still next to me in my brown paper bag was Jose. A sip wouldn't hurt, right? I've eaten and I am not getting drunk, just numb.

I left Jose in the bag and twisted off the top. One swig, and the burn flowed down my throat. "Ah my friend, you and I have had some good times," I said, lowering the bottle and holding it out in front of me. It required another swig, just to make sure it wasn't bad or anything.

I got myself up and back to the hotel before I was fully intoxicated. Jose and I were catching up very fast. My stride was still straight as I went up the back stairs and sat down on the top step. My body felt so warm and fuzzy, so much that I kept drinking.

I can always tell when I've had too much, my lips will start tingling and become numb. I was way beyond that point. I was almost drunk. Almost? Yeah, no, I was on my way to full blown drunk. But my head forgot about Susan's death and all my problems. Jose was a good friend of mine. He helped to forget.

CHAPTER 12

I DIDN'T KNOW JUST HOW LONG I'D BEEN SITTING ON THE stairs but from the feel of my bottle, it had been a while. Jose was becoming rather light. Probably not a good thing for me.

Fuck it, I didn't care right now. Didn't give a fucking care in the world. Hell, the world could end right now, and I wouldn't have a clue. Sitting with my legs apart and holding the bottle between them, I felt a presence come up behind me. I knew the footsteps all too well.

Lincoln had found me.

"Hey, there you are! I've been looking for you," he said, upbeat.

I turned up to look at him with the world starting to spin. "Well, you found me. I had to get some food." My words were slurring badly. Then I looked down at my bag and took another swig.

Lincoln sat down beside me and I hung my head, still holding the tequila by the neck in the paper bag. He looked at my profile and then at the bag in my hands. "I see you found a friend." I could feel the disappointment in his voice.

"Yes, he has been helping me cope." I took a breath and my emotions weighed on me. "I wanted the pain to go away and have nothing to worry about. The agony." I have no idea if I was making any sense.

"I can tell, but it is only temporary. As you know"

"I know that! But right now, it's working. Not my best decision, but Jose is my friend."

Another swig and then I angled my friend toward Lincoln. I was way beyond drunk.

"I see." What Lincoln did next surprised me, he took my bottle and swigged some for himself.

I gazed up with him and grinned from ear to ear. "That-a-boy!" I slurred out. My head was feeling like a bobble-head doll.

My gaze never left Lincoln, and when he looked my way I leaned in and kissed him. His lips were so plump and juicy I couldn't help myself. There was no resistance from him, but suddenly he put his hand on my chest and pulled away, leaving me hanging.

"Jess, no. This isn't right. You've been drinking, and that's not..." He paused. "I don't want to take advantage while you're drunk."

I couldn't believe what I was hearing. I was suddenly horny as fuck, and he was turning me down? What the hell? And yes, okay, I was a little drunk. No, make that way drunk. But you can probably figure that out. Often, drunk sex is the best sex. There is no judgement and your body is relax to feel all the sensations.

"Why, it never schtopped us before," I pointed out in a slur. "And if I remember, it'sch unbelievable while we were in-*toxxxx*-icccated. Mind blowing. Not that it isn't alwaysch." Boy am I slurring. But I really, really wanted this. "Sex was one of many things we never complained or argued about." I look at him with puppy dog eyes, pleading.

"You have had a rough couple of days. It wouldn't be right. You're not thinking straight." Lincoln was resisting me.

"So?" I kissed him again on the side of the mouth. "I have been wanting this since I walked through your door." I continued kissing his mouth, moving from one corner to another.

Then I landed in the middle; there was no resistance.

"Me, too, but I want this when we're both thinking straight." He let me continue kissing him.

I pulled back for a second and handed him my bottle. Can't beat them, join them! He took the bottle from me and took another swig. My libido was cranking into high.

"I am thinking straight. I want this." I whispered into his mouth, taking my Jose back. "Please." I tried not to beg, but my buzz was becoming more and more cloudy. And I did want this, badly. Lincoln was no newbie in the bedroom, and he made every moment incredible, no matter the time or how drunk either of us was.

I leaned back, kissing him on the mouth again; no resistance again. In fact, he was kissing me back. Gently, until his hands moved around my back and pulled me in closer. His lips put so much emotion into the kiss, it wasn't hard to get enveloped by them. He pulled away and helped me up to me feet. My hand was still clutching the tequila. Lincoln took my face in his hands and kissed me harder, deeper. We kissed and slowly walked to our room.

Opening the door, neither of us letting go, we pushed our way in, and everything became more amplified. I set the tequila down and Lincoln shut the door with his foot, releasing my face briefly. In that moment, I reached down and stripped my shirt off over my head, leaving me in just my bra. I was so turned on, my nipples hardened. Lincoln turned and looked at me, then stripped of his shirt as well. Then we rejoined and continued our kissing, pressing our bodies against each other. Skin on skin was so intoxicating, beyond my Jose intoxication. I could feel Lincoln becoming hard against me.

I lowered my hands from his face, unbuttoned and unzipped his pants, plunging my fingers deep down. I grasped his erection in my hands and began stroking. The more I stroked, the harder he grew, and the more fevered he kissed. He parted from me enough to release a moan. I kept my hands moving up and down, getting more moans. It turned me on high. Lincoln moved his hands off my cheeks and around my back to unhook my bra. I had to let go of him long enough for it to fall to the floor. In that time, I knelt, took hold of his pants, and lowered them and his boxers to the floor.

As I was down low, I grasped him again and teased him with the tip of my tongue. Swirling around his ego, I gently sucked and then claimed him with my mouth. Just enough to make him groan and gasp. His hands ran through my hair as I continued sucking and teasing his cock. How I missed this—the intimacy, the sex, the lust. I couldn't get enough. Pulling him out of my mouth, he tasted so good I wanted more, but Lincoln hoisted me up and grasped my face again. Our kissing became more involved, from soft kisses to hard with tongue. My arms wrapped around him and my naked breasts pressed into his chest.

Lincoln walked me over to the bed and laid me back on it. He glided his fingertips down over my breasts and continued down to my pants. With ease they came off, and Lincoln teased his fingers all the way down. He then reached my feet and switched to light kisses, starting at my feet and progressing back up my legs. With hands of silk, he moved upward, placing kisses on me up to my inner thigh. My legs slid apart and his fingertips played between my legs, finally finding my clit and circling around it. My body went into hyper-sensitivity, and finally he inserted a finger inside me. I was so wet from his touch; I couldn't control myself. I began to moan and pant for him. He was pulsing his fingers, and I was going crazy.

He pulled his finger out and resumed kissing my inner thighs, progressing up to the apex. His tongue moved to my clitoris and licked circles around it. My back arched as he caressed my very wet center. I wanted more. The tone of my moans changed, Lincoln stopped, knowing my limit. Then he moved on top of me. Our kissing reconnected, and within seconds he pushed inside me. The bare contact sent an energy surge throughout my body. The rhythm of our bodies was so in sync, every move sparked a new sensation. Sliding in and out, our nerves fired with every new thrust.

As Lincoln pulsed with me, my body went into hyperdrive and my orgasm was beginning to build. My breathing quickened and I moaned louder. With my change in volume, Lincoln's did too. His pace quickened and we both began building toward explosion. We both knew how the other liked it, so I tightened with my Kegel... and that was the spot. His breathing intensified with mine, and we both exploded. We orgasmed together and the yells that came from us were loud and deep. They seemed to last eternity, and with every slight movement my body felt like it was being ripped in half. But in a good way. I screamed with intense pleasure. Lincoln's release was just as powerful.

As we tried to reclaim our breathing, Lincoln laid on top of me to recapture himself.

"Holy fuck!" I blurted out; my breathing still heavy.

Lincoln pulled his head up with a smile and planted another kiss on me. His eyes met mine and they glistened. "Yes, holy fuck is right!"

Lincoln eased himself out of me and rolled onto the bed next to me. Our breathing slowed to about normal and our bodies remained touching. I rolled inward toward Lincoln. I eagerly wanted more kissing, more of everything. Making up for lost time without him.

"God, I missed you," I said to him.

"I know, I know." Lincoln replied, wrapping his arm around my head and pulling me into his chest. His fingers twirled strains of my hairs as I melted into him.

My body was giving up, and I began to pass out from either tequila or exhaustion. In my haze, Lincoln was whispering words in my ear I couldn't understand. I faded away after an emotional day and reconnecting with Lincoln. My only worry as sleep prevailed was...

Will I remember this in the morning?

MORNING APPROACHED AND MY WORLD WAS IN A DOWN-ward spiral. I could feel my world spinning, and as I opened my eyes, a painful pounding started in my head and eyes. Quickly closing my eyes again, I tried to push the feeling away as the agony grew bigger. I began to pull myself up in bed, but the moment I moved, the sensation of vomiting approached. In the nick of time I hurled myself for the toilet, I vomited. And vomited and vomited some more. Damn, the tequila tasted better going down. Once there was nothing left to throw up, I found myself sitting back and breathing. Holy hell Batman, I feel like shit. I took the T-shirt I was wearing and wiped my mouth. I needed to get back to bed.

I edged my way out of the bathroom and noticed my bottle was sitting on the table. I inched my way over to see just how much I'd had to drink. The bottle had about an inch left in it. *Oh shit, no wonder I feel horrible and have not a clue what happened yesterday.* Setting the Jose bottle down, I moved over to the edge of the bed, put my head between my legs, and breathed.

I sat there for a while, not wanting to move. Then the door swung open and in came Lincoln.

Lincoln had on his sunglasses and carried a paper bag. He noticed me barely looking up at him and said, "Good morning, sunshine!"

"Ugh," was all I could get out.

"I brought you some breakfast." Lincoln reached into the paper bag and took out a wrapped-up greasy breakfast sandwich. That was my go-to hangover food, with orange juice. And low and behold, Lincoln produced a bottle of orange juice. Good man. Lincoln stepped over and handed both to me.

"Thank you." God, I was grateful for this right now. I unwrapped the sandwich. The smell was nauseating but I took a bite anyway. Chewing slowly and with a hard swallow, I asked, "Hey what happened last night?" Everything was a blur after I drank about half the bottle.

"You don't remember?" Lincoln asked, puzzled.

"No, I remember making my way back here and sitting on the steps. How I got inside and to bed, I have no clue," I admitted embarrassed, but I was able to take another bit of my sandwich. Go, me!

"Ah, well, when I came back, you were sitting on the top step drinking, and I got you inside. You had most of the bottle gone, so you were feeling pretty good."

"Yeah, I must have been pretty drunk considering how I feel right now."

"You definitely felt good." Lincoln paused, waiting for a response from me. When it didn't come, he said, "Ah well, we need to get on the road today and make up for lost time. Between the storm and...well..."

"Susan's death and my night of drinking," I finished. "Yeah, I want to get this place far behind us." I felt my stomach getting a little queasy and full. I puffed my cheeks out for confirmation. "I'll go change so we can head out. Thank you for my hangover cure."

"You're welcome. It has never failed you yet," Lincoln said almost coldly but with a forced grin. It was like he had something else on his mind.

I changed into real clothes, tried to brush my teeth, but the gag reflex almost made me vomit again, so I reemerged from the bathroom, feeling like death. My gear was still in good shape and not scattered around the room. Pawing through my bag looking for my sunglasses—which I can never find—the bear made his way out again. I brought him up and gazed at him. More memories resurfaced that I didn't want to relive right now.

Lincoln came up behind me, holding my sunglasses in his hand. "Looking for these?"

I turned to look at him and tears escaped my eyes. "Thanks," I responded, taking the glasses from him.

"Hey," Lincoln opened his arms and I collapsed into them. He held me for a minute so I could release and then gather my thoughts. It was so comforting being in his embrace, I didn't want to let go.

"It's going to be okay," he said with reassurance in his voice. "We're going to be okay." He lifted my chin with his fingers for me to look in his eyes. He had confidence but I was doubtful.

I just nodded my head, giving him my acknowledgment, and then he kissed me lightly on the lips. Time had taken a toll between us, but it wouldn't take long to mend my mistake.

"Here, you might want this too." Out of Lincoln's back pocket he took his ball cap. "The sun is a little bright and you're suffering enough." He grinned as he put the hat on my head.

"Thanks." I adjusted the hat and looked down at my bear.

We gathered our things and made our way to the Mustang. The bill for our room was paid, and soon we were ready to hit the road again. Lincoln was correct about the sun, but he'd left off a small detail. It was blazing hot out. There was no chance we could keep the top up. On a normal day I be thrilled, but with my horrendous hangover, I was screwed. I had put myself in this torture, so I'd have to live with.

I let Lincoln drive and I rode shotgun. In my clutches, I held the bear. He was giving me reassurance, which had always been his purpose, but today I appreciated it more. Lincoln's lead foot would help us get back on schedule and I didn't say a word. Just don't get pulled over was all I said to him. That was the last thing we needed. I wanted this mission to be over. I held my bear very close to my chest and the four words Susan last said to me buzzed through my mind. "Be still my heart." I recited it silently over and over. What was she trying to tell me? In my hangover fog, it persisted, and sanity would soon leave. I just squeezed the bear tighter.

She had told me to seek out Lincoln and take care of him. She made a point to say that.

The Bear. Lincoln had given me the bear. Which I found in her closet.

I have the bear and Lincoln. Come on, focus. Put the pieces together.

Be still my heart.

Be still my heart.

Be still my heart.

Holy Fuck, my heart! Fuck, my head! Susan's words binged in my head like a bell. She was giving clues. The location of Aries, perhaps? I ripped off my sunglasses. Damn, bad idea. I put my sunglasses back on and turned my bear over. Inside the back of my bear is the small mechanism that made the momma heartbeat. The batteries were in a box that controlled the sound. The box just clicked in, so it was easily removable. I took off the backing and batteries.

"Lincoln!" I looked at him and tapped his arm. "Pull over," I commanded.

"Why? Are you going to throw up again?" He wasn't impressed.

"Just do it!" I barked and he complied.

"What is this about?" Pissed Lincoln was coming out.

"Look," I leaned over to show him.

What we saw changed our whole attitude and direction, everything. Aries!

CHAPTER 13

THERE IT WAS, TAPED TO THE BACK OF THE BATTERY COMpartment.

Aries.

It wasn't very big. Just a chip the size of a battery with the mini scarlet letter "A" printed on it. Clever, Susan. A data chip that could revolutionize any organization for unlimited power. Aries was small and simple, but the knowledge it held was infinite.

Lincoln got a good look at it and said in surprise, "That's it?"

"Yes, that's it, and if you knew how much information this little chip held, you'd fall out of your seat or piss yourself." I tilted the device to get a better look at it. Susan was clever to hide it in a place only I would find. Her last words were the final clue, and I just had to put the pieces together. Anyone searching her belongings wouldn't think to look in a stuffed animal, let alone behind the battery pack. Most would presume it would be in a locked case, protected with high security.

Nope, this was not so.

"Really? Piss myself?" Lincoln said doubtfully. "Yeah, probably not."

"This little chip holds more information about weapons, information that could feed the hungry, producing more food, making clean water, etc. In the right hands, this can do so much good for the people around the world, but with the wrong people, well, let's just say war, power, and greed."

"And how did Susan play into this?" Lincoln asked.

"Susan was assigned some time ago to steal the device from an archive facility that was protecting Aries. She, with all her charms successfully obtained Aries. I had my orders from Division to infiltrate the Federation, climb the ladder, and to steal Aries back. I'm to return to the Division and place it in a more protective facility. She knew what my operation was from the moment I contacted the Federation, and she assisted me in getting promotions to climb the ladder. It wasn't until she realized the power the Federation would obtain with this little device that she decided recently to go rogue. The Federation had its good aspects and bad. Aries would tilt the scale toward the bad power. Susan wasn't about harming the innocent. The rest, you know." I looked over to him. That was it in a nutshell.

"So, now what do we do with it?" Lincoln asked hesitantly.

"Now..." I paused. "Now, we go see Mitchell."

Lincoln looked back at the road and huffed. "I had a feeling you were going to say that."

Lincoln pointed the car back on the road, and we headed toward Washington D.C. It would take us less time to reach than if we continued to Vermont, which was where the Emissary believed we were going. With that thought, I took out my Federation cell and tossed it out of the car. It smashed into many pieces as it hit the ground.

My turn. I was going rogue too.

THE DAY IMPROVED THE CLOSER WE GOT TO THE NATION'S capital, and my hangover diminished. The six or so hour drive was shortened thankfully by Lincoln's lead foot. My head still hurt like hell but now I had direction. It gave me the willpower to continue. Believe me, it sucked, but I'd gotten myself into this mess and now I was going to pay. Dearly!

Lincoln remained focused on getting us there. I sensed his anxiety level rise after I mentioned a visit to Mitchell. Something had happened between the two of them after I left, and from the features on his face, it wasn't good. I had a feeling the conflict had originated with yours truly. Mitchell was my boss and best friend. Lincoln was my lover and Mitchell's brother. See where this could go wrong? I can. And now we were about to reunite for the first time in ages.

Lincoln knew his way around the city of D.C. as we got closer. We both did, but I let him take point. Before I knew it, we were pulling into the parking garage of the Division building where, last I knew, Mitchell had his office. Granted, this was many, many months ago. We entered the parking garage. Lincoln was not Division but used to assist us here frequently being a local detective. I had been gone for so long, so of course the guard asked for ID. Luckily, I had my old credentials in my backpack. Reaching out to the scanner, my breathing quickened. Was this going to work? Or had Mitchell shut down my authorization?

A glance over to Lincoln and the card went into the scanner. The scanner processed for a second, and the gate opened.

We parked and went to the elevator, proceeding up to the finale. I hoped. I was still holding tight to the bear, not letting it go from my grasp. To on lookers, it appeared I was like a child clutching her beloved toy, scared to be in this place, and Lincoln was my escort. Up and up we went, when finally, the elevator opened on the sixteenth floor.

The doors parted and we stepped out into a well-lit corridor with nice carpet and crisp white walls. Many offices led off from the corridor, and we got many looks as we stormed by.

Well, Lincoln stormed by. I just brought up the rear. The looks may be because of me; I did go MIA for some time. For all they knew,

I'd left. Seeing my return prompted suspicious looks, which were war-ranted. Boy, wouldn't I have liked to yell down the hall and say, "Hey assholes, yup, I'm back!"

But I played the part of "I'm a damaged little girl" even though it was difficult.

We reached the end of the corridor and an assistant sat at a desk outside another large door. What the hell was up with this? This is new. Both my bosses have similar offices. Mitchell never used to have his as-sistant outside his office. Unless. Unless, he was promoted. I have missed so much. Lincoln didn't care, he was going to bull his way through.

"Is he in?" Lincoln sternly asked without stopping his approach.

"Yes, sir, but you can't go in there without an appointment. Mr. Johnson is busy now," the assistant stood up and blurted out to Lincoln.

"Well, he'll make time for this," Lincoln answered, opening the door to Mitch's office.

The assistant took one look at me and gasped. She knew who I was, and it had been a long time since we'd seen one another. This was going to happen a lot, so I'd better get used to it.

Lincoln opened the door and strolled in like he owned the place. I, of course followed in his wake, but making sure I wasn't the prime culprit. The brothers had something going on, and I wasn't going to be the first target.

If only. I was the reason they had to reunite—me and Aries.

I shut the door behind us and made sure I stayed in Lincoln's shad-ow. I am not a person to cower behind a man, but this moment wasn't the time to take a stand.

"What the hell?" Mitchell stood up from his chair, not anticipating the intrusion. At first the look on his face was confusion, then migrated to shock.

"Hello, Mitchell," Lincoln said with confidence.

PART II

CHAPTER 14

"LINCOLN."

Mitch's voice finally registered who the intruder was. His own flesh and blood. The look on Mitch's face was priceless. "Who the hell do you think you are barging into my office like that? You think you own the place?" Mitch doesn't usually raise his voice, but the few times I've heard him was directly at his brother...and mostly I was involved somehow.

Fights between brothers usually involve something serious—at least to them—sports, tools, cars, women, the usual stuff. Of course, when I met Mitch, he wasn't into chicks and there would be no fighting over me, not in that manner. Thank God, men can be such idiots when they fight over women. Anyway, Lincoln and I had been seeing each other for about six months when one day I overheard them bickering about something. The brothers are so different there wasn't much they could fight about. Except maybe me. Mitch and I became so close over the years that we could tell each other anything—how good our sex lives were or what clothes to wear. He was my best friend.

So, once I had been having a bad night and instead of going home to Lincoln, I sought out Mitch. I mean, we knew everything about each other, wouldn't you go to the person you trusted the most? Duh! Well, we ended up—or I should say *I* ended up—drinking a little too much wine and I needed a ride home. Mitch offered and I accepted. When we walked in the door, Lincoln was panicked something had happened to me. I was so buzzed I was like, meh, and walked away. Mitchell on the other hand, didn't back down. They bickered about me and how I was Lincoln's problem, blah blah blah. Mitchell ensured I was all right, and I was confident he would make sure no one hurt me, including his brother. Then, Lincoln said the same on the flip side. Oy vey. I'd had enough. I finally spoke up and let the two idiots that I loved most in this world to shut the hell up! I was fine and would stay fine. That was the end that time, but their fights usually occurred around me.

If I didn't like men so much, I'd say fuck 'em.

"Mitchell, I have something you seem to have misplaced." Lincoln turned around to me still clutching the bear.

A gasp came out of Mitchell when he got sight of me. "Jessy, Jess!" Shock echoed in his voice, and he came around his desk to get a better look.

His figure hadn't changed since I saw him last, but he had gotten a little grayer and a few more lines had appeared on his face. He was still my Mitchell and I had missed him.

I stepped forward to Lincoln's side and out of the shadows. "Hello, Mitch." I was trying my best to hold my tone.

"Oh my God! It is you!" Mitch was already on the verge of tears when he practically ran over to me and we embraced. The moment we touched my eyes swelled up. I was so excited to see my best friend and to be home. Don't get me wrong, I love Lincoln with my whole heart, but my love for Mitch was different—best friend and brother. Lincoln was my lover and my best friend, but one thing about Lincoln I could never change, he loved girls and Mitch didn't. So, I got the best of both worlds.

As we hugged with the bear sandwiched between us, I answered, "It's me, I promise it's me," back through teary eyes. "Lincoln helped me get back home." Mitchell let go of me and held me at arm's length.

"Are you okay? I have been so worried about you since you went dark. When contact was lost, it killed me not knowing," Mitch said, babbling on.

"Yes, I will be okay, but so much has happened," I said.

Then I looked up to Lincoln.

"Well, I knew my brother wouldn't be able to stay away." Mitch looked over at Lincoln as well. "Even after I told him to drop the issue."

Lincoln stepped closer to us and said, "Actually, she found me."

I just smiled at him.

"Well, I am glad. No matter how you're back, I'm happy." Mitch shot me a smile, but his eyes were snide toward his brother.

I can't wait until I find out what happened between the two of them.

"Well, I have a present for you." My words pulled Mitchell back to me and I smiled at him through blurry eyes. The cost of Aries was high, and knowing Mitchell, he will want to hear my debrief soon.

Mitchell gave me an inquisitive look as I held out the bear. I handed him the bear and he gazed at it. "Wait. Isn't this the bear Lincoln gave you?"

"Yes, he is. Susan was the last one to have him. She kept him safe until I came to my senses," I answered as Mitch walked over to the other side of his desk and leaned on it. I followed and sat down in one of the visitor chairs. Lincoln followed me over and stood behind me.

"Okay, so why am I holding the bear?" Mitchell asked.

"Susan was clever." I paused and glanced up at Lincoln. As I turned back to Mitch, Lincoln put his hand on my shoulder for reassurance.

His touch helped me hold it together. "Look in the back of the bear and you'll understand."

I watched Mitch turn the bear over and open him up. He was giving me a look that my sanity was failing, but I nudged him on. He got to the battery box and I urged him on. Opening the battery box, a huge smile grew on his face when he looked inside. A good huff came out of him as he nodded his head.

I sat in my seat feeling motionless.

"You found Aries!" Much pleasure was in Mitchell's voice, but I just sat solemnly.

"Yes. Or I should say, Susan did. I followed her clues before the Federation could." I was very cold with my words, for Mitch had no idea what I'd had to sacrifice for this. My body and soul, my sister, my relationship with Lincoln, all for peace. It was all eating me alive. Knowing that Division had Aries now, my time with them will be short. The Federation would soon be after me, and I will be executed for my betrayal. Just like Susan.

"You should be happy about this." Mitch said walking over to the other side of his desk. He sat in this chair. "We have Aries now and you can come home. Why do you look like I just signed your death sentence?"

"I am relieved to be home, but the cost it took to obtain Aries was very high." My emotional strength was starting to fail me, and I chewed my cheek and swallowed my emotions.

"Oh, well I guess we better get a debrief going before we move you." Mitch had turned back into a boss and more serious. "Linx, I am sorry, but I am going to have to ask you to wait outside for a bit."

"Why?" Lincoln's snotty attitude came out. "I was with her for the last week and I know everything that has happened. Anything she says isn't going to faze me." Lincoln raised his voice, annoyed.

"It isn't about what Jess says, it is about her classified assignment, and I need to debrief her. It isn't anything personal, it's my job," Mitch stood up with authority and barked at Lincoln.

"Your job! Your job took her away from me and put us in this mess. Now, she so upset with what happened, that it will take months maybe years to get my Jess back," Lincoln said angrily.

"Yes, Lincoln, I am aware of what happened, and you were not the only one to have her taken away. She is my best friend and your girl-friend. It wasn't my decision," Mitch shot right back. "But right now, I need to do my job and debrief her."

I was saddened with the argument going on between Mitchell and Lincoln. I looked up at Lincoln with sad eyes, knowing what I needed to do. I was an agent and I knew the procedure. Lincoln, being a detec-tive, should know that too.

"Lincoln, it okay. I'll be fine. I'll come find you in a few minutes," I said looking up into his eyes. I knew that what I had to say Lincoln shouldn't hear. It would infuriate him, and right now I needed him with me, not for him to go out seeking revenge.

"Fine, if you are sure."

"I'm sure. I don't think Mitchell will hurt me. And if he does, I know some of his deep dark secrets to use against him." I looked over to Mitch with a smile.

"Okay, I'll wait outside for you," Lincoln answered, patting my shoulder and finally turning to leave.

Once the door was shut, I turned back to look at Mitchell, and he did the same. We both took a deep breath and proceeded with the debrief.

CHAPTER 15

"HE LOVES YOU VERY MUCH." MITCHELL STARTED OFF, breaking our silence.

"Yeah, I got that. It seems you two have something to sort out," I added.

"Nothing that won't be resolved now that you're back."

"What happened after I left?" I pushed wanting answers before we proceeded. I knew Lincoln would give me a blunter explanation, but Mitch would be more detailed. A difference between brothers.

"Well, after you left for California and were hired by the Federation, Lincoln sought me out and wanted answers. There was so much I wanted to tell him, but I had to pick what I could reveal. Of course, my brother was furious that you were picked for the assignment. I tried to explain to him that it wasn't my decision, it was Conrad's." Mitch paused for a second, took a breath, and continued. "Lincoln being Lincoln, stormed out of here pissed off, and last I had heard, he'd left the police department and moved. Where did you find him?"

"That's why he left the department?" I was shocked. Lincoln was so good at being a detective and loved his job. I never would have imagined he'd just up and leave. I suddenly wondered if he was still a cop, in Albuquerque, or if he'd quit altogether. I'd always assumed he'd always carry a gold shield.

"That's what I heard. I lost all forms of communications with him after that. He just dropped off the map." Mitch was a little baffled.

"I found him on the outskirts of Albuquerque." Still processing the information Mitch had said.

"Albuquerque. Wow, he was out to find you. I never would have thought he'd go out there. Knowing him he found information on the Federation and would get as close as he could."

"I never knew. Susan was the one who found him, and I just followed her guidance."

"Well, I'm glad she did because that means we have you back and mission completed. But anyway, shall we begin your debrief before we both get a little more emotional?" Mitch was my emotional friend; he was starting to fall apart.

"Yeah, I have a feeling we'll be catching up more now. You won't be able to get rid of my ugly rug." My comical comment wasn't so comical. But Mitch grinned at it.

"You can count on it." He took out a iPhone so we would be official and on the record. I didn't want to spill my guts, but I couldn't keep it all hidden forever.

Mitch pushed the record button. "This is Mitchell Johnson debriefing Jessy Connors. Please tell me about your undercover assignment with the Federation."

"Well..." Here I go. My sordid truth was about to become public, and I was sweating like a pig. "My assignment was to infiltrate the corporation known as the Federation, work my way up the ranks to become friendly with the man they call the Emissary. My assignment was to make sure they "the Federation" never acquired the device known as Aries. I made my way in with a contact."

"Who was this contact?"

"My contact was my sister Susan. She had worked for the Federation for a sometime and help move me up in ranks quickly with her influence. She had taken the name Susan Bowman, and with us being twin sisters, my alias was Jessy Bowman. As Jessy Bowman, I became the Emissary's new favorite toy. With the advice of my sister, if I wanted to get close, I had to be a willing sacrifice."

"What do you mean, sacrifice?" Mitch asked.

"I had to be willing to do anything the Emissary wanted. Which meant...anything." I paused. Even with my best friend sitting across from me, whom I have told everything, I was ashamed.

"Anything?"

"Yes, anything. I had my first interview, and with my skills, I could sense what he was thinking. Eyes say a lot. So, I had to let the Emissary..." Deep breath. "I had to let him rape me. I lost a piece of my soul that day, and from that day on, I learned how to weasel my way closer to him. The Emissary wasn't a man you say no to, I learned very quickly." I hung my head down shamefully.

"I moved up in the ranks quickly with small assignments, but every time I got something, I had to give something. With my ability to interpret, I worked my magic."

Mitch and I went on with the debrief for about another half hour before my brain had turned to mush. I needed a break, and Mitch could sense it. All the of the information and discussion was becoming overwhelming, especially the sexual encounters with the Emissary. We only touched briefly on the capture of my sister and how her clues lead me to the discovery of the Aries device. I was glad Mitch didn't push this topic more now.

Her death was so still recent and vivid in my brain; I wasn't sure if I'd be able to hold it together if I talked about it.

"I think we can pick this up tomorrow," Mitchell finally said, and I blew out a sigh of thankfulness.

We both got up and proceeded to the door. Opening the door, who did we find pacing? None other than Lincoln. He glared at us as we came out into the waiting area. I can only assume he was driving Mitchell's assistant crazy by the look she was giving us.

Mitchell looked at him and back to me. "I can take you home now. We can pick this up tomorrow."

I nodded my head in agreement...then the word lit my brain up like lightning. Home! The only home I had was the Federation home. The loft I used to have in D.C. was long gone.

"Home?" I inquired to Mitchell.

"Yeah, home," he answered with a reassuring grin.

Half an hour later, we walked up the stairs of a three-story apartment building. I had gone up these stairs hundreds of time; they were the stairs that had led me to a loft apartment at the end of the hall on the top floor. I was just out of college and Division's orientation, I was dirt broke, when I stumbled upon this place. It wasn't much, but I fell in love with it. The place had been offered as a rent to own deal when I signed the lease, and within a few short months, the owner asked if I would like to potentially purchase the place. Of, course I would. A place of my own, hell yeah. I made sure he knew my predicament. It was the last apartment at the end of the building, and I took advantage of the location. You'll see when we walk in. How in the hell was it still here? With my absence and Lincoln leaving too, this place should be gone.

Mitch opened the door using none other than my old set of keys. I knew that from the key chain he held. It was an old metal spoon from Ben & Jerry's ice cream place in Vermont. When I graduated high school, Susan and I went on a road trip to anywhere. And that was one of the places we stopped. I had a bad habit of buying key chains from just about everywhere I visited. Some people collect shot glasses, coffee mugs, T-shirts. Me, I collected key chains. I was an odd duck. Anyway, the spoon key chain was tarnished, and I was one of the few who could still pick out the worn colors on the ice cream at the end of the spoon.

I was allowed entry first and a gasp came over me. My place—sorry, *our* place, yes, Lincoln lived here too. It hadn't changed from the last time I was here. I put my hand over my mouth in disbelief. Scanning the room, I saw all our pictures were right where they had been, and the moss green blanket was still on the back of the couch. Everything was as it had been. It just had a musty smell.

"Mitch, how is this possible?" I asked, recollecting myself.

"Well, when you were reassigned to California and Lincoln left, I kept your place. I knew someday you'd come home, and wouldn't want some stranger's place, but home." He tapped the key in my hand. "While you both were gone, I'd come by once a week and make sure the place was still standing. Seeing pictures helped remind me that someday you'd come home." Mitch took a deep breath. "I needed re-assurance that my best friend would come back." His voice faltered slightly. He'd had it rough in my absence too.

So, as you walked in, the kitchen is to your right. It's small but it has a counter with a stove and room to prep food. The opposite side had the sink, dishwasher, and fridge. A dining table was on the left side of the entrance door, with the living area behind that. It was a favorite spot of mine. Between the fireplace and the balcony, it was a tough choice. The mantel held my same pictures. Many of Lincoln and me, a few of Mitch and Lincoln, Susan and me, and one of all of us. I grew up in a household with very few photos. There was so much resentment from my dad toward my mom, he'd never wanted anything that re-minded him of her. We had been part of that reminder. So, no pictures.

But when I moved away, I made sure I had pictures everywhere of the people most dear to me. Notice, dad nor mom aren't here.

I gazed at all my photos as I slowly walked around. I didn't want to miss a thing. It had been far too long. A quick glance out my window to the balcony, and I continued. Lincoln and Mitchell were just a blur to me in the doorway; they were there but not. Heading to my small bathroom, I peeked in, and everything was still there, as if I had only left for the weekend. Behind the bathroom was a spare room we had used for an office and storage. It did have a twin bed against the wall in case someone had to stay. Unfortunately, there was no door. I had put up a shower rod and a cloth shower curtain to conceal the room. It never had a door and I didn't feel the need to add one. Finally, I came to the stairs that led to my loft bedroom. They were wrought iron stairs, and one of my favorite parts of my place.

I ascended the stairs to see my bed was all made, dressers with draws shut, and on top of the dresser was my usual running attire. I wasn't a heavy runner when I left for the Federation, just occasionally went for a run. But as I got deeper into the Federation the mental and physical wear was trying, so I found running to be my outlet; my release from the pain I had to hide. Staring at the sneakers, I realized this was a time for some release. The last few days had been horrendous, and I was due. Lately, running was the only way I knew how. Taking the initiative, I changed into my capris and T-shirt and laced up my old friends. The clothes were a tad too big, but my sneakers were perfect. Right now, I was going to run. Even my old iPod and headphones still had life.

Trotting down the stairs, ready to leave, I walked into two very strange looks.

"Where do you think you're going?" Lincoln asked me.

"I'm going for a run," I announced to both Mitch and Lincoln. The looks I got in return were far from pleasant. Mostly they were, "Over our dead bodies, you are."

Mitch, the smooth talker said, "Right now, I don't think that is wise. Not until you have someone with you."

"Excuse me?" I was beyond pissed. I had to have a babysitter to go for a run. Did either of them realize what my life has been like? *Pure hell.* And right now, I needed to run. "What gives you the right to stop me? I have been through a hell of a lot more than the two of you will ever know, and I now need a babysitter to go running. Fuck you!" My disciple began to crumble; I was about to blow.

"We want to keep you safe," Mitch put in.

"Safe? I have been on my own for months and had to deal with everything myself. I had no protection. The only way I was able to keep going was to run. Living through being someone's sex toy, torture, and watching the things I have or done, I had to find a way to cope. So here it is. After this week, I need to run."

I was about to screaming level when I pushed past the men to the door.

"If you two are going to try and stop me, I suggest you lock me up. Because God only knows how long I will have before the Emissary comes after to me and brutally kills me. I will be lucky if it's a week. So, screw you both, I'm going for a run." I opened the door and slammed it shut behind me, leaving Mitchell and Lincoln in disarray.

I plugged my headphones in and found my bad day mix. Loud pounding music pulsed into my ears and I headed down the stairs before the boys could catch me. Pushing open the door, I turned up the music and hit the pavement sprinting. My feet pounded the ground and I went as fast as I could go. Any thoughts in my head disappeared.

After forty-five minutes of running, drenched in sweat, I returned to the loft. Knowing the brothers, if I was gone too long, they'd hunt me down. My reason came back after about thirty minutes of running, and I felt like a new person. I panted as I stood outside my building, catching my breath before heading up. Not knowing what I was going to walk into, I prepared my brain for anything as I trotted up the stairs. I opened the door and what I saw amazed me. Lincoln and Mitch were talking to each other, not at each other.

I strolled right in as if nothing had ever happened. They both look up at me in surprise, not sure what to think.

"Well, I'm glad to see the two of you are speaking again," I interrupted them as I walked over to the fridge and grabbed a bottle of water.

"Yes, we are." Lincoln answered.

"So, what are you guys going to do with me?" I asked, taking a swig of water.

"We have a plan." Lincoln paused. "We are going to kill you!"

Holy shit, that wasn't what I was expecting.

CHAPTER 16

"Excuse me?" I was in disbelief. They are going to kill me, and they weren't joking either. Both faces were painted seriously.

"You heard me," Lincoln said.

Mitch stepped forward and took control of the situation before Lincoln and I came to blows.

"Well, actually, we are going to kill Jessy Bowman and her associate." Mitch said.

"Ah. You're going to kill Jessy Bowman? Huh!" I thought for a second and took another swig of my water. "Well, I am Jessy Bowman, so I guess you're right, you're going to kill me."

"We are not actually going to kill you, of course. We are going to kill the Federation version of you to keep Jessy Connors safe."

Mitch had a plan, or the brothers had a plan. Well, at least they were working together.

"The Federation has many outlets," I said. "They will see right through whatever plan you have in mind. I know, I have been there. We found people who thought they were invisible."

Lincoln decided to come into our conversation. "Well, if you die and there is no way to confirm the body, then how will they find you?"

"Linx and I have come up with a plan for both of you to be killed in a freak accident. They happen every day, and you just happen to be at the wrong place at the wrong time." Mitch was giving me the blow by blow.

"Okay, let's hear this plan." I will admit I was curious.

"A news bulletin will be release about an eighteen-wheeler having a tire blow, losing control and crash. The crash will have taken the lives of two people traveling whose car was unable to avoid the crash. Their vehicle crashed into the eighteen-wheeler and burst into flames. Nobody survives and the few identifying marks left will identify the body of one Jessy Bowman. A high advisor to the Federation." Mitch described his plan, but I still wasn't completely convinced.

"Your plan sounds good, but how are you going to get the evidence to pull this off? It will take a lot of preparation."

"If you haven't forgotten, we are Division, and I will make it happen. We have an agent whose life is in potential danger and we will work to correct that. If that means we need to blow up an eighteen-wheeler, then we will. Plus, I haven't gotten to play much lately. Should be fun." Mitchell was always the smart one and I could tell from the expression on his face, he was completely serious.

I set my water down on the countertop a nodded my okay. Let's hope Mitch can pull this off, or I will have very little time left on this planet. "Okay, what can I do to help?" I was going to be involved.

"Nothing," Lincoln said.

"Nothing?" I questioned.

"Yes, Jess, nothing. I need you to take care of you right now. You will have an escort at all times when you leave the loft, even for running." Mitch was now in boss mode. I was about to protest but he kept going. "There will be someone downstairs around the clock until we get this situation under control."

"So, I am to be babysat, is what you're saying?"

"Yes, for now, until we know you are out of the woods. You are also ordered to mandatory therapy once a day until you are cleared." Mitch walked over to me and put his hand on my arm. "I am not trying to punish you. It took some convincing for Conrad to let me have this much. I need you, and I will get you through this." Mitch looked over to Lincoln for confirmation. "We both will. All right?"

I relented. "Sure, yeah, okay. But please keep me updated. I don't like being in the dark or lied to."

How could I have agreed to this? The plan was crazy, and now I was to sit back and let it all happen with no involvement. I had been part of the plans during my whole service to the Emissary and now I was rock bottom. This sucks!

"I'm not lying to you, and I of course will keep you informed." Mitch answered and hugged me. "I have to go, but we will get through this. I promise." He pulled back and turned to walk out the door. He glanced in Lincoln's direction but said nothing.

Both Lincoln and I watched Mitchell walk out and then looked at each other.

"You can go too." I ordered. All I wanted was solitude right now. And possibly a shower.

"Is it true?" Lincoln asked, ignoring my order.

"Is what true?" I asked.

"What you said the Federation did to you?" His eyes showed concern and sadness.

Oh. That. "Yeah, it is." I answered with shame. It hurt to admit.

Lincoln walked closer to me. His face was hard to read. I couldn't tell if he was disappointed or upset with me. "I wish..." He paused.

"Why didn't you just leave? If they treat people like that..." His voice was starting to break. It saddened him what had been done to me.

"I was in too deep. Once it all took place, I had gained recognition from the Emissary and couldn't leave. I was alone with all this on my shoulders, and I used every advantage I could to move up in the ranks," I admitted, but held my eyes down.

Lincoln was the last person I wanted to explain this to. Mitch had let it slip that Lincoln had left to come look for me. If I had gotten wind of that months ago, I wouldn't have asked him for help now.

"Once I was in, I couldn't get out until I'd completed my assignment," I added, bringing my eyes up to investigate Lincoln's.

Lincoln leaned his forehead to mine and held it there for a few moments. "I would've protected you, or at least been there for support. I could have helped."

I pulled my head back to look at him. "I couldn't risk your life. No one should have to go through any of that, and if they'd found out I had you, they would have killed you." My voice at a breaking point. I needed to regain myself and cut the emotional shit. That is one thing the Federation did to me, it made me strong and rid me of my emotions.

Lincoln didn't say a word, and he didn't have to. I could see what he was feeling, and it was breaking my heart.

"I am going to take a shower now." I retreated from Lincoln's space and turned to go. "Feel free to let yourself out."

I was walking over to the bathroom when I looked back at him. His face was sad, and I wanted to embrace him. Instead, I headed into the bathroom. "In case you had forgotten, I live here too." Lincoln called out and I turned at the door frame to respond.

"I'm sorry." My heart truly meant it, and I shut the door.

CHAPTER 17

A FEW DAYS PASSED AND I HAD BEEN ASSIGNED AGENTS TO watch me. I knew all of them, some better than others. My longtime friend Reilly O'Grady was part of my detail. During the day, if I needed to leave the loft, he went with me. I usually only left the loft when I went to my therapy session or to run. The first couple days, I was a huge pain in the ass toward my protection. In the mornings early, I snuck out to go running. As a teen, I'd learned the tricks of evading my father.

I would sneak out through windows or just wait until he was drunk enough to forget or pass out. I was only caught a few times and the consequences were severe. So, I learned from my mistakes and was more cautious.

It didn't take long for Mitch to hear about my escapes. On day three of my potential evasion, I was able to sneak past Lincoln, who had taken to sleeping in the small spare room bed, and out the door, when I was caught red-handed. Sam Maxwell, whom everyone called Max, met me at the door at 5:30am and informed me if I tried that trick again, I'd be locked away.

Sure. Believe it when I see it. But once I examined Max more carefully, I saw he was dressed in running gear. A smile stretched across my face. Max was doing me a favor and became my running partner.

Sam Maxwell. What can I tell you about him? Oh yeah, years ago he'd had feelings for me and asked me out. But cute as Max is, I was already taken. He wasn't unattractive to look at by any means, and he was in unbelievable shape. He had another one of those baby faces that I can't resist, with short cut sandy brown hair and very soft brown eyes. No question, if Lincoln hadn't scooped me up first, Max would have had no problem. Built like a brick shit house, who knows what he could do. But as I said, Lincoln got to me first, so Max and I became friends. He never came out and actually ask me out; he didn't want to put a damper on our friendship. In fact, we tended to challenge each other. We both like to run, so we often teamed up for races. It was nice having a running buddy. Lincoln wasn't much for running, so Max pushed me.

Anyway, after my third escape attempt, Max and I set out every morning around 5:30, and at first, he let me go full out. He did keep up with me and even challenged me. I had been running so much in the last few months that every challenge felt revitalizing. It is the best feeling after a workout. My body and mind were clear, and my thoughts were returning to me with guidance. I think Max felt the same way; we both had the same glow—workout glow, get your mind out of the gutter—you get afterward a hard workout. Only the thoughts going through his brain were a lot different compared to mine.

We made sure we stretched and said our goodbyes for the day. Neither he nor I knew if I'd see him again that day. Reilly swapped out with him. I was thankful Mitch had put together a team of agents that I knew and trusted. Newbies, I would have picked apart and spit them back out. I can be rather crude.

I made my way back up the stairs to the loft, and from outside the door, I could smell it.

One of my most favorite smells of all. Coffee! Lincoln usually had it made before I returned from running. Never did I ask him to, he just did it, and I made sure I thanked him every time. The poor man had been through so much, and I had been a huge bitch to him, but I am trying. Between the lack of sleep, constant watching, and therapy, I was a little on the bitter side.

Opening the door, the aroma lifted me to another world. Ah, my favorite! And to my surprise, Mitch was here, drinking coffee with Lincoln. Wow! They both turned as I came in, sweat and all, they looked up one side and down the other. I guess I looked rather ravishing, ah yeah, not! Being drawn to the coffee, I bypassed both and helped myself to a cup. Just like yesterday, and the day before, and practically every day, I inhaled the aroma and fell into nothingness.

"Coffee-gasm?" Mitch asked me with a smile and a twinkle in his eyes.

With a deep breath, I answered, "Mmmm! You know it."

"I guess some things never change," Mitch said with a chuckle. "You have done that for as long as I can remember, and it is still amusing to watch."

"I will do it until I die or there is no more coffee!" I remarked.

Both Lincoln and Mitch chuckled at my comment.

I was coming off my coffee-gasm, opened my eyes, and looked over to the boys. "So, Mitch, what brings you here this early? I can't believe you are here to make fun of me."

"As much as I missed your reaction to coffee, I came by to bring you this." Mitch took a newspaper from in front of Lincoln and slapped it down.

The headline of the front page— *Shit!* It read:

Second IN Command To Federation Killed In Car Crash

Holy shit, he did it!

I continued reading.

> *Tuesday, an eighteen-wheeler vehicle blew a back tire, losing control of the rig, resulting in a multi-vehicle crash on the highway. Many injuries came about, but only two fatalities. After their vehicle was struck, it burst into flames and both occupants were unable to make it out. Later, evidence showed the deceased was a Federation second in command, Jessy Bowman, and an associate who has not been able to be identified. Only partial remains were able to identify the body, but with the help of dental records, it was a positive identification. The vehicle and its contents were a total loss. The Federation has given no comment at this time on the situation.*

Holy shit was right! Mitch had really given me an out. But my gut was telling me the Emissary wasn't going to buy it until he performed his own investigation.

I looked up at the brothers with some excitement and slight hesitation. The article went on regarding the crash and details of the blown tire. Mitch had done a fantastic job, and the article was very believable. If I didn't know what the circumstances were, I'd be totally convinced by this article that two people had died in the crash.

My grin emerged into a smile. I was speechless. I could feel two sets of eyes gazing at me.

"I thought you might want to read that," Mitch commented, taking a sip of coffee.

"Yes, thank you. I am not sure what to say." I was not the kind of person to be speechless, but I was now.

"This gives you your life back and we can move on. And maybe you can actually get your real hair back." Lincoln was confident with the getting back to normal thing, and the *we* can move on part. The comment about my hair, well, Jessy Bowman dyed her hair much lighter to blend in. I am a much darker redhead, not a strawberry. Lincoln has never been a fan of blondes. He always said they look fake.

"Ha ha," was my reaction to the hair remark. I shifted my body more toward Mitch. "So, does this mean I can actually go out by myself? No more escorts?" Fingers crossed.

"No. Until we know the Federation is satisfied with these findings, we can't risk your safety. I'm sorry." Mitch's explanation was sound, but I was still disappointed.

"It was just a thought. But I understand. Knowing the Emissary, the way I do, he will be pissed off and will conduct his own investigation. Losing Aries will set his world into upheaval. I wouldn't want to be anywhere near him when he finds out." My disappointment was palpable, but I understood why I wasn't out of the woods yet. Aries was safe, but with myself as a traitor, I was not safe. At least Jessy Bowman was dead...for now.

Mitch took a last swallow of coffee and put the cup in the sink. "I know this isn't easy, but this is good news. The rest is precautionary. I don't want to risk losing you again."

"I know. I'll be okay." I gave Mitch a smile, but it was a halfhearted smile.

Mitch came up and hugged me, "We'll get through this, I promise."

I nodded to him, and Mitch started toward the door while Lincoln and I held our positions.

"Oh. And Reilly won't be around today."

"So, I get out of therapy?" Please!

"I'm afraid not."

Damn!

"Another person has been assigned. Reilly had an engagement with his daughter."

"Understandable. He deserves time with his daughter after dealing with me. Who is the poor schmuck with me today?" I didn't need some newbie.

Mitch looked over to Lincoln. I followed his eyes.

"Looks like you are stuck with me," Lincoln said.

Another smile from Mitch and he grasped my arm, leaving. "Please don't kill each other!" And he was gone.

I glanced over to Lincoln, and he was trying to hide a smile while drinking his coffee. I returned to my coffee and we both held the silence for a moment. "How did you get so lucky to have me today?"

"I volunteered," Lincoln answered bluntly.

"Well, I have to be at Kirkman's office soon, so I'm going to shower." I was changing the subject.

"Yeah, sure." Lincoln seemed nervous. I headed toward the bathroom when Lincoln's words halted me. "If it's all right with you, after your session, I thought we could spend some time together. Just the two of us. Celebrate a bit."

I was taken aback by his words, but I understood his nervousness. "Sure, sounds nice!"

CHAPTER 18

ONCE I HAD COMPLETED MY SHOWER, I FOUND A NICE comfortable dress to put on. Since I had come back from my run, I could feel the temperature had risen and the sun was shining bright. I had the jitters badly. I have no idea why I was so nervous. This was the first time since I came home that I will be with Lincoln for pleasure. Not that! But spending time with him. We used to do it all the time, I am not sure why now I would rather crawl up in a hole and hide.

Lincoln dropped me off at Dr. Kirkman's office about forty-five minutes later and would return in about the same time. I gave him my thanks and headed in.

Dr. Suzanna Kirkman was the therapist I was assigned to. Of course, she was, and guess what? We have history. Shocking! Suzanna and I went to college together and were in multiple classes together. We even competed for top of our psychology classes. She came out on top and got her pick of jobs. Even though the race was neck and neck, I was the better loser (ha ha, no not really). We had very different techniques. I would analyze people by their expressions, which is a rare skill to have. Suzanna was your norm. I went on to the Division and she didn't. I think there are times she envies me, but in this situation with her as my counsel, I think she made the right decision. I am so fucked up in the head, some days I don't know what I've been through or done.

She was also a very attractive woman. But with her curt attitude, it put her across to the world as a bitch. Kirkman had an hourglass frame with many curves. Her shoulder length hair made her face round and brought the features of her face out. It was the cut for her. A light brush of makeup and glasses made her professional. Suzanna Kirkman could easily scare someone from her scowl. Not me, she is all talk.

Dr. Kirkman was briefed on my situation. About the Federation and all my experiences. Talking about them isn't the easiest. I have only been to a few sessions, but knowing the drills and methods of therapy, I wasn't impressed. I didn't want to relive the abuse. It was hard enough the first time, and now it was even harder. Knowing my experiences and coping, I should be in a psych ward. I am so glad I am not in Dr. Kirkman's shoes right now. I am a horrible patient.

Kirkman's office was your typical office. Lots of books, a couch, couple chairs and a desk. Like most therapist offices it wasn't a place people wanted to be. And for me, I was ordered. If it was my office, I would want to feel comfortable and homey so people can relax and be honest. Yeah, not here. When I came into her office, she could automatically tell I was nervous. I mean, how couldn't you? I just had to get through this hour and then the rest of the day.

I can hide later.

"Good morning, Jess. You look very nice today," Kirkman said with a smile. Sometimes, I just wish people would just say what they wanted to say, their faces and body language do.

"Good morning, Suzanna." I said I pleasantly even though I really didn't want to be here.

"Thank you. The weather is beautiful, so I thought I'd enjoy it."

Kirkman gestured me to come in and sit down. I wasn't a lie down kind of person, so we sat in the armchairs. Uncomfortable ones at that. I tried to get situated but my nerves wouldn't let me settle. At first, we caught up on the day before and how my night was last night. This was our usual opening discussion, where I must go once every day for two weeks, get evaluated, and then I get downgraded to two to three times a week. Yeah, go me! I explained that I was still having nightmares and waking at any point in the night. But every morning I was up with the sun and ready to run off my horror.

It was about halfway through our session when Kirkman changed topics almost mid-thought. "You are looking very nervous and apprehensive today. What's going through your mind?" she asked me very bluntly.

I wasn't sure what to say or where to start. I was used to most questions, but this one caught me off guard. "My normal routine for the last couple days was changed this morning, and I am very apprehensive on how the rest of my day proceed," I admitted, but without giving too many details.

"Why has it changed?" Shrink talk.

"My normal person wasn't able to be here today, so I have a different one."

"And who is the substitute?"

"Lincoln." One word and I was done.

I wish.

"Lincoln. Lincoln is *on duty* this afternoon." Kirkman used finger quotes when she said on duty.

"Yes, he volunteered to help out. He asked me if we could spend some time together. Just the two of us." My voice was becoming unsettled.

"And why do you act as if this is a bad thing? He used to be your person, your lover and best friend. Why is spending time together such a bad thing?" Kirkman was curious.

"I don't know!" I got up and walked around the cramped office. "I am unsure what he will think of me."

"Why? From what I have heard from you, and from Mitchell when he encouraged me to take your case, Lincoln loves you very much."

"I believe he still does but..." I stopped to catch my breath. "I think he will see me differently after he realizes I am now damaged goods." A bubble caught in my throat as I got out the last two words. It was the first time I admitted out loud that I felt like damaged goods.

I was damaged, and I didn't want him to have to deal with the emotional stress I have.

"Yes, you have been through a great ordeal, but I saw the look in his eyes when he dropped you off. He loves you, and I don't think he sees any of what you see. I believe he sees his lover, his person, as very lost. Wishing he could help," Kirkman explained.

"I just don't want him to get hurt." Tears started welling up in my eyes. "The Federation will punish me when they find me, and I would die a thousand deaths if they did anything to him. I already lost my sister. If they took Lincoln or Mitchell, what's the point?"

"Lincoln and Mitchell are adults and can make their own choices. They have chosen to stand with you. I truly believe they feel the same way you do. They would sacrifice their lives for you. Now, they want you to come back into their lives."

"They don't need to know about the cruelty and abuse. It would tear them apart. I don't think I could stand it." My face was wet from my tears.

"How do they feel seeing you?"

"I don't know. Their expressions have been muted lately. Lincoln often looks sad, and Mitch is conflicted."

"Why do you think that is?"

"I won't let them in," I admitted, and let my head fall.

"When a loved one sees another loved one in distress, they are drawn to help. Lincoln is hurting just as much, and he won't give up until he knows you are recovering." Kirkman was just hitting all the right spots. Damn her, I don't like crying in therapy.

I lifted my gaze up to the ceiling and put my hands on my hips for a moment. I needed to collect myself. After a couple deep breaths, I looked at Kirkman. "What should I do?"

"I think you know what you need to do," she answered.

"I need to let them in. But I fear what will happen."

"Take one step at a time. Take the afternoon and just roll with it. Try to relax, enjoy the day. You never know what will happen, and Lincoln may be just as nervous as you." Biting down on my lip and nodding my head, I agreed with Kirkman. But I was still terrified.

We spent the rest of our time just calmly talking about nothing. I trying to calm my nerves and relax for the afternoon. Before I knew it, Kirkman was showing me to the door. "Jess, try and have a good afternoon with Lincoln. Remember what we talked about. I want an update tomorrow." She gave me a smile and I was out the door.

Today was turning out especially hard...and the day was just beginning.

CHAPTER 19

LINCOLN WAS LEANING ON THE MUSTANG WAITING FOR me. He was scanning the area and was looking mighty fine in his sunglasses. When he realized I was approaching, he stood up and stepped over to me.

"How did it go?" Lincoln asked.

"Just like every day. We talk, I cry, and we move on. Same ol', same ol'" I replied. The gentleman that he was, Lincoln opened the door to the Mustang for me. Top down of course. I hopped in and Lincoln closed me in. Once he was in the driver's seat, we set off. I had no idea where.

We had driven about half an hour when I asked, "Where are we going?"

"You'll see." Short and sweet. Lincoln wasn't giving away nothing.

Five minutes later, we drove into a small town that nestled along the oceanfront. It was a breathtaking sight. All the colors of the ocean and beaches brighten up my day. I smiled behind my sunglasses and enjoyed all of Mother Nature's beauty. We parked and both exited the car. It was nice to go on a drive but even better to stop. The view took my racing mind away and I was enveloped in it.

"Come on," Lincoln called out to me with an outstretched hand.

Kirkman said I needed to try, and as much as it unnerved me, I took Lincoln's hand, and we walked down to the shore.

Reaching the beach's edge, I had the urge to take off my flip-flops and let my feet sink between the sand. Removing them, Lincoln look down at me with a smile, and it was a smile of happiness. He looked much more relaxed than I felt, but I was rolling with the punches. Years ago, we would do this kind of thing—drive until we found a small town and just stroll. It was our time to do nothing, not think of work and just be Jessy and Lincoln. Today seemed like a flashback to one of our trips. Lincoln in his lightweight pants and white cotton button down, and me in a summer dress. Time just seem to revert. I picked up my sandals and took Lincoln's hand, and we strolled down the beach.

I admired everything around me and how simple it was. Kirkman is a hardass and a pain in my butt but I believe she was right about giving in and not letting my fear consume me. I need this kind of nothingness to clear my head.

"Hey, whatcha thinking?" Lincoln asked, halting our stroll.

"About nothing, about everything," was my response. I lowered myself to the sand and sat with my ass down and knees up. Lincoln sat down beside me. He sat close enough, but not all over me.

"Actually, I was thinking about..." I paused.

He looked at me, urging me to go on. "It's okay. You don't have to tell me."

Yes, I do. I thought. You need to know.

I looked over at him. "I was thinking about how life would be right now if I hadn't miscarried. What our lives would be like. Have you ever thought about it?"

"Yeah, I think about it every day. I thought about it more after you left, wondering what I had done to push you away. And if our kid would be here with us now, playing in the sand or bouncing in the waves. It hurts to think of what might have been."

Truth was coming out of Lincoln, and I owed him the same.

Pursing my lips together I nodded in agreement. "I think about it all the time too. I blame myself for not being able to hold on. If I had, life would be so...unbelievable. I wish it hadn't happened, and that he would be here now with us. Instead, I suffer from PTSD from the hands of the Federation, and it will most likely ruin me. If they don't kill me first."

Seconds passed before Lincoln responded. "The Federation can't control you anymore not with me around. We will get through this, together. I'm not going anywhere." His worlds melted my heart.

He had moved closer, with his arm propping him up behind me, but his body was fully exposed to me.

"I know, I'm just scared. I would never forgive myself if something happened to you, or to Mitchell. I already lost my sister; I can't lose you too." My truths were opening, and I tried so hard to keep it together.

Lincoln's hand wrapped around my back and he cradle me with assurance. I leaned into him and lay my head on his chest. His head rested on mine, and then he began to rub my back.

Moments passed and finally Lincoln broke the silence. "You said he would be with us." He looked down at me. "You thought the baby was a boy?"

"Yeah, I did. He was going to be the spitting image of his dad."

"Did this handsome little man have a name?"

"Ray." I smiled sadly. "Ray because he was my little ray of sunshine. It always brightened my day thinking about when he'd get here."

"Ray, huh? Not a bad name. But what if he ended up being a she? A little one like you."

"Rayna. I bet she would give her daddy a run for his money." I chuckled, thinking how Lincoln would react to a girl. But I truly believed I would have had a boy.

"Many guns!" He smiled and pulled me back into his embrace.

It was safe in his arms and felt the tension finally letting go.

After a while of just sitting in the sand, we got up and strolled some more, hand in hand. It was nice and relaxing to escape our—my—troublesome lives, and we even played tourist for a while. I went into a small shop and bought a book. A real book with pages, not on a screen.

When I came out, Lincoln asked "So, did you get anything interesting?"

"A book." I was quite tickled with my purchase.

"A book?" Lincoln was not impressed.

But I was so proud that I handed him my bag to show him what it was.

He pulled out my book and smirked. "Harry Potter! You got a Harry Potter book?"

"I wanted to get as far away from this reality as I could. No murder mysteries or romance, but something that wasn't real. So, Harry Potter it was." I beamed with delight.

Lincoln just smiled and shook his head. I giggled at his reaction.

We continued stroll and Lincoln went off without me for a moment. What was he up to? I could still see him, but his back was turned so I couldn't scope out the situation. Ever so briefly, he'd turn back and make sure I was still waiting. Finally, he turned and approached me with two different ice cream cones. Another one of my weaknesses. It wasn't as powerful as coffee, but it was a close second.

"Why Mr. Matthews, is one of those for me?" I asked like a little schoolgirl on her first date.

"It could be." Lincoln took a massive lick off one cone and then the other. My mouth gaped. He saw the expression on my face and almost spit out the ice cream. I giggled again. Then he handed me one. Even though it had yucky boy cooties on it, I licked it anyway. Besides, I liked Lincoln's cooties.

Ah, chocolate. My favorite! It was so dark and creamy, there was no other kind. "You remembered my flavor."

"There are two things that have been lasered into my brain about you, which I will never forget." It was if Lincoln was making a speech.

I just proudly licked my ice cream. "Oh yeah?" I asked with a whole lot of sarcasm.

"Yeah, and those two things are...drum roll please...coffee and chocolate." Lincoln bowed with these final words. He was so cute when he played around.

I laughed more. He was so funny. With my laugh, Lincoln's eyes twinkled and his face glowed. He was filled with what? Happiness? I hadn't seen it for such a long time, I had to process this.

Suddenly, he went blank.

I lowered my ice cream, caught off guard from him expression change. "What? What did I do?"

"You laughed," he said softly.

"You were funny," I answered.

He moved in closer to me, inches away. "No, *you* laughed. The real you. My Jess came out, and it took my breath away."

Ah, he is so sweet.

He leaned in and kissed me, very gently. When he pulled away, only inches from my face, he said, "Don't let her slip away."

I put my free hand on his face and said, "I am working on that."

I looked into his eyes and could see pain reflected in them. It was never my intention to hurt him, but the result was, I had. I have a lot of ground to make up.

He nodded and touched his forehead to mine.

It wasn't long before we needed to head back to the city. It would be getting dark soon, and I was anxious to be back in my safe zone at the loft. Plus, I was exhausted. Usually during the day, I get time to take a nap. They are only brief, but I can sleep some. Between the night terrors and running, my body feels as if the plug had been pulled.

The ride back to the city didn't seem to take as long as the ride out and once we were back at the loft, my anxiety level reduced some. We had a great day and it was what the doctor ordered. I was relieved that the day went to well and been nervous for no reason. Maybe I believed he wouldn't accept me after all the horror I'd been through. I felt damaged, and those who are damaged usually get pushed aside or thrown out. Lincoln didn't do that and is assisting to repair my damage.

With all my activities of the day, my body was exhausted. All I wanted was to curl up and not move. Coffee wasn't even going to help. Shocking, I know. Coffee is the cure all drug for me. Not this time. Almost as soon as the door shut, I took my book over to the couch and curled up. Lincoln sensed my exhaustion and never said a word. It had hit me like a ton of bricks. Even though the book was one I had read many times, I was thrilled to be reading it again. Harry and his friends would help my mind escape from the nightmares of my life.

As the pages turned, my mind tuned into the world of Hogwarts, and before I knew it, Lincoln came over to me.

"Is it all right if I sit with you?"

"Sure." I sat up enough for him to sit down.

Lincoln sat down, and like a broken record, he lifted his arm and I settled back against his chest. He then put his arm around me, and I continued reading as if nothing had ever changed. This was our usual nightly routine before I left. I'd read leaning back against him, and he'd find something to watch on TV. Even though we hadn't done this for ages, it still felt like the right spot to be in. I relaxed for the first time in a long time. Like really relaxed, which is hard for me to do. There is always something I need to do instead.

I'm not sure how long we lay like that, but I sensed myself drifting off. I felt Lincoln's arm around me rub my arm, and it was comforting. With my heavy eyes, I let my book fall onto my lap and sank into a deep sleep. My body had given in and my mind went blank. My brain was fried from the day, but now I felt as if I was floating. Almost as if I was high on drugs and just floating around like a cloud. Until I realized what was going on. Still mostly asleep, I wrapped my arms around Lincoln's neck as he carried me up the stairs to bed.

I was done for the day.

CHAPTER 20

SUDDENLY, I BOLTED UPRIGHT IN BED, GASPING FOR AIR. I was drowning and I couldn't get enough oxygen in my lungs. Wheezing and gasping to the point of hyperventilation, and it scared the shit out of me. I began to cough as if I had taken water into my lungs. Mini screams escaped though my coughs and gasps. Moments later, Lincoln bustled up the stairs. I saw him but I couldn't focus on him. I need to get as much oxygen in as I could, or I'd drown.

"Hey, hey, it's okay. You're dreaming," he called out to me as he sat down on the edge of the bed. All I could do was look at him, panic taking over.

"I'm drowning...I was drowning!" I cried.

"Look at me, look in my eyes."

I did as he told me.

"You're okay, it's just another dream. You're not drowning. I'm right here." Lincoln patiently grasped my face with his hands, helping me regain myself.

118

From his touch, I was able to get my breathing under control and slow it down. I was still on the edge of another panic attack, but as I slowed my breathing, the anxiety began melting away. Lincoln took his thumbs and wiped away my tears.

"I'm okay, I'm okay," I repeated quietly, still a little panicked

"Yeah, you're okay," Lincoln assured me.

It took me a few minutes before I could really speak again. Lincoln released my face and put his hand on top of mine. Another lovely nightmare, courtesy of the Emissary and the Federation. Thanks a lot, assholes. I have a wonderful life of horror.

"You want to tell me about this one?" Lincoln finally asked as I came back to normal.

"What do you mean this one?" I was puzzled by his words. I have had a nightmare almost every night, but I wasn't aware Lincoln knew about them.

"You have had them since Albuquerque. Every night, something new. Most of the time you never woke up, but I heard the screams." He explained as his thumb rubbed my hand.

"You heard me all this time?" I was kind of embarrassed.

"Yeah, I'd sit with you and rub your back until they eased. To see all the anguish, you went through was painful. I never said anything. Not until you were ready for me to be here."

"I'm sorry I didn't want you to see me like this. I didn't want to frighten you."

"I'm not going anywhere." Lincoln's words pierced my heart. Those were his words and he meant them.

I nodded gratefully.

"I'm no therapist," he said, "but I learned from a beautiful Division agent who happened to be in the psychology field that it helps to talk about dreams. Get them out so they can be analyzed."

Wow. Mr. Matthews had been listening. Nice play.

I smiled and knew he was right. Kirkman and I talk every day, but it was getting to the point our talking was making my dreams more intense and more revealing.

"The Emissary had to test three advisors. We were taken to one of our facilities for this particular test. I was one of the three," I explained as the memory came back to me.

I HAD BEEN ESCORTED TO ONE OF THE FEDERATION'S FA-cilities outside of the city. It was more like an old farmhouse than a warehouse. We had many of them. It was unclear to me why I was there, until I walked into what appeared to be an empty living room. In front of us, were three chairs, and we were encouraged to sit. *Ah shit, this can't be good.* In front of the chairs were three big horse troughs filled with water. My other counterparts began to panic when they saw what was in front of us. But I calmed myself and tried to show no emotion. This was just another test to show what the Federation did, and what would happen if you even remotely pissed them off. I hated these tests. This was number two for me.

From the left side room, The Emissary came in along with— I was taken aback when I saw my sister Susan come up beside him. We made eye contact, and Susan tried to give me a warning. Her eyes grew big and so did her nostrils. I could see that she was taking deep breaths. With a minimal nod, she was telling me to do the same. As she silently instructed, I began to take slow, deep breaths to start to open my lungs.

"Good day, my lovely associates. I am sure you are wondering why you are here today." The Emissary sounded like he was a talk show host, buttering people up. "Well..." His voice changed to serious. "As you know, here at the Federation, we like to put our employees through a number of tests to ensure loyalty, and to enhance their knowledge of the consequences in case you decide betray us."

My gaze followed him as he walked around us.

As he spoke, he sneered at every one of us as if we were filthy animals. The other two women began to cry and whimper. I tried to remain still, scanning the room and him for any angle I could get. And kept up my breathing.

"As you see, Susan and I have selected the three of you to receive this example."

More sobs came from the other ladies.

"We will see just how well you all do in water. If you're able to survive, you pass."

Holy fuck, this guy was trying to kill us. I forced myself not to shift or make any move, except my eyes. Keep. Breathing. The more air in, the longer you will last.

I looked over to Susan in search of something I could use, but she wouldn't meet my eyes. She had given me a tip by her breathing. Take deep breaths.

Before I knew it, three guards came up behind us and cuffed our wrists together with zip ties.

This is going to be bad. Two of us will die. I cannot be one of them. I am in excellent physical shape so my lung capacity should help me, plus the fact I am still taking deep breaths. I run every day sometimes twice a day, I will be the survivor. I hope.

I didn't know much about my opponents. Wait. They were not my enemies but colleagues. I guess now we were in competition. One was a heavier set lady and the other was tall and lanky. I should stand a good chance.

Once all three of us were tied up hands behind our backs, it was only a matter of seconds before the plunge. I remained as calm as I could under the circumstances. The others were not. They whimpered and whined. Pleading the Emissary not to do this. They'd do anything or they don't want to die. I kept my mouth shut.

"I expect all of you to survive," the Emissary ordered, paying no attention to the other lady's plea. With wave of his hand our guards stepped closer.

My guard grasped my hair with a yank and hauled my body out of the chair. *Keep breathing deep, keep breathing.* I could not panic, not yet. Eternity passed, and then I was pushed face first into the water. It was so shocking as I hit it. Being held down face first, my impulse was to push upward and out, but the more I struggled the deeper I was pushed. Time has no meaning when you're drowning.

Hours passed in my brain as I felt my lungs begin to burn and crave oxygen. I screamed as loud as I could, but the water muffled it, so it was not projected. Feeling my lungs filled with water, this was my race against my death—death by drowning. A very unpleasant way to go.

I began to feel my life drain out of me as I was hauled out of the water and put back in my seat. How long was I in there? Inhaling as much air as I could, my lungs burned and ached. My body shock uncontrollably from the torture and horror of the trauma and lack of oxygen. Holy Fuck! My brain was trying to regain its clarity so I could keep my composure. My hair flopped over my face, soaking my entire body.

As I continued to shake, I felt a hand on my shoulder and my whole body froze.

"Ah my dear, I am so pleased you survived," the Emissary said sweetly over my head with a slight tinge of heinousness. "I have become quite fond of you and would have been sad if you had perished."

I glanced over to my other associates. Their heads lay face down in the water, motionless. Guilt flooded my body along with relief, for I was the one who'd survived and would live another day.

"Yes, it was regrettable these two didn't survive." The Emissary glanced their direct and back to me. "Guards take our new advisor, clean her up, and show her the reward."

I didn't utter a word as the Emissary and Susan left. What have I done? I don't deserve a reward. I just survived and my coworkers did not. Screams raced through my brain, but they never escaped my mouth. There would be another time for that.

I HALTINGLY TOLD LINCOLN THE STORY. IT WAS AWFUL, and to see the look on Lincoln's face broke my heart even more. He was devastated and helpless as I numbly recited my ordeal. He just sat on the bed rubbing my hands and not moving or saying a word. When he looked down at my hands, I could read his anger and sadness.

"I'm glad you told me," he said. My heart tore even more when I saw his eyes. I was embarrassed and angry with myself and tried to push away my horror.

"Will you stay with me?" I asked knowing right now we both needed each other. Even though I'm sure I needed him more.

"I'm not going anywhere," Lincoln said once again with a little smile. Those words were only for me and Lincoln always spoke them when I need reassurance.

He crawled in beside me under the blanket and sheet, and I lay back down. Without any prompting, he wrapped his arms around my body and pulled me in close to him. We spooned together, making sure the other felt safe.

Just knowing someone was there was enough for both of us.

CHAPTER 21

THE NEXT FEW DAYS WERE ALL VERY MUCH A REPEAT OF every other day. I run with Max in the morning, return for my coffee-gasm and then I'm escorted to Dr. Kirkman's office. Later I return to the loft, read, wrote notes, eat, sleep, and then come the nightmares. They have eased a bit as the nights have passed with Lincoln beside me. Every time I am abruptly awakened, he is there to comfort me, either to listen or just to be there. Kirkman has me talking about all aspects of my "tests," and if I have them in my dreams, we analyze that too. I seem to relive every detail of those awful times, and sometimes they are on a repeater loop. I will have the same dream multiple times, and each time is as vivid and terrifying as the first.

Many nights later I woke up unexpectedly, preparing myself for the side effects of a bad dream…but nothing. Nothing popped up. My body had become so acclimated to waking that I had done it automatically. A slight sense of panic flowed over me, and then I looked to my left to find Lincoln sound asleep. Seeing him sleeping so soundly put a smile on my face. He had been there every step, and never expressed any negative feelings toward me. I couldn't have asked for more.

Seeing him lying there, something sparked within me. Going with my instinct, I lowered myself down slowly and kissed him, letting my lips linger on his skin. Moments passed, and I felt a reaction. I gave him another kiss, followed by another.

Through sleepy eyes, he glided his hand up my face and cheek, and with fluttering eyes, he gazed at me. "Hey," he said sleepily.

"Hey," I answered.

I leaned back down and kissed him again, meeting with no resistance. Understanding my actions, Lincoln reacted and grasped my face with both hands and kissed me harder. We continued for long moments, then suddenly he pulled away and looked deep into my eyes.

"Are you sure?" he asked, for permission.

"Yeah, I am," I answered, feeling my libido kick into overdrive.

He gave me a look and I nodded my head with assurance. That was all he needed, and we started kissing again, but passionate kissing. It was gentle but confident. I knew he wouldn't hurt me, and I needed to be close to him. Removing my shirt and panties, I exposed my naked body to him, and he eased me down onto the bed. In a split second, his boxers were stripped off and fell to the floor. With his gentle touch, he began running his hands up and down my body, making every one of my nerves tingle.

We kissed slowly, reconnecting. Lincoln slipped his fingers through my hair and I relished it. He looked at me with twinkling eyes and lifted himself on top of me. On all fours, he continued kissing me, on my lips, cheek, throat, and ear lobes. The throat is my sensitive spot and he knew it. My back arched and Lincoln kept going. It was pure bliss from just a simple touch.

He pushed inside me, and we made love for hours that night. Very slow pulses and rhythm were all we needed. Lincoln was so gentle and my heart ached for missing so much time with him. Slow thrusts and tender kisses. All I had ever felt for this man filled my body. I loved him more today than I ever had.

After a time, we both began to crave the end game. I was the first to build, and with my moans growing, Lincoln's also grew. He was close to his orgasm, and I was too. I could not hold out any longer. My insides began to rip apart with intense pleasure. As I began, Lincoln also exploded.

Breathing and panting heavily, we both collapsed. I was on the bottom and Lincoln lay on top. I realized what had just happened. I had found a part of myself I'd lost.

Lincoln must have felt something because he pushed himself up and into my eyes. "Hey, why the look?" he asked softly, unsure.

"I never realized how much I needed you until now."

He ran his fingers through my hair again and rubbed my cheek with his thumb. I nuzzled it.

"I missed you more than you know." My words escaped.

Lincoln leaned down and imprinted a kiss on my lips. "I know. And I'm not going anywhere." He rolled off me.

I tucked myself under his arm, rested my head on his chest, and found his hand. He gave me another kiss on my forehead and we just lay together.

I'm not sure when we fell asleep, but my alarm went off at its normal time of 5:30am and Lincoln was passed out. I extracted my naked body from the bed and dressed in my running gear.

Sam Maxwell would be here soon, and I was pumped for our run.

Max arrived and we took off. My energy level was off the chart, and I felt like a new person, reborn. We ran our usual route and I left him in the dust. When we came to our halfway point, I stopped to catch my breath. Max caught up to me, huffing and puffing.

"Holy shit, Connors, your killing it this morning. What's come over you?" Max asked, bending at his waist to help him recover.

"I finally slept! Can you tell the difference?" I asked with a huge smile.

"Ah yeah, you've had something." Max replied with a small chuckle. I chuckled along with him. "Shall we?"

"Yeah, but this time will you slow down?"

We kept running, and this time I stayed with him...or he stayed with me. I felt free and refreshed when we reached the loft. He said he would be with me today and would be back in a bit. I nodded and proceeded into the loft.

It was a few minutes earlier than normal. The place was quiet and there was no coffee made. Lincoln must be still sleeping. Odd. He almost always had coffee made before I got back. So, I took the incentive and made the coffee. I love the smell and with my killer good mood, my day was going to be the first good one in a while.

After the coffee finished brewing, I poured two cups and added cream and sugar for each cup, slipped off my shoes, and made my way up the stairs. When I reached the bedroom, I could see Lincoln was still sleeping. He looked so peaceful I didn't really want to wake him. He had been dealing with me and my crazy nightmares. Our sleep schedule being so very erratic, we both needed sleep. I watched him for several minutes then sat down on the edge of the bed. I placed both coffees on the nightstand and leaned in to kiss him. Worked before, should work again.

Lincoln stirred from my kiss and woke up very slowly.

"Hey, good morning," I quietly said to him, letting him wake.

It took him a minute, and I took advantage of that minute to drink my coffee. He gazed up at me, then slid up to sit, and I handed him his coffee.

"Ah, thanks." He took a sip and savored it. "You're back earlier than normal."

"I beat Maxwell today bigtime. He wasn't expecting me to blow him out of the water." I was tickled and I lit up with excitement.

"I can tell. You're beaming," Lincoln said with a big ol' smirk on his face, also still a little sleepy.

"I had a good run." Mirroring his look, I held in my pride, then burst into laughter.

"Only a good run?"

"Well, there may have been other factors," I teased. "I need to go take a shower. I'm pretty gross." I stood up.

Lincoln just looked at me. I waggled my eyebrows at him as I descended the stairs very slowly. He never took his eyes off mine.

"So, are you coming?" I called up as I reached the bottom.

Before I knew it, I heard a herd of elephants coming down the stairs.

I squealed as Lincoln followed me into the bathroom.

CHAPTER 22

OVER THE NEXT SEVERAL WEEKS, I MADE TREMENDOUS progress. Dr. Kirkman advised Mitchell and Conrad of my progress, and recommended I was ready for sessions to be moved to twice a week. If I was up to it, I should be allowed to consult on cases, but only paperwork, no fieldwork. Mitchell was pleased with her report, and I was ecstatic.

Lincoln and I were moving along just as fast. There wasn't a time when my libido didn't take over when he was in the room. I felt like a teenager again with her first lover. My body craved him all the time, and I mean all the time. If we had a spare moment, guess what we ended up doing? I think you know. And the sex was never disappointing.

Or I should say, from my end it wasn't. Lincoln might differ, but I doubt it. We're just making up for lost time.

The Federation seemed to have bought the story of my death in the car accident. Mitchell said there had been no intel reported about my defection or death. We assumed it was safe to pull back on my security. It wouldn't totally be gone, but not twenty-four-seven. I was okay with that.

I'd grown accustomed to Max and Reilly over the last month and our friendship together had blossomed. Max and I both wanted our morning runs to continue, maybe even train for a half-marathon. I was very excited by that idea.

One morning after my run, I came back to the loft to find Mitchell waiting for me. He and Lincoln were chatting over coffee. And damn it, that little shit was using my cup. They both grinned when I gave Mitch a dirty look.

"I told you it would be the first thing she noticed," Lincoln said to Mitch, and they both chuckled.

Damn shit heads.

But they were my shit heads.

I stormed over and grabbed my backup cup. It wasn't the same, but it would have to do. After pouring myself a cup, I returned to the boys. "So Mitchell, what brings you here beside my cup?" I asked sarcastically.

"Well, now that you have partial clearance, I brought you over some photos to look at." Mitch tossed me a file. But I could tell there was more he wanted to say. When he holds back something, I can spot it a mile away.

"Uh-huh, sure. Why are you really here?"

"God, you're a pain in the ass sometimes." Mitch hated when I called him out.

I grinned. "And yet, for some reason you keep coming back for more."

He smiled at me and glanced at Lincoln.

"Spill it!" I barked.

"All right, well, now that you are somewhat stable—"

I rolled my eyes at him. "Ha ha."

"—I want to introduce to you someone I have been seeing and get your advice. You have always been the one who can pick out the bad ones with that lie detector thing you do."

Now, the truth comes out. I was his wing man, and he needed reassurance. You would think his own brother would step in, but no, Lincoln held back and watched the show.

In the past, Mitchell was kind of a man whore and fooled around a lot. And I mean a lot. If I hadn't been around to shoo off the bad apples, I don't know what Mitchell's life would be like now. He was too good a man to be like that, so if I could help set him straight, I always did. Lincoln wasn't much for Mitchell's taste in men, or any man. He did accept Mitchell's lifestyle when he came out, but it was hard for Lincoln to live in it. So that job was mine.

"Okay, what did you have in mind?" I asked.

"How about we meet for dinner? Nothing to fancy, just casual." Mitch was nervous asking me. He must really like this one.

I looked over to Lincoln, hoping for backup in my answer and I got nothing. "Sure, *we* can," I said with emphasis on we.

Lincoln gave me a nod as he stood up and placed his cup in the sink. "Yeah, we can do that." He came back over to me and kissed the top of my head. "I have to go help an old buddy of mine on a case, but I'll be back this afternoon."

"Okay, have fun." I told him.

"Oh, I will. And you girls have fun chatting."

Lincoln was making fun of us. Well, it was warranted, especially when Mitch and I got together and talked. Having a gay best friend was the best.

"We will, thanks. See you later!" I called after Lincoln as he walked out the door.

I turned back to Mitchell. I wanted details. Like two schoolgirls talking. I missed this so much.

"So, does he have a nice ass?" I asked, making Mitch blush.

"Direct, aren't you?"

I grinned. "Ya think?"

"Yes, he does have a nice ass. What is with your glow today?"

"I'm feeling like me again," I lied, knowing Mitch would call me out.

"Bullshit!" *Told ya.*

I gaped at him, pretending to be shocked.

He narrowed his eyes. "You got laid. And don't lie. I can tell, that's morning-after glow."

I pretended to be shocked. "Maybe..." I said playfully.

"Oh, come on, I know he's my brother—ick—but you are glowing so much, it's too bright." Mitch pretended to shield his face.

"Yes, he is your brother, and I have gotten laid more times in the last month than I can count. Is it that obvious?".

"Ah yeah, it is. And I am a little jealous. Not that I want to have sex with you—yuck—or my brother—double yuck." He made vomiting faces at me which made me giggle. He could always make me smile.

We chatted like that for about a half hour, then he had to leave for work. I informed him I would look over the photos and let him know my findings. I'd see him later for dinner and vet his new friend. I'd let him know what I thought.

Today was my first day with no therapy, and I was going to enjoy my freedom.

LATER IN THE EARLY EVENING, I WAS GETTING READY FOR our dinner date with Mitchell and his new beau. Lincoln wasn't very enthusiastic about meeting Mitch's newest beau, and surprisingly, I was a bit anxious too. Mitch was very excited about this new relationship, and I wanted him to be happy.

I was deciding on my outfit and Lincoln was tinkering down-stairs. I held up two outfits, both causal, but I still wanted to make an impression. Who knew? This person could be my future brother-in-law. I held up my favorite black dress in one hand, and my fitted blue jeans and flowing top of black and white stripes in the other. Hemming and hawing, I finally decided on the black dress. I could dress it down some with some accessories and lite makeup, possibly some low flats too.

I was taking my time with my makeup and I could hear Lincoln below playing music. His choice of songs always put a smile on my face. I finished up, slipped on my shoes, and headed downstairs. Lincoln was leaning up against the kitchen counter when I came down.

He turned to look at me. "Wow!" He gazed appreciatively at me. "You look amazing. Radiant."

His compliment was making me blush. I felt good, and I wanted to look good too. Judging by Lincoln's comment, I'd succeeded.

"Why, thank you," I said with a bow of my head and halted in front of him with a bubbly smile.

Just then, one of my favorite songs came on.

"May I have this dance?" Lincoln asked, gesturing with his hand.

I nodded and took his hand.

Al Green—I love that man's voice, and Let's Stay Together is one of my all-time favorites. It was the first song Lincoln and I ever danced to.

Lincoln held me close as we danced, holding both of my hands in his on his chest. I rested my head on his chest and let him lead me around the living room. I looked up at him, he kissed me, and twirled me out and back again. Many more twirls and a couple dips later, I was smiling from ear to ear. As we moved, my hair danced around with my body, and as I gazed into Lincoln's eyes, he beamed at me.

"You know, if we weren't due to meet my brother, I'd do this all night long with you," Lincoln said, smiling down at me.

"Just this?"

"Okay, and maybe a few other things..." He held me close as we swayed.

"That sounds amazing."

Lincoln leaned down and kissed me. "I probably don't say this enough." He released me and looked into my eyes again. "But I love you."

He was so romantic, my heart melted. It was the first time he'd said those three words since I came back.

Touched, I said, "You have no idea how much I love you." My voice broke. There were so many things I wanted to say to him. "You are my everything."

Lincoln held my hands tighter and kissed me again. When he released me, he made sure to swing me to add laugher to the moment. He always knew the perfect thing to do. It was time to go, and if we'd kept dancing we would never leave.

WE ARRIVED AT THE RESTAURANT THAT MITCHELL HAD chosen, a casual bar and grill. I was totally overdressed. But who cared? I felt pretty, so I should look pretty. Lincoln and I made a handsome couple, whether we were overdressed or not. Screw the world! The hostess asked how many and as we were about to say something Mitch came around the corner.

"OMG! You look amazing," he greeted me with outstretched arms. If I didn't know him inside and out, I would say he was high as a kite. But I do, and Mitch is very excited and nervous. When these factors come into play, his inner girl comes out more. I love every minute of it, but it makes Lincoln a little unsettled.

"We have a table in the back. This way."

We followed Mitch to the back of the restaurant, and as we passed the bar Lincoln's gaze drifted. "I am going to need a beer," Lincoln whispered into my ear, holding my hand as we table-danced our way to the back.

At a round table, a man who look vaguely familiar sat alone, and stood up when he saw us approach. He was an average-built man with dark brown hair and a long face. It was going to be a piece of cake to scope him out. His features were very distinguished, and from the look I saw between the two men, I hope I came to a good conclusion.

Mitchell introduced us. "Mark Wallace, this is my brother Lincoln." Lincoln shook his hand. "And this is my best friend Jessy." Mitch almost sounded proud.

I shook Mark's hand and watched for a reaction as we looked at each other. His smile was genuine, but his eyes were not. "So, this is the Jessy I have heard so much about."

We all took our seats. I am faking my smile to keep up the appearance. From the touch of his hand shake, my neck hairs stood up on end.

Mark continued, "Mitchell has told me so many stories about the two of you. I'm so glad I get to meet you." He said it sweetly, but the tone of his voice had a different meaning behind it. I was starting to get a bad feeling about him.

"I can tell you make Mitch very happy. He's done nothing but glow lately," I remarked.

Lincoln sat down beside me and immediately put his hand on my thigh. I am not sure if he was trying to prove he was straight or was horny. Maybe both. The instant the server came over, he was the first one to order a beer. That gave it away, he was nervous. Men are so easy to read, and tonight for Mitchell, I was on duty.

Not feeling like drinking—shocking I know—I ordered a club soda with lime, and you would have thought I had two heads. Lincoln and Mitch looked at me strangely. I shrugged it off and browsed the menu. I was going to indulge tonight and have a burger. I was craving the protein after all my exercising lately.

We chatted as we waited for food. I opened with, "So, where did you two meet?"

"Mark is a new analyst from Nevada. It wasn't long after we met, well, it just all fell into place," Mitchell explained with stars in his eyes.

I took a second to process this information as the two men nuzzled each other. Nevada sparked my brain and it would go away. There was something about Nevada I just couldn't put together at this moment. Lincoln took another swig of his beer and Mark looked in my direction with warning in his eyes. This made the back of my neck tingle even more, which isn't a good sign. But for Mitch's sake, I'd keep an open mind for a while longer.

Lincoln glanced over at me. He must have felt my tension level rise when Mark looked at me. I gave a tiny shake of my head and he let it go. Finally, the food came. I tried to shake off my uneasy feeling and keep a nice, smiling face while we ate. But deep down, the warning flags were flying high.

We dug in, but as soon as I took a bite my appetite vanished. The burger looked and smelled so good, but I turned my nose up at it. I was very uneasy with what I was seeing in Mark, and it was going to break my heart to tell Mitch. Throughout the meal, I was getting furtive looks from him and deception from the crooks of his mouth and corners of his eyes. Something was very off about this man. Feeling queasy, I got up and excused myself to the ladies' room. To get away, to think.

I wasn't far away from the table when I heard someone following me. I figured it was Lincoln checking on me, but to my surprise it was Mitch. How in the hell was I going to explain this one?

"Hey, are you okay?" Mitch asked, catching up to me.

"Yeah, um no. I'm not." I was at a loss for words. I was expecting Lincoln.

"What's up? You don't look so good."

"I just needed some air for a minute," I lied.

"Isn't Mark great? I mean, I am head over heels about him. I know you figured that one out." Mitch was so bubbly and now I had to pop that bubble. "I came to find you to see what you got out of him. Is he the real deal?"

I really wanted to skirt around the truth and was trying to figure out how, but Mitch knew me too well.

"Ah, shit, what is it?" He knew bad news was coming and I'd never even said a word.

"He is hiding something," I stated as if I was profiling someone. "I wouldn't trust him with any secrets."

Mitch was frustrated by my answer and started to fidget. I was feeling guilty, but I couldn't lie to him.

"Are you sure?" he asked hopefully.

"Yes, the way he has been looking my way all night, he isn't being truthful, and he knows something that we don't. I just haven't figured out what yet," I answered. "Mitch, I love you too much to see you hurt. And professionally? Be careful what you tell this man. It could cost a lot you more than a broken heart." I leaned in to give Mitch a hug.

I walked back to the table by myself. Mitch was going to need a minute to deal with the information I just gave him.

CHAPTER 23

"HEY, YOU LOOK HORRIBLE. WHAT'S UP?" LINCOLN ASKED me as we walked into the loft after dinner.

"Mark. There is something I can't shake about him. I know he is hiding something, but I feel like I am missing something important. The way he looked at me, it made my skin crawl." I shivered at the memory.

"I could tell. You got all tense and didn't even eat. I knew something was up when you wouldn't touch your burger." Lincoln was being a smartass as he put my leftovers in the fridge.

"I'm sure it will taste as good tomorrow. If it is still there." I gave Lincoln a look of, "Don't you dare touch my food."

His answering grin said, "Maybe, maybe not." After closing the fridge, he walked over to me and opened his arms.

I went into his embrace and his warm body melted me.

He wrapped me like a blanket with his arms and body, and we just stood there. Me, frustrated, and him trying to calm me down. I wrapped my arms around his back, surrendering.

"Maybe the awful feeling will reveal itself," Lincoln said. "I know you told my brother. I could tell when he came back. He knew something was up."

"Yeah, I couldn't lie to him, but what I had to say wasn't what he wanted to hear." I tilted my head up to look at Lincoln. "I wanted Mark to be real for Mitchell, but he isn't."

"Listen, it isn't your job to fix Mitchell's love life. He asked for your opinion and you gave it to him. My brother is a smart man, he won't disown you. How can he? You are unofficially part of the family."

At those words, a small smile came out. I had been in the brothers' lives for far too long to be kicked out. I imagine one day I'll be true family, if Lincoln decides to keep me around. I leaned my head back on his chest. The toll of the day was taking my energy away.

Lincoln squeezed me a little tighter. "Want to go to bed?"

"Yeah, I do." I felt so confused, and my level of energy was zapped.

Lincoln unwrapped me from his embrace and put his arm around my shoulder, leading me over to the stairs. "Maybe I can help you out of that dress," he suggested as we climbed the stairs.

"You never know." I winked at him.

THE REST OF THE WEEK SEEMED TO FLY BY. I KEPT MY routine in check—I had my runs in the morning, and had a few sessions with Kirkman, which were becoming more intense. We had progressed past my time with the Federation and now we were coming into the events with Susan. This was frustrating to discuss because I had to relive every moment of my discussion with Susan leading up to her death.

My brain was still spinning after that dinner with Mark and Mitchell. There was something missing. Mark was stuck in my brain, and some other uneasiness floating around. Kirkman was helping guide me through my thoughts, but this was something I need to figure out on my own. With my brain on high, my body was taking the toll. I was exhausted all the time. It seemed whenever I had a spare moment, I'd lay down. It was getting out of hand.

One afternoon after my visit with Kirkman, I came home and flopped onto the couch. I was so flustered about everything. I couldn't focus on the photos Mitch gave me, or the notes I was scribbling down about the Federation. I just lay there with my hands covering my eyes, trying to focus. Ah. I wanted to scream. I stayed there a few minutes, until I couldn't take it anymore.

Fidgeting around, I decided it was time for me to clean. Better that than start to pace. The bathroom was probably in need of a good scrubbing, and it would keep me occupied until Lincoln came back. He had been asked back to the Metro PD to consult on a couple cases. Which was a good move for him. He was still a great detective and he needed to keep his 'foot in the door' to keep some sanity. According to Mitchell, Lincoln had left the department so he could find me, but in the end, I'd found him.

Anyway, I headed into the bathroom and opened the cabinet...and froze. What I saw in the bottom cabinet took my breath away. I stood still as a statue. There was a box that stood out and my jumbled brain suddenly became clear. *Holy crap.*

Tampons!

PICKING UP THE BOX OF TAMPONS, I SAT BACK ONTO THE toilet in shock. I had been feeling overwhelmed and anxious for about two weeks. I'd figured it was all the memories being dredged up and the stress of talking about them. Memories and stress can cause a person many side effects, especially if the memories were traumatic. I am a prime example.

But this... This halted me in my tracks.

This week, Kirkman and I talked about my sister's death, right? Right. I explained to her the sequence of events leading up to Susan's execution, which I'd been forced to watch. I'm repeating myself, I know, but it helps me focus and line up the puzzle pieces jumbled in my head. After Susan's death, what the hell did I do? I— I— I remembered the bathroom, and lots of sobbing. Oh, how could I forget the vomiting? Not pleasant. But there was something else I was missing...

Closing my eyes, I tried to go back to the days after Susan died. Something was coming back to me. A flash of memories popped in and out. A Jose Cuevo Bottle which I presume I drank. That would explain why I didn't remember anything. It was empty when I woke with my lovely hangover. But... I was sitting on the hotel steps... And Lincoln was sitting next to me.

The memory was fuzzy, but my subconscious worked overtime.

I kissed him, really kissed him. And then...?

God damn it, this fucking sucked! I can't remember.

I opened my eyes and looked down. In the back of the cabinet, something else caught my eye. I leaned in and grabbed it. With the other box in my hand, my memory sparked, and I knew what had happened. My brain had been leaving me clues, but I was so focused on other things I had missed almost all of them. There were so many questions suddenly in my mind, but I need to get one out of the way. A big one. I spent the afternoon mapping out my course of options, but there was going to be nothing done until I spoke with Mr. Matthews.

I sat on the on the couch waiting for Lincoln to come home. He'd said he would be back around six-ish, that way we could still enjoy the evening. A few things needed to be discussed before I could go any further, and my goal was to remain calm. My investigation of the day had ended in a very unexpected result, and I need to confront it before it drove me crazy. My memories had finally returned, but my brain was still going ninety mph.

Lincoln came through the door around quarter to six. When I heard the door shut, I popped up from my prone position on the couch. I watched Lincoln go over to the fridge and grab a beer. He unscrewed the cap and took a swig.

"Hey," I called out to him.

Lincoln swallowed his beer and answered, "Hey, how was your day?"

"Well..." I looked down at my lap. "It was an interesting day. A memory resurfaced today, and I wanted to discuss you about it."

"Yeah sure, anything." Lincoln circled around the counter and came closer.

"So, I went to see Kirkman today and we started to discuss my sister."

"Ah man, I'm sorry. I'm sure reliving that isn't easy." Lincoln was always very supportive.

I had to pull my gaze up to look at him and let him see the fight in my eyes. "No, it wasn't the best day, but something did come up that I need help figuring out."

"Sure, anything," he repeated.

Okay, you can do this.

"My memory was foggy about the days around Susan's murder. There are things I couldn't piece together. But after talking, some memories sparked, like snapshots."

He looked at me but didn't say anything. Oh shit, permeated his face.

"The bottle of Jose Curevo was one, and a few others." I paused to try and figure out how I was going to ask this.

"You drank pretty much that whole bottle," Lincoln said.

"Yeah, I know. But there's more. I remembered...seducing you." I looked at him, worried about his reaction. He didn't say anything to that, so I continued. "I kissed you and you tried to back off. But I

142

insisted. Things, many things progressed and from what I recall, the sex was unbelievable."

He looked at me with sadness and guilt, which isn't what I expected. "Yeah, it was," he said.

"Why didn't you tell me?"

"I was going to, but then we found Aries, and things sort of took off. You and I were good as we were, and I didn't want to ruin that. You were healing, and I was afraid I would somehow damage you." He grimaced.

"I think I am more hurt that you didn't tell me than I am about that night. From what I remember, it was completely my idea, and you pushed me away more than once. What bothers me more that I had to piece my memories together without any recollection. If I'd known, then the first time I *thought* we'd had sex wasn't the first time, I wouldn't have been so scared." My words were even moving me. I was not pissed but a little hurt.

"I should have told you, and I'm sorry." Lincoln said, coming over to the couch. He sat next to me, still clenching his beer.

"It is what it is. I'm not mad, just unsettled. Now, I remember, it puts a lot of things in prospective."

"What do you mean?"

"My brain has been so jumbled lately I wasn't picking up on the signs. But now—" I pulled out a small bag from behind my back. I gave it to Lincoln.

"Open it," I ordered.

Lincoln set his beer on the table and took the bag. Puzzled, he glanced into the bag and finally pulled out the two things inside. The first was a small white shirt which had embroidered on it, "I Love My Daddy." The second was my pregnancy test, reading positive.

The shock on his face was all I needed to spur me on.

"I'm pregnant," I said nervously.

I looked at him, waiting for some kind of reaction. He just sat there looking at both objects. The little onesie was one I had bought the first time I was pregnant. The test I'd found in the back under the sink. From the last pregnancy. All I wanted was to hear him say something, anything, to give me a clue what he was feeling. My nerves started to rise at his continued silence.

"Lincoln, say something please." My voice broke.

Still no response.

"Look at me please. I can't do this alone." Tears began to roll down my cheeks.

Lincoln finally broke through his stupor. The moment he saw my face, his world awakened and the objects in his hands dropped. I started to get up, but Lincoln placed his hands on mine. I held his hand and I could feel my anxiety lower.

"You are not alone, I promise," Lincoln finally said. With the words a faint smile appeared. From his smile, mine grew through tears. "We're going to have a baby," Lincoln stated with joy in his voice.

"We are going to have a baby," I repeated with a giggle. "Yes!"

In a single moment, Lincoln grabbed my face and planted a wet one on me. We kissed, and it lasted for what seemed like minutes. When he released me, the smile on Lincoln's face gave me so much happiness. I had been so frightened and seeing him with so much excitement filled my body with warmth. Everything was going to be okay.

THE WEEKEND WAS UPON US, AND MY BODY THREW UP the white flag. The stress and anxiety from the last few weeks officially caught up with me. There was no way in hell I was able to do anything. All I wanted to do was sleep. More often than not, Lincoln would find me asleep either on the couch or in bed. He was so good about letting me rest. I would feel his presence nearby and wake just long enough to receive a kiss or a few snuggles. A couple of times I got tea in bed.

Coffee would have been better, but I'd take herbal tea if I had to. I felt so lazy, but my brain was denied any activity. Baby Matthews wasn't tolerating any amount of movement.

After two days of rest, on Monday morning I was back to my routine. I ran with Max and got myself prepared for the day. My sessions with Kirkman had been more intense lately, but with fewer sessions per week. I was grateful I didn't have to see her every day, but each time we did get heavy in discussion. Any topic we chose was picked apart and analyzed. By the end of our time, I was mentally and physically worn out. Bringing up Susan was probably the hardest, because there was nothing I could do to help her. When the pain was inflicted on me personally, I could cope. But seeing your own flesh and blood die... Helpless was the only thing I felt. Now I'd added guilt to the mix. I am a hot mess.

Later in the week, I took the plunge and went to get my hair fixed. Meaning back to a more normal color for me. It was time to change from California to back to the east coast. I knew Lincoln wouldn't care; he was partial to my norm anyway. It might even turn him on. *Wink, wink.* We all know I don't have a problem of getting any. I can just look at him, and *boom. Wham, bam,* thank you ma'am. I love him to pieces for it.

It wasn't until the end of the week that I revealed to Kirkman the news regarding my uneasy feeling. I'd explained to her in previous sessions how I felt like I was missing something. Indeed, I had been. Baby Matthews on board. I expected her to show more excitement, but a happy smile was all I got. That was enough, it was her. She'd never been much for emotion, now or then.

Before I went into my session, I had the urge to call Mitchell. I was still pondering the Mark Wallace thing, and I needed more information. Such as where did he come from? What kind of analysis was he doing for Division? That sort of thing. His facial expressions gave him away, but I couldn't complete the puzzle until I spoke to Mitch.

As my phone dialed, I was very aware of my surroundings. More so than normal. Today, my security guard was going to be Sam Maxwell after my session, but right now it was Reilly. I'm not sure what I'd do without them as my shadows.

Mitch didn't pick up, so I left him a voicemail. "Hey love, it Jess. Call me back. I have a few things I need to ask you." And that was it, short and sweet. He would call me when he could.

My session with Kirkman was the final time this week. I was thankful for that. In the last few minutes of our session Kirkman finished up, then out of the blue decided to walk me outside. In our weeks previous, she had never done that, and it wasn't something I was expecting. But I rolled with it.

We stepped outside her building, and as we walked into the sunlight, I turned to thank her. And she gave me a huge hug. Holy shit, I didn't think Suzanna Kirkman was capable of hugs.

"I am very happy for you. Everything is falling into place for you now. I hope you realize that," she said, releasing me.

With her kind words still lingering in the air, my cell rang. Mitch was returning my call.

"Hey, I've been trying to reach you," Mitch said on the other end.

"I was in session." I mouthed over to Kirkman, "Sorry," and held my finger up in a just-a-minute gesture. "Hey, what part of Nevada did you say Mark was from?" I needed to move this along.

"Mark is from an office in Carson City." At Mitch's answer, I froze.

Shit! Carson City was where the Federation had offices.

My brain was finally putting the pieces together. I knew I had seen him before. It was when I was being administered one of my torture tests. He was my guard.

Mark wasn't a Division analyst. Mark was Marcus. *Federation Marcus.* And that only meant one thing.

At the realization, I slowly dropped the phone to my side, stunned, while Mitch was trying to get my attention back.

"I believe you will be a great mother!" Kirkman said to me, bringing me back to reality.

In my stunned state, I never saw the bullet fly by.

Not until it went right through her head.

CHAPTER 24

OH FUCK!

Kirkman was dead before she hit the ground.

I stood motionless. Suddenly, more shots ricocheted all around my head and body. Reilly was waiting for me in the car when the bullets started flying. Without hesitation, he bolted out to cover to me. I was just ducking down behind another car when I saw him take a bullet in the shoulder. He went down like a ton of bricks but managed to roll to cover.

I was still clenching my phone and, in a panic, yelled into it, "Mitchell, Mitchell. They found me. We need back up *now*."

More shots bounced off the walls around Reilly and me, but we managed to avoid being hit. I was unarmed, and Reilly was hampered because of his injury.

Scoping out what our next move would be, I glanced at Kirkman. There was no saving her; blood and gray brain matter was seeping out onto the sidewalk. Our sharpshooter had either been aiming for me and missed, or he'd meant to miss.

Either way I was fucked. The Federation knew I was still alive.

As the bullets flew, it seemed like eternity before Reilly and I got any backup. A car blazed around the corner. Bullets pinged into the vehicle as it squealed to a stop close to us. Our savior had arrived. Rolling out from the car, Sam Maxwell had his gun drawn and stayed low in a defensive stance.

"Jess are you hit?" he yelled, making his way closer to us.

"No, but Reilly is, and Kirkman's dead," I yelled back, swallowing my panic.

Max scooted his way over to Reilly, hoisting him up and moving him to relative safety. I stayed low and tried to move toward them. More shots whizzed by my head. *I had to get to Max.*

From the phone in my hand, Mitch screamed at me to get out. "Get out of there!"

Minutes lasted hours, until I gathered my courage and sprinted over to Max and Reilly. My breathing was fast, and my heart wanted to blow out of my chest from all the adrenaline.

"We've got to get him to the car!" Max barked at me. I nodded and we helped Reilly up. At Max's signal, we moved as one. The distance was brief, and we kept low. With a burst of speed and adrenaline, we all made it to Max's car. I threw open the back door, shoved Reilly in, and Max dove into the driver's seat.

More shots pelted the car as Max squealed away from the curb. I kept my head down and held pressure to Reilly's wound. Once we were out of range, my breathing slowed enough to get my brain to revive.

"Sam, where are we going?" I blurted out in desperation.

"Somewhere safe." Max was driving like a maniac and didn't give a fuck about anything but escape.

"They found me Sam, they found me!" Emotion welled up as the realization flooded through me, along with all the implications.

"I know. I came as fast as I could when I found out," Max said.

"Found out what? Sam, what?" I yelled in confusion.

He glanced back at Reilly and me, making sure we were still okay. I have never seen Sam Maxwell as panicked as at that moment.

"Aries was stolen. We believe someone on the inside stole it. Meaning—"

"Meaning, I am now their target," I finished. *Oh, God.* "Where is Lincoln?" I needed him desperately.

"When I found out, I called him. We both went looking for you." Max jerked the steering wheel. "How's Reilly?"

I went from shock to action. Reilly was losing blood from his wound, but I was able to hold pressure on it. I leaned him forward and saw an exit wound. He's be okay but needed medical attention asap. "The bullet went through, and there is a lot of blood loss," I answered shakily. "He should be okay, but we need to get him to the hospital."

Reilly was getting a little tipsy in my arms from the blood loss, but I kept him upright and pressure on the wound.

"I will. As soon as I get you to safety."

"Sam, where are you taking me?" I asked, panicked again. I knew I'd never be out of danger again. Not until the Federation killed me.

Max was driving hard and fast, using every evasive maneuver he'd been taught. "I've been ordered to take you back to headquarters for evacuation." Max kept looking back at me in the rearview mirror.

"Evacuation? What the hell?"

"You are to be taken out of the city and go into hiding, until..." Max paused

"Until what? Damn it, Sam, tell me!" I was agitated.

"Until Aries is recovered, and/or the Federation is dismantled. I'm sorry."

Dismantled? That would never happen. And the recovery of Aries could take months. Hell, years. Panic was flowing all over me. The implications of the situation were pounding at my brain, but I had to hold it together long enough to get Reilly medical help.

"I need to see Lincoln. Sam, I can't go away without him." I was yelling through my tears. Being pregnant wasn't helping with the emotions on top of everything.

Sam drove like a bat out of hell to get to the Division building and zoomed into the parking garage. Waiting for us by the entrance was an ambulance and two medics, who swiftly went to work and took charge of Reilly's care. In less than sixty seconds, the ambulance sped off, sirens blaring.

An agent I was unfamiliar with stood with Mitchell waiting for us by the door. My hands were covered with blood, but I didn't give two shits right now. I wanted Reilly to be okay, and I wanted answers.

"Maxwell, come with Jessy and me so we can get her processed for departure," Mitch ordered.

Max and I were swept into the elevator. As it ascended, I could feel my body start to collapse. I stood as still as I could, trying not to show my anxiety, but Mitchell and Sam Maxwell knew better. All Mitch had to do was turn to me, and I fell into his arms, shaking.

"It's going to be okay, I promise," he said, holding me firmly. He wasn't my best friend right now. Right now, he was my boss trying to get hold of the situation.

I wiped my tears away as the doors opened and we stepped out into the hallway. It wasn't a hallway I ever wanted to walk down.

This was the one that lead to Conrad's office.

CHAPTER 25

MITCHELL NEVER KNOCKED WHEN WE ENTERED CONRAD'S office, he just went in with Sam Maxwell and me following behind. Conrad was hunched over his desk examining something when we barged in. He was an average-built guy with short graying hair and wrinkles to match. He was so dry that even a cactus would die of thirst. He looked up at us, not too pleased. Conrad was never pleased. He was a fucking bastard asshole who hated the world. There was nothing Conrad cared about, and there never would be. Prick.

If you can't tell, I seriously dislike the man.

"Sir, we need to immediately implement Connors protocol, for her safety. It's in place, and the team is be standing by for your orders to make her disappear," Mitch informed Conrad.

"Has the situation really become necessary for this?" Conrad asked.

"Yes, sir. An attempt was just made on her life. Her team was able to get her out safely, one casualty, and one of ours was wounded." Mitchell was all business now.

"Understood, have her out on the first chopper."

"Wait, What?" I stepped up and interrupted. I was hearing their words but not fully understanding what was happening.

"Connors, you are to be moved to a safe location and put into protective custody until further notice," Conrad barked.

"Protective custody? I am already in protective custody. Now, look!" My anger was beginning to bubble to the surface.

"Yes, protective custody. As you can see, what we set up wasn't enough, and now the Federation has retaken the Aries device and put a hit out on you. So, it is time for you to disappear." Conrad was just as pissed as I was. We never go along but as he was my boss. Following orders wasn't so easy when the guy giving them was an ass.

"I'm not leaving without Lincoln Matthews," I demanded, holding my ground.

"You need to leave now, Connors. Lincoln Matthews isn't Division's problem. You will be on that chopper and heading out within the next thirty minutes," Conrad ordered.

I glanced over at Mitch for some support and I knew I would get some help...but I had to give up my newfound condition and the new information. "I need him to come with me. He is a detective and can assist with my protection. I request he be assigned to my detail immediately." I was holding firm. I needed Lincoln.

"Excuse me? I am the one who gives orders around here, not you."

"Sir." Mitchell finally stepped in. I hoped his words would be enough. "Matthews is a well-trained officer and has experience in these matters. He would be a great asset to Connors' protection team. He has my approval."

Conrad was fuming. We were questioning his orders. But I was not going down without a fight. He knew I was the one person on our side who knew how to use the Aries device, and they needed me alive for it. The Federation had many who could work Aries. I was one of their defectors, which meant I needed to be eliminated, so they had all the control.

"Johnson, Lincoln Matthews may be a cop, but he is not Division, and hasn't been cleared by our department. I will not approve him."

"Conrad, I have information on the theft of Aries. If you want it, I need him to be a part of my team," I pleaded. "I wouldn't have gotten this far in my recovery without him." My cards needed to be shown if I wanted to get Lincoln with me immediately, and not wait for possibly months while the Division got their shit in order.

"Ah, I see. Let me guess, he's your lover. And you won't be able to survive without him. I get it. Well, too fucking bad." Conrad had thrown it back in my face. "If you are at least as smart as you proclaim, I suggest you reveal your information." I needed to reveal my hand. But to do so, I needed Lincoln on board.

"Not without Matthews." Stand firm.

"I'm only going to say this once and once only. He isn't my problem, you are. Give me the information and get the hell on the chopper. Do yourself a favor and cooperate." Conrad began to stand up and braced himself hunched over on his desk.

I knew what he was trying to do. I was in danger and yes, I was his problem. More time without Lincoln would cause more set back and my psyche wouldn't withstand the pressure of a pregnancy alone.

"I'm pregnant!" I blurted out, and that brought the room to a sudden standstill. Not one word was uttered.

Mitchell glanced over at me in disbelief, and I could see his eyes widen from shock. After all, he was going to be an uncle. Conrad froze in place and pondered my words for a second. His head tilted upward, and I could see the wheels turning.

"If I were to say he is my husband, would that make a difference?" I gritted out.

Conrad came closer to me and lowered his head. "I assume he is the father?"

"Yes, he is, and I need him at my side," I demanded.

"If he were your husband, I would have no choice but to comply. But since he is not, and not here, I cannot approve him. Not yet." Conrad had a tweak of compassion in his tone. Shocking, I know. He grasped both my upper arms and held me in place. "Mitchell, do we have everything in place for Connors?" Conrad looked over to Mitchell.

I closed my eyes sadly.

"Yes, sir. The chopper is due here in a few minutes," Mitchell answered.

Conrad released me and walked back to his desk. On top of a stack of files was an envelope that he retrieved and gave to Mitchell.

"Sir, may I request that Maxwell accompany me?" I asked hopefully. Max and I had grown close in the last few weeks, and I trusted him as much as Mitchell or Lincoln. If I had to choose someone, I'd chose him for my protection, and I know Lincoln would approve, as well.

"Request denied," Conrad snapped.

"Sir, Maxwell is Division and has been on my detail since my arrival back. May I ask why?" I went from sad to pissed again in about three-point-two seconds. Not good for the pregnant lady.

"Maxwell will be needed here to help investigate how Aries was taken from our custody. Special Agents Anderson and Davis have been briefed and will be taking over you detail. You are to do what they say, or I will lock you up myself. Is that clear?" Conrad was done with this conversation.

"Crystal!" I snapped back.

"Go get cleaned up before departure. You look like you slaughtered a pig." And that was it. We were dismissed and had to get the hell out. "And Connors," Conrad said as I headed for the door. I turned my head and glared at him. "I sorry the circumstances aren't better, but... congratulations." Then he turned back to his desk and I walked out hoping not to see that fucker ever again.

MITCHELL TOOK ME INTO A PRIVATE CONFERENCE ROOM with an attached bathroom. I was able to clean myself up as much as I could with what I had. My clothes still had blood on them, but I was able to scrub my hands and arms. I was close to mental collapse, but I was still seething over Conrad.

Mitchell leaned up against the long table as I came out of the bathroom.

One look at him, and the flood gates opened. I collapsed into his arms and cried on his shoulder. "I can't do this," I mumbled between sobs.

"It will be all right. I'll take care of everything, I promise." Mitch wrapped me in his embrace and held my head. I usually wasn't a weak person and one who was so emotional.

"I can't go without Lincoln. Mitch you must help me. I can't go through this pregnancy alone. What if it happens again—a miscarriage? Last time it tore me apart, and Lincoln was there," I said, still crying.

Mitch pulled me out and looked deep into my eyes. "I will get him to you, I promise. But I need you to take care of my future niece or nephew." Mitchell nodded down at my soon-to-be baby belly. "You will be in the best hands I could find. Tegan and Xander will be there every step. They volunteered when we came up with this continency plan."

Tegan Davis and Xander—short for Alexander—Anderson were probably the two people in the Division that Mitchell and I trusted the most. Tegan and Xander were seasoned agents when Mitch and I came to Division, and they were assigned to be our mentors. I learned so much from each of them, and when they were reassigned, Mitch and I were very disappointed. But they felt confident we were ready for action.

I thank each of them every day, especially Tegan. She made me branch out and assured me that a woman could do anything. No man would take away my abilities. Using her words, I grew as a person and in my profession. She knew it would be hard, and as a woman of color, she'd said, "If I can conquer anything, then you can too." I never forgot that, and whenever I felt lost, I always came back to her words.

Xander was Mitchell's mentor, and reassured Mitch that as a gay man, he should not change how he performed. Xander didn't have the same struggles as Mitchell or Tegan; he was your average guy—handsome and always with great hair. Mitch and I had grown very close to them, and to this day, they were willing to help.

Mitchell's words captured me, and I focused on them. "Tegan and Xander are coming to get me, and take me where?"

"A safe house. They have been briefed on the situation; they were my first call when we decided on this backup plan," Mitch explained. "Both of them assured me they would do anything for either of us. All I had to do was get you there."

I nodded. "Okay." We knew these people, and I knew he was right. My time was running out. Before the chopper arrived, I needed to pull myself together.

"And Lincoln?" I asked.

"I will get Lincoln to you. I might need some time, but I will," Mitch promised.

I nodded again. "I need your phone." I sniffed and held my hand out.

"What for?" Mitch asked, but reached for it in his blazer pocket.

"I need to tell Lincoln I'm okay."

"I'm not sure that's a good idea."

I looked at him with puppy dog eyes and licked my lips. I needed to do this. I'd left Lincoln before without any word, and I wasn't going to do it again.

"Please, Mitch. I left him once for stupid reasons. I don't want him to think I did it again."

Mitch handed me his phone.

I brought up a new text and began to type,

MITCHELL: Linx, it's me. scared but safe. Hiding. Help MJ 4 me. ILY. Sys <3 JC.

I tried to put what I could into simple code, knowing Lincoln would decipher it. I pressed send, tilted my head back, and waiting for a response. I had to make sure he knew I was safe and to help MJ—meaning Mitch—and I loved him. That was the most important thing to make sure he knew. If he had heard about the shooting— which he would because he'd been at Metro—he would be bouncing for information.

About a minute later, Mitch's phone lit up with a message.

LINCOLN: Good. be okay. Luv you too.

I teared up at Lincoln's message and sucked on my lower lip. I was never afraid, but I was scared shitless right now. I handed the phone back to Mitch and took a deep breath.

"Thank you," I said as tears stained my cheeks.

Mitchell once again took me into his arms and held me. I didn't move, sobbing onto his shoulder. Trying to inhale some air to quiet myself, I could feel Mitch squeeze me tight. A beep came over his phone and we broke apart.

"It's time to leave," Mitch said in a low whisper.

I nodded, wiped my face, and closed my eyes. "Let's go.

MITCHELL AND I MADE OUR WAY TO THE ELEVATOR AND ascended to the roof. As the doors slid open, the wind from the chopper blades blew us around. It was always a shock when one was faced with a chopper ride. As we stepped onto the roof I saw two figures emerge from the helicopter. Tegan and Xander. They were here to take me to my new undisclosed location for who knows how long.

Mitchell turned to me, opening a file folder and handing me a regular size envelope. "Here's one of you alias packets. Passport, driver's license and a cover story in case someone asks."

I opened the envelope and found exactly what he said. Taking out the passport, I opened it to find my name had been changed from others I had. It was standard for any person working for Division to have multiple forms of identification for situations like this allowing them to leave the country. This name I was given took me by surprise.

"Jessica Matthews." My voice broke as I said the words.

"I know Lincoln won't mind, and someday I imagine it will be right anyway. It works," Mitch said to me with sad eyes.

I sucked in my lower lip, holding my emotions together. "Yeah, it has a nice ring to it." I looked up at Mitch. "Now, I just need my prince."

"I promise I will get him to you. But promise me, you'll take care of baby Matthews. My brother will never forgive us both if something happens to either of you."

"I promise." I hugged Mitch tightly. I was losing my best friend again due to my bad choices, and I didn't know if I would see him again.

We released each other and I held tight to my new identity as I walked out to greet my new protection detail. Mitch was behind me carrying the file for them. As we struggled through the wind to reach the helicopter, I was greeted with a hug from both my former mentors. They knew what was at stake and how emotional I was going to be. Mitchell gave Xander the file and shook his hand.

"Take good care of her," Mitch said, holding against the propeller wind.

"We will. She is in good hands," Xander reassured him.

Tegan placed her arm around my shoulder, guiding me into the chopper. It was time to depart. I looked back at Mitchell with blurry eyes and watched him stand there. My best friend had tears running down his face also. Stepping into the bird, I took my seat between Tegan and Xander, buckled up, swallowed my emotions, and rested my head back. Tegan handed me my headphones and I put them on. Xander adjusted his and spoke at me through the comm. "Hey, it's going to be okay." Then he patted my leg, trying to help.

Right now, I was so lost, and just wanted to crawl into a hole and hide until this whole catastrophe was over. But the end game would only result in my death or the Emissary's, and mine was more likely. The chopped lifted and we were off to my new home, God only knows where.

PART III

CHAPTER 26

TEGAN AND XANDER HAD TRANSPORTED ME TO A LITTLE
two-story Cape Cod style house in the boondocks of Kentucky. That
was about the extent I was told at first, and no outside contact was allowed. It was just the three of us. I was introduced to my new home a
few hours after I left Division headquarters and two stops in between.
Just precautionary, in case we were followed.

Tegan and Xander gave me the grand tour. The property was
fenced in and isolated, so I could go outside. They gave me the upstairs
so I could have some privacy. This included a small bathroom and an
adequate size bedroom. At least the bed wasn't a twin but a queen.
Probably for my growing belly. Welcome to my new home.

It was taking me some time to acclimate to my new life in captivity.
I mean, I wasn't a prisoner or anything, but I felt like a six-year-old
having to have a parent go everywhere with me. I wasn't allowed even
to go for a walk by myself. It was absurd. But under the circumstances,
it was necessary. I had to accept it.

But I had other things to deal with on top of my new living situation. Once my adrenaline lowered after my day of excitement, my

pregnancy was taking over. The nausea was kicking me in the ass at full force. Between sleeping and wanting to puke all the time, I was a pleasure to be around. I'd wake up, nauseous; I'd walk around and feel like I'd puke everywhere, and then I'd sleep. My favorite thing in the world wasn't even possible—coffee. It could only be decaf but was is the point that. The smell of it was so bad, I'd stay up in my room while Tegan and Xander had theirs. It was a devastating ordeal.

Within the first week, I had been scheduled for my first OB appointment. Tegan would be accompanying me, and we would follow the cover story Mitch had provided for us. I was rather impressed with what Mitch had come up with. I was an army wife and my husband had been recently deployed. Of course, Tegan and I did not look anything alike—our skin color was a dead giveaway that we were not blood relatives. My best friend had taken care of that, as well. Since my husband was not around and I was a potential high-risk pregnancy, I had been left in the care of my aunt and uncle. Xander could pull off being my uncle, so nothing was suspicious about that. Tegan and Xander portrayed a happily married couple taking care of their niece. Mitch was thorough and I was impressed.

Anyway, Tegan accompanied me to my first visit. The small town clinic never questioned our story and treated me like any normal army wife. Playing this part was strange but I would adapt. The doctor was very sweet and took her time with me. Being in my situation, I knew I had to be careful about what I was at liberty to say. I did tell her I had been pregnant before but miscarried. The last weeks had been stressful with the departure of my husband, and now the lovely first trimester side effects were in full force. I was given my exam and even got to hear the baby's heartbeat.

The moment I heard the thump of baby Matthews, my heart melted again. Tegan held my hand as I listened and wept. I wanted Lincoln to be here to hear this, but I would have to live it for both of us. Even

Tegan was moved by the sound and was the best support I could have. The doctor determined I was around nine weeks pregnant, and due to my past history I wasn't allowed any strenuous activity. That ruled out running. The Federation was going to answer for that one. I was allowed to walk as much as I wanted, but it wasn't the same. Running was my outlet. Baby Matthews was top priority, and I would not jeopardize that for anything. The baby was all I had of Lincoln right now, and I would do anything I was instructed to do.

As the days went by, Tegan and Xander were so supportive of me. Through my pissy face to times of crying, they were always there to give me a hug or a rub on the back. They took turns taking me for walks many times a day so I could get some fresh air. I took many little catnaps and ate very little. Ginger and lemon tea had become my new best friend, although many days I longed for coffee. I sat outside in the sunshine most afternoons in my new favorite fenced-in yard and tried to not dwell. Days ran together and I was getting more bored with each passing day.

There were days I read through books like crazy and others I couldn't get past two pages. I needed to keep my mind busy. Back when I was seeing Kirkman—rest her soul—I had plenty of things to keep my mind occupied. Here, I was having difficulties. One day, I wandered through the house and found a notepad. I began writing. There were many things I could put down that might help put away the Emissary if I happened to disappear. The Federation had numerous secrets and I needed to put what I knew into writing. *Fuck you, Emissary, I will haunt you from wherever I am.*

Before long, Xander had to go buy me more notebooks and pens because I was going through everything I could find to write on. Time passed, and I had accumulated stacks of notes. Hopefully if I happen to disappear, they'd come in useful.

With my new occupation of writer, the days seemed to pass by a little faster. I was still walking at least three times a day and sleeping off and on. But the nights were the hardest. Every night, if I didn't cry myself to sleep, I would wake up from a recurring nightmare. I was reliving memories again from my time with the Federation, or I would have awful scenarios of my future. Either way, sleep wasn't my friend. But writing kept me busy during the days and took away some of my anxiety.

About a month into my new life, my body had become adjusted to the baby growing inside, and thank God, the nausea eased up. I was able to actually smell coffee one morning and not want to vomit. The next step would be drinking it—decaf would have to suffice. I couldn't wait. I was also able to eat a little more food. Xander was so excited when I had a bit of an appetite that he would make me anything I wanted. And these days, I wanted nothing but chicken wings. I couldn't get enough crispy chicken wings. I know, crazy. But they made my mouth water every time.

ONE SUNNY AFTERNOON, I ACTUALLY WAS FEELING GREAT, no nausea and full of energy. Taking advantage of this, I grabbed a chair and put it smack dab in the sunshine. I was going to soak up as much rays as I could, because who knew how long this feeling was going to last. It wasn't long into my sunbathing that Tegan came in with a bag full of groceries, and a box. I didn't think anything of it. She came out onto the patio and got my attention. Xander followed her outside.

"Hey, what's up?" I turned in my chair and asked. It seemed suspicious.

"You have a package," Tegan answered, beaming.

"Me? How would anyone know I where I am?" This was making me uneasy.

"Oh, don't worry, it is from Mitchell. He is the only one who knows where we are, and he told me we would be receiving it," Tegan said.

They both came closer to me and I got up to meet them halfway. Tegan placed the box on the patio table for my inspection. On top of the box was a label with Tegan Davis on it and a P.O. box number in a town miles away. Xander handed me some scissors and I opened the box. Just a tiny bit of excitement bubbled inside of me as I opened it. I removed the padding and I was stunned when I glanced inside. I pulled out my Lincoln bear. Mitchell either had found him, or Lincoln had been involved.

Removing the bear, I looked deeper into the box and found my favorite picture of Lincoln and me. Squeezing my bear, I took our photo turned it over. On the back, I found a sticky note.

I'm not going anywhere.

Tears blurred my vision as I read Lincoln's words. These were from him, and I wasn't going to be alone. He was here with me whether through the baby or in my heart.

Tegan was also teary as she looked at me and asked, "What's the note say?"

I couldn't say it, but I showed them.

"You both are so happy!" Tegan commented as she looked at the picture. She handed it off to Xander and he smiled.

All I did was nod my head, took the picture back, and hugged my bear tighter. Xander was looking at me rather strangely when he asked, "What is that around his neck?"

His question startled me, and I inspected it immediately. Around the bear's neck was a necklace with a ring dangling from it. It was an old necklace I'd left behind when I left him for the Federation job. Lincoln must have found it and sent it along. Without hesitation, I took off the gift and put it around my neck. As it dangled, I rubbed it, taking strength from it, and then I kissed it. If I couldn't have Lincoln, these things would have to do until I could.

A MORE TIME PASSED, AND I HIT A MILESTONE. I WAS cleared by the doctor to go to work. My weeks of pregnancy had passed without issues. I had gone past the time when I'd miscarried, and the doctor said I was in great shape. I had been on restricted activities until I passed my previous date. Of course, my OB didn't know I didn't have a job and I was in hiding. But with any luck, I'd be able to convince Tegan and Xander to let me do something. At this point, I'd do anything. Some time out of confinement would be fantastic.

Luckily, Tegan and Xander weren't as hard to convince as I thought. They agreed and had gotten the go-ahead to let me have limited time out and about. I was shocked that I was going to be able to work and get out of this Godforsaken house. It's a great house, but I had spent a lot of time here and I was grateful to be released.

The next day, Xander took me around to possible places to apply for work. Whatever we chose, I had to make sure it was secure. There were many places in our little town that had help wanted signs in the window, but the one that grabbed my eye was a little diner. Xander wasn't crazy about the idea of a pregnant woman under protection waiting tables. I understood, but the moment we entered the place, Xander agreed I would be okay here. I interviewed with the owner and was hired for limited work. Excitement flowed through me and I felt as if I was glowing.

Knowing that tomorrow I was going to work made me feel on top of the world.

Many things had been conquered in the past few weeks. I'd made it passed my miscarriage date, food was edible again, my old friend coffee—decaf of course—had returned, and I was able to sleep a little more at night. All my doctor's appointments were right on schedule, the baby was growing, and so was I. My small frame showed a baby belly much quicker than I had anticipated. There was no hiding it any longer. Soon, I would have to rearrange my life for Baby Matthews, but now I took one day at a time.

The only thing missing from all of this was Lincoln. I missed him tremendously, and many nights I lay awake with a wet pillow.

The three of us made our days memorable and sometimes eventful. Tegan might get a little wild and crazy by having a glass of wine, or a whole bottle and start singing. They say laughter is good for the soul, but Tegan's singing made my gut hurt. She was hilarious. There was even times Xander would join her and seeing them smile and giggle helped me not feel so lonely. But I wouldn't mention any of this. Everyone was supposed to be acting professional, and our silly moments were far from that. I was so grateful for these two and what they have done for me. I will never be able to repay them.

CHAPTER 27

ONE LATE NIGHT, MY BRAIN WOULD NOT SHUT OFF. IT kept turning and sleep was pushed away. The wheels never slowed, and I thought I might scream in frustration. Lying in my bed was no longer an option, so I got up with difficulty— my belly was now much bigger—and downstairs I went.

As I tried to walk down the stairs quietly, my feet protested. I thumped all the way down, most likely waking the others. I made the bottom step and headed toward the kitchen. To my surprise, I found Xander perched in the chair in the living room reading the paper.

"Can't sleep?" he asked, not moving his paper.

I knew my steps had been too loud.

"Between my brain churning and my belly doing somersaults, sleep wasn't an option. So, I thought some herbal tea might help." I answered, patting my belly. It was about the size of half a basketball and growing rapidly.

Xander looked at me inquisitively as he lowered his paper. For some reason, I don't think he completely bought my story. "Yeah, I don't think that is the reason. I mean, I believe the baby has something to do with it, but there's more." He was able to distinguish my feelings by my expressions, as well as, if not better than I can.

"No, that's not all of it," I confirmed feeling let down.

I went around to the couch and squatted down, angling myself at Xander. This was going to be quite the conversation. I had his full attention.

"Have you ever had a time when everything around you was going good, but you felt so lost?" I asked.

"Yeah, I have." Xander placed his paper aside and leaned closer to me. "I felt very much as you do right now after I lost my wife, Kathy."

"You did?" I asked, stunned. I never knew Xander had been married. He never talked about it, so I assumed the job had always ruled his life. That's what happens when you assume.

"I remember feeling so lost after she died. Kathy was the love of my life. When the car accident took her from me, I wanted to hide and shut down. My world died the day she did."

"I'm sorry, I didn't know. I bet that was horrible."

"Yes, it was. Pieces of my heart and soul were ripped out and trampled on. Like you, I felt very much alone. It is a miserable feeling, and I'm sorry for you." Xander looked at me with true intentions. He leaned forward in his chair. "I know how much you miss him."

"Very much. I'm hollow without him. Way more this time."

"I know. I see the pain in your eyes and hear your cries every night. There are days when I miss Kathy so much, I just want to break down. But knowing her, she wouldn't want me to. She would want me to live, and to live up to my potential." This was a side of Xander I wasn't expecting, but I was glad.

"I know Lincoln would want me to do the same, but its restricting here, hiding."

"Yes, it is. But I know he would want you and that baby safe. Nothing else matters." Xander was correct. Lincoln would protect me in any way possible.

"He's a good guy." I smiled at that. The truth sometimes hurts but will also heal.

We both took a moment to collect our thoughts. I thought about the things Xander had said, that he'd had a wife. She was the love of his life and then was gone. I can relate. Except my lover is still alive, as far as I know, and can come back to me. Kathy Anderson could not. I could see in Xander's eyes that the memories of Kathy still saddened his soul, and I truly felt sorry.

"Hey, did you know that I was supposed to be your mentor all those years ago?" Our moment of silence was over and Xander was changing the topic.

Xander's comment took me off guard. "You were? How come I was assigned to Tegan?"

"When we got word that new recruits were coming our way, you were assigned to me. Both of us share a skill that most people don't." He paused for me to ponder what we had. "You and I are very good people readers. We can read a person's face or body and know what they are thinking. Our psychology training helps us distinguish these different emotions. Not many can put those two things together, so you were assigned to me."

"Why was I never told this?" I was a little confused.

"I requested that you not be told, and Tegan and I were able to swap. Mitchell was better suited for her, but you were..." He paused. "You reminded me too much of Kathy. When I saw you, it was as if I had gone back in time. Kathy had a lot of the same features as you, and all I saw when I looked at you was her. With it being so close after the accident, it was too troubling for me to see her in you every day. And I am sorry for that now. I could have helped you in many ways if I'd stuck with you."

I leaned closer to Xander and placed my hand on top of his. "I am sorry about your wife, and I am sorry I resemble her, but I'm not sorry you are here right now with me. Helping. You and Tegan gave up your normal lives to protect me, and for that I am truly grateful." I was getting emotional now.

"Well, if I had been there for you in the beginning, maybe we wouldn't be here now. You'd maybe be having a baby with the person you love instead of being in hiding." Xander held my hand tighter. "But I promise I will get you home safely, and, the Federation will not exist anymore." He seemed sure that would happen.

"I really hope you're right, Xander."

We both sat in silence for a brief time, pondering everything we'd each expressed. I hadn't shared a heartfelt moment with anyone except Lincoln for a long time.

"Have you heard from Mitchell? Anything?" I asked, breaking the silence.

Xander looked up at me and sat back, getting more comfortable. "Not for about a week. He was able to inform me there is a rather large bounty on your head."

I looked away. "No surprise there. The Emissary is out for blood—my blood. How about Aries?" I was hoping Xander might accidentally spill some information.

"Well, from the briefing I got, Aries was stolen from headquarters and according to Mitchell, it was an inside job."

I stared up at the ceiling. All of this was my fault. If I had stayed with the Federation, this would never have happened. I'd be out in the sun, working and alive. Now I am pregnant and in hiding, all because I had orders from the Division. Hurt the ones I love to keep others safe, or the Federation would hurt even more people by using the Aries device. It was a no-brainer. My life was forfeited, but the life of my child was not.

"Yeah, Mark Wallace. He was able to infiltrate headquarters and steal Aries. I knew it when I met him, that he was Federation. Only I realized it too late. I tried to use the knowledge of the thief to Conrad before my departure. My bargaining chip for Lincoln. It obviously didn't work."

"Wallace was the mole? Somehow that doesn't surprise me. Just remember Conrad is a ass but he is good at his job. They will find him."

"But there is one thing the Emissary doesn't know." This, I was proud of.

Xander looked at me inquisitively. "Really? Do tell."

"I was able to reprogram Aries when I discovered it. I am the only person who able to operate the device. No matter how much he tries, the Emissary will not be able to open it."

"When did you do that? It was handed over as soon as you reached DC." I had gotten Xander's attention.

"I was examining the device and I tweak it. Therefore, I am actually more valuable alive than dead."

Xander's body relaxed and a huge smile formed. "That's my girl!"

As my time went on, my belly grew rapidly, making my waitressing job more difficult. I was still working at the diner, but my load was on the light side. I'd met some of the nicest people in the world and made new friendships. The problem was, I was living a lie, and these were not people I wanted to lie to. My coworkers were so generous about my life and accepted me with open arms. They all believed my cover story about being an army wife, and there wasn't one thing they wouldn't do for me.

But today, I could feel something was up. Entering my thirty-second week, I became more limited in what I could do, and that realization made me rather sad. Soon I would have to give up my time with my diner companions. Baby Matthews was making things more difficult. When pregnant people tell you about the waddling and you shake it off, yeah, don't. I have the waddles bad, and it's not a walk in the park.

But there was something going on, and Xander and Tegan were in on it.

I dressed in a maternity shirt and got ready for the ride to the diner. As I suspected, there was something up. Both Tegan and Xander felt the need to drive me there. Um, yeah, as if that wasn't a dead giveaway. When we pulled up to the diner, it was as if life never existed inside. All the lights were off, and the place looked abandoned. The place should be hoppin' by now.

Suspiciously, I got out of the back slowly and waddled my way to the door. It took me a little longer to get there. It seemed overnight my feet had swelled, and my belly was twice as big. It was going to be a long eight weeks. I hesitated when I reached for the door, but overcame my uneasiness, sliding it open and ringing the bell.

The place was deserted.

"Hello, Marge. Jerry. Anyone here?" I called out, spying around.

"Surprise!" My coworkers jumped out from hiding and yelled.

My heart and the baby jumped, and I screeched slightly. Surprise took my breath away.

The lights came on and I held my hand over my mouth, catching my breath and giggles. Emotions flooded through me as I gazed around the room. All my coworkers and many of my fond customers were present, and the room was decorated in baby attire. I was speechless.

"Oh my, this is so...amazing." My heart felt so much love. "You all put this together for me?"

Jerry, the owner of our little diner, stepped forward all smiles. "You have become part of our family, and with a little one on the way and you being away from your love, we thought we'd surprise you." He was so jolly as he came over and hugged me. I could feel his emotions feeding into me when he hugged me.

"Everyone here chipped in to throw you and the baby a shower. It only seemed fitting!" Marge said in her southern accent. Marge was an older lady, possibly in her late 50s or early 60s. She had been waiting table most of her life. I couldn't have asked for a nicer lady to be my confidant.

"I am so thankful for all this. You all mean so much to me. I— We are so grateful." I rubbed my belly. "There are not enough words." I had to stop and inhale.

Marge came over and rubbed my shoulder. I took her hands and held on. No words were needed.

"Ah, let's get this show rolling. We got gifts and food." Jerry was always able to turn something serious into fun. "I've got cake!" He smirked at me, holding a delicious-looking cupcake up to his nose. Jerry was teasing me, and he knew it.

I am a sucker for sweets. I snatched the cupcake and took a bite in satisfaction. It was so scrumptious. I may have eaten more than one. *Whoops.*

Since I hadn't found out the sex of the baby, the diner and gifts were decked out in greens and yellows. It didn't feel right finding out without Lincoln. I was going to need him soon for my sanity, and for the baby. Whether I'm in hiding or not. Plus, I was so Goddamn horny, Lincoln was needed to solve that problem as well.

Mitchell better get his ass in gear or momma bear won't be nice.

Everyone at the diner told me congrats, and many said they can't wait for the little one to arrive. Unfortunately, I knew I wouldn't be here much longer once the baby was born. Risking the lives of these wonderful people wasn't an option. The Emissary would give no mercy to any acquaintances who might have helped me.

I unwrapped gift after gift and stuffed my face with way too much food. Jerry even got me laughing so hard I almost peed myself. Small bladder plus baby plus Jerry equals watch out bathroom line. Pregnant lady goes first.

After an hour of unwrapping piles of diapers, wipes, outfits, and many gorgeous homemade quilts and other things, I was pooped. Nap time anyone? Yes, me.

"Thank you everyone, so very much. We are ready for anything now!"

"Not so fast, missy!" Jerry said from behind me.

I turned. Jerry was holding one last gift with a dozen long-stemmed roses and a note taped to the vase. The elegant roses were dazzling and smelled wonderful. My first instinct was they were from Lincoln, but as I pondered, I realized the color was not right, and the roses were far too perfect. Pink Roses? Lincoln knew I wasn't a fan of pink.

"Oh, Jerry, they are beautiful. You outdid yourself," I boasted to Jerry.

He loved every minute of it, but said, "Sorry my sweet girl, I wish I could take credit for them. I would have done a great job...and probably be broke by the look of those beauties." Jerry was a jokester and a gentleman. And he was correct. These flowers were so perfect they would have cost a fortune.

Peering around the room, I was able to catch Xander's eye and give him a brief warning.

Then I smiled at Jerry and reached for the package and note. My pulse took off as I took out the card and read it.

> *My sweet darling,*
> *I am pleased that you are healthy and are taking good care of our child. We will be reunited soon, and I am anxious to meet our beloved miracle. You and I are in need of a conversation. In the package is a secure line for us. I await your call.*
> *R.E.*

The blood drained from my face and my body was immobile. I once again caught Xander's eye, and he knew I was scared.

How the hell did the Emissary find me?

He thinks the baby is his. Of course, he would. I am probably the last person he fucked. I snatched up the package and pretended it was

177

time for a bathroom break again. I needed to hear what the Emissary wanted. Xander wouldn't be far behind, after seeing my expression.

Between the bathroom doors was an exit to the back behind the diner. I sneaked out. Unwrapping the package, I found a burner cell phone with just one number programmed. The Emissary's. With shaking hands, I hit speed dial.

The Emissary answered the first ring. "Well, my dear. I see you received my note and the roses."

"Yes, I did. They are lovely. Thank you. What can I help you with?" Patience was not one of my virtues, but I was trying my best to be pleasant.

"I was ecstatic when I heard of your pregnancy, and knowing the child is one of the Federation's, I felt I needed to reach out. I now understand why you defected. You should come home, and we will care for you."

"How can you be so sure the child is yours?" I asked, controlling my tone.

"Jessy, I know the child is mine because no one else would want a little slut like you. You had it so good here, but then you decided to betray us. This news must have been alarming, and running was thought to be your only option. I am offering you a chance to come home and give our child a wonderful life. All will be forgiven, as long as you come back willingly."

Wow, he had given me so many insults and kept a pleasant voice. Jackass.

"There is no guarantee the child is yours. You just called me a slut, so the possibilities are endless. Also, I do not believe you will greet me with open arms if I choose to return." My voice was solid, but my insides were burning up.

"For the safety of the child, I give you my word no harm will be done to either of you. No one will hurt you. I swear."

"Sir, even if I wanted to return, I am restricted on any length of travel. No major changes in my living arrangements will be allowed until after the birth. My body will not handle it." It wasn't all a lie, but not all was true either.

"Is that so? Then I will send someone around to keep an eye on you and my new prized possession. See you very soon." That was it, the call went dead and he was gone.

The call may have lasted only a few minutes, but a lifetime flew by before my eyes.

With a jitter of my hand, I dropped the phone and it smashed on the ground. Stunned and terrified were the only things I could feel. I was paralyzed.

No emotion Jess, you have a building behind you full of people who care about you. All you did was go pee. Get your ass back in there, and then get the hell out of there. Xander will be looking for you.

My brain always gave me a pep talk when I needed it.

So, I went back inside.

CHAPTER 28

In the diner, Xander and Tegan were both waiting for me.

I went straight to them, still clenching the Emissary's note. "I could use a nap. Would one of you take me home?" I asked trying to be normal, but there were too many breaks in my tone.

"What's going on?" Tegan asked with concern.

"I am a little overwhelmed, but I don't want to spoil everyone's fun," I lied.

Xander knew better and read right through my lie. Tegan wasn't buying it, either.

"Please, I want to go home," I pleaded with them.

"Okay, I'll get the car," Xander complied.

"We can come back for the rest of the things." Tegan patted my upper arm and left me standing there.

I was able to hold my self together to say good-bye to everyone, giving many hugs and thank yous. Everyone understood that baby Matthews was wearing me out and I needed a nap. Even some smartass comments from Jerry got a giggle out of me. He and Marge had done a fantastic job, and I felt guilty that I wasn't able to stay longer. The conversation with the Emissary had frazzled me. I just wanted to get home, wherever that was.

The one thing I took with me for show was the roses. Everyone believed my husband had sent them to me. But really, I need something to burn. It was a shame to destroy them, but I needed to take my frustration out on something. We arrived back at the safe house, which now had been compromised, and I clenched the flowers and note. The whole ride back I was silent and wanting solitude. Xander had sensed my apprehension and left me alone.

"I'm going to lie down," I blurted out and proceeded up the stairs. I could feel both sets of eyes staring at my back.

I went up the stairs, closed the door to my room, and with every ounce of strength, I chucked the vase of roses against the wall. "*God fucking damn it!*" I screamed in fury as the vase smashed.

I grabbed my bear and sank to the floor by the window as tears streamed down my face. It wasn't long before a knock came at my door. Both Tegan and Xander had heard the smash and were checking on me.

Three knocks and Tegan said, "Jess, is everything okay?"

Without an invite, both my mentors entered my room.

I looked over at them, a complete mess, and said nothing. Tegan looked down and saw the smashed vase and roses scattered on the floor. She bent down to pick up one of them.

I stopped her. "Don't. Who know how much poison is on them?"

"Who are they from?" Xander stepped forward and asked me bluntly.

I held up the note and he took it. His look said it all when it registered the flowers were not from Lincoln or Mitchell.

"He found me. It's only a matter of time before they come for me," I said in shock.

"What is she talking about?" Tegan asked Xander.

Xander handed her the note and she also scanned it. "Who is R.E.?"

Tegan was a smart lady, but at the moment, I thought she was the dumbest lady in the world.

"The Emissary." I squeezed my Lincoln bear tighter.

"What was that phone call about?" Xander asked. He meant business now. My friend and mentor was on duty.

"The Emissary was congratulating me on our child, and said if I came back willingly, I would not be harmed. Whatever that means."

That was all Xander needed to hear. He was out the door with phone in hand. He was a planner, and this wasn't part of the plan. I needed to be prepared to move again, but it wouldn't make a difference now.

Tegan came over to my bed and sat down, inviting me to sit with her. "I know this is not a question you want to hear, but...are you sure the child isn't his?"

The question shocked me, and I can guarantee my tear-stained face showed my disbelief. "What? Yes, I know for a fact the baby isn't his. He isn't the only one who has secrets," I answered, looking away. My brain was exhausted, but it wouldn't rest. "There are things about his medical history that he doesn't believe. Things I shouldn't know."

"I believe you, but I had to ask," Tegan said a little guiltily.

"I know. Don't you think that hadn't crossed my mind? But one of the first times I encountered the Emissary, I learned something important."

That was when one his biggest secrets was revealed to me...

I ENTERED THE EMISSARY'S OFFICE IN SURPRISE. I WASN'T expecting to meet with him this early. I had only been working for the Federation for a few weeks. I had seen more and experienced more than I ever had in my previous job. I had undergone a few strenuous tests and been given mountains of work. I seemed to be holding my own according to Susan and making a good impression around the corporation.

Today was a warm day, so I'd chosen to wear a skirt and a light cotton blouse. The air conditioning hit me with an arctic blast when I entered the Emissary's office. *Holy*. But I didn't let that faze me. Today, nervous, I was hoping for praise from the Emissary for all my accomplishments since I'd been with the Federation.

Closing the door behind me, I waited for an acknowledgment from the Emissary. He was busy hovering over his desk, so I waited patiently.

"Come in, Ms. Bowman. Thank you for meeting with me," the Emissary greeted me, and gestured over to one of the chairs in front of his desk.

"Good day, sir. It is a beautiful day. I hope you will get outside to enjoy it," I responded.

"I hope to. Sit. I wanted to talk to you about your performance over the previous weeks."

I took a seat and properly placed my legs and hands to cover my bare legs. "Of course, sir. I appreciate the opportunity the Federation has given me." I needed to butter him up before I either got bad news or praise.

"I have been impressed with your performance since you got here. My staff raves about you and your skills. You have performed admirably." The Emissary moved out from behind his desk and closer to me.

"Thank you, sir."

Before I could say any more, the Emissary place his hand on my shoulder and his fingers began to creep south. "So many good things have been said about you that I want you to work under me now. You will go far in the Federation with my guidance." His hand began to rub me while moving closer to my breast.

My body froze and stiffened as I analyzed his actions. My intuition told me this wasn't a situation I wanted to be in. His hands moved down and into my shirt.

"I believe we will work wonders together," he said, caressing me.

I was so uneasy. "Please, sir. I don't want to do this. I am not that kind of person," I pleaded, but his actions did not stop.

"Oh, yes you are. If you want to advance your career here, this is your only choice." The words whispered in my ear were pure evil. I could feel his breath upon my neck, and it made my body shiver.

"No! It isn't." I blurted out, stiffening.

In a flash, a knife whipped around to graze my neck. The Emissary was fast with the weapon, but he never broke the skin.

The move was unexpected, and I felt a rush of panic.

"I suggest you do as you are told, or this lovely neck is going to be damaged, and every time you see one of the scars, this moment will haunt you." He pulled my hair, lifting my chin and exposing my neck. I swallowed hard but said nothing. "Do we have an understanding?"

I nodded, but also added, "For the record, I am saying no. But as you hold the knife and I am defenseless. I have no choice."

"Good girl. Now *get up!*" the Emissary commanded, never moving the knife from my neck.

As he grasped my hair in one hand and the long knife in the other, he pulled me up off the chair and guided me to the front of his desk. I felt the tension lessen on my hair as he pressed his body against me, holding me in position.

"Now, that's better." The Emissary released my hair and moved his hand up my thigh.

"Please stop," I begged as a tear steamed down my cheek. His hand was at the apex of my thighs and began to invade my panties. The cold steel of his knife sent a shiver through my body.

"I suggest you hold still. I wouldn't want to damage your beautiful appearance." With a swift move of his hand, I heard his zipper and button of his pants release.

His body pressed harder against me and I could feel his erection against my backside.

"Please," I whispered one last time.

In one movement the Emissary thrust into me from behind. I wanted to yelp in pain but held back my cry. Any movement would do more damage. With every thrust, more pain filled my lungs and tears fell. As the Emissary pushed harder, the knife upon my neck loosened, but the damage was done. Thrust and pull, thrust and push, he held my hips and did his damage. I tried to move away but when I tried, a nick appeared at the side of my neck.

Because I was cut, the Emissary's speed increased. He got even more turned on.

I was terrified.

Minutes seemed like eternity as he continued his assault. I just wanted it to end and find a place to hide. Rape was never something you forget, and I was now a victim. Time slowed to a crawl as he began to climax. I just wanted it all to end. He had done his damage to me physically and mentally, but if I was to continue at the Federation, I would need to find a way to cope.

I had my orders from Division, and I was damn sure going to get the job done.

Finally, the Emissary pulled out and pushed me away with force. I almost fell to the floor but grabbed the desk to steady myself. He zipped himself back up and pulled my hair to bring me back to standing.

I could feel his breath on my neck again, still restrained as he whispered, "I'd say you're a decent fuck." The Emissary released me and shoved me away. Before I faced him, I made sure I showed no emotion. Nothing could be evident to him that this had affected me. Nothing.

"Go clean yourself up. I promise the next time will be more pleasurable." His devilish eyes pierced me, and his words were twisted.

I smoothed my skirt and left the office with my head held high.

"Why wasn't any of this in your briefing?" Tegan asked me to bring me back to focus. "This could explain your pregnancy and also why you've survived."

Xander had reentered the room as I recited my horrifying experience.

I held my head in shame but answered, "Because this was over a year ago, and I haven't finished the whole story."

"Please tell us," Xander pushed as he leaned against the door frame. "It may be the only way we can help you."

The instant I left the Emissary's office, I went straight back to my place to rinse my hatred and the essence of him off my body. When I walked through the door, I wasn't expecting my sister to be waiting. The moment I saw Susan, I wanted to punch her and scream.

"You knew!" I barked at her.

She came over to me slowly with depressed eyes. "I saw the way he looked at you when you first arrived. It was only a matter of time. We all go through the same thing." Her tone was one of concern and sorrow.

"You could have warned me so I could have mentally prepared myself. How could you be so callous?" My temper was flaring.

"If I'd told you, would you have been able handle it without giving away your knowledge? The Emissary isn't stupid, Jess. Keeping you in the dark was to help preserve your true intentions and identity."

I knew Susan was correct, but the truth stung, and the damage was done.

"All I will say is, if he believes you are as smart as you are, this will continue, and you better find a way to cope," Susan said and turned away.

"I have to complete my assignment, Susan," I called out to her.

She turned toward me again. "I know. And now I'd recommend you shower and go see Dr. Edward. He can help you." With that advice, Susan walked off.

I did as she'd instructed.

An hour later, after standing in the shower for as long as the hot water lasted, I was in the office of Dr. Ross Edward, one of the Federation's doctors.

"So, what can I help you with today?" Dr. Edward asked me, very straightforward. Edward, a tall man with thinning hair and a lean build. He was so tall I felt like an ant as I looked up. His light brown eyes showed concern and his posture showed interest.

"I need the morning after pill," I said quietly.

"I assumed when I saw you that this might be the situation," he responded.

I was shocked. "How could you possibly know my situation?"

"Just by looking at you. You're very pretty and petite, just the Emissary's type. I assume you have the smarts, or you wouldn't be involved with the Federation." His words had me in complete disarray.

"Apparently, I am. I take it this happens often?" I asked, already suspecting the answer.

He came around his desk, but instead of leaning up against it, he sat down next to me. "Yes, it does, but only to a select few. I believe I remember seeing another person in here who looked almost like you some time ago. At first, I thought you were her, but you have a slightly different appearance."

I looked at him. "That's my twin."

"Yes, Susan. I am sorry you were to be his next victim." Edward actually felt sorry for me.

"Any suggestions? I have been informed this will happen again, and I need to cope with it. I don't want to get pregnant with that monster's baby." The thought sent fury coursing through my veins.

"The coping part, I suggest something form of exercise or booze. The first time will always stay with you, but seeing the look in your eyes, you'll get anything you want from him. It will be your job to determine how to use him to your advantage. I see much rage and determination in you." He paused and I just watched him. There was something about him, almost as if I could trust him and confide in him.

"And the second?"

"The second part about getting pregnant isn't as much of a concern."

"Wait, what?" I demanded.

"I can give you the morning after pill, or information." He was giving me an option. Like hell, I wanted the pill. "Hear me out."

"Okay, but what could be so important that you give me this unacceptable choice?" I was on the verge of losing my cool.

"This is a breach of doctor patient confidentiality; I will take the consequences should this surface. You should know the Emissary isn't able to procreate."

This got my attention. "What? You're saying the Emissary isn't able to have children? He's sterile."

"Yes, that is exactly what I'm saying." I saw a hint of a smile on Edward's face. This was a game-changer. "When he was a child, he developed a severe case of the mumps. He ended up hospitalized and suffered many side effects. Sterility was one of them."

"But he was erect and got off. How is that possible?" All this was panicking me.

"There are issue with his swimmers. The testicles don't produce sperm. Simply put, the equipment works, but he is shooting blanks," Edward explained.

All I felt through all my hatred was immense relief.

"I can still give you the pill for your peace of mind, but I have run multiple tests and can assure you of the diagnosis."

"Does he know?" I was baffled by this news.

"He knows, but he is convinced there is one person who will bless him with a child. My experience tells me it will never happen, but he insists on keeping his fantasy."

Man, I was starting to like Dr. Edward.

"Ok, um, I guess you have given me what I want." I got up from the chair.

Edward rose as well and looked at me. "Hey, I know this isn't easy, but I have a feeling you will be someone to watch out for in this organization. The Emissary may not know what he's dealing with in you." He smiled and led me over to the door. "If anytime you need to chat, feel free. My door is always open."

"Thank you, I appreciate that," I said, and looked into his eyes. The eyes were kind, telling me this was a person I could trust.

I CAME BACK TO THE PRESENT AND FINISHED THE STORY for Tegan and Xander.

"Edward and I became good friends after that day, and I confided in him a lot. The information he gave me proved to be true. Susan confirmed it. So, I know this child isn't the Emissary's even though he believes it is."

I had explained enough. I was done for the day. Lincoln was the child's true father, not the Emissary. Nothing and no one would ever going to change that.

CHAPTER 29

I was starting to feel like a beached whale as another week passed. I made up the excuse to Jerry and Marge that I was just too exhausted to work a shift anymore, and to my surprise, they totally agreed. I could work the counter for a few minutes, but other than that, nada. After the conversation I'd had with the Emissary a week ago, I was happy not to go anywhere.

In my profession, I learned through many hours of training that you should not get frazzled. But after the chilling talk with the Emissary, I was frazzled and very nervous for the baby. My fate had already been decided when I took the Federation assignment. But I'd be damned if I'd let my baby suffer the same fate, or worse.

In any case, my beached whale status left me waddling and struggling with everything. If I fell, it was unlikely I'd get back up without assistance. At least I had been promoted to top prego status, and I could ask for just about everything at any time. Being the person I was, I still tried to do as much as I could myself. I was bitchy if I couldn't manage.

After telling them about my conversation with the Emissary, I knew it was only a matter of time before Xander and Tegan received backup. I suspected that Xander had gone out of my room that day to tell Mitchell about the development. As much as I wanted to talk to my best friend, or anyone from the outside world, it would be prohibited. I was unsure when we'd get help, but it shouldn't have taken this long. Mitchell was usually very prompt.

Today was beautiful outside and I was taking full advantage of it. My comfy lawn chair was out of sight in our very secluded backyard, so I could sit there with my belly in the air and very comfy clothes. My dress today was light and airy. With sunglasses on, I floated away in the quiet.

"Hey, Jess." A hand nudged my shoulder. It startled me, and then I realized it was Tegan.

"Oh, hey, what's up?" I asked sleepily. I must have dozed off. The sun and air had felt so good, and I was so tired that I'd fallen into a nice slumber.

"Xander has returned with more agents for your protection. We figured you'd like to meet them," Tegan said, standing in my sunlight so I could see her.

"Yeah, okay." I started to rise. Started was the key word, because this beached whale was going to need assistance. "Hey, Tegan. Little help here," I called out to her since she had already headed back into the house.

A little chuckle came out of her as she came back to help me up. Many grunts and groans later, Tegan had helped hoist me up. It was a struggle, and I was almost completely out of breath, but I made it. I took a minute to collect myself, smooth my belly, and adjust my dress. Man, I was not sure how much longer I could keep this basketball inside me.

Tegan turned back toward the house and Xander waited for me in the kitchen as I waddled my way in.

"Hey, so where are the poor souls that got assigned to babysit me?" I was trying to make light of the situation even though I was worried.

"One is waiting in the living room, and the other is grabbing a few things out of the car." Xander responded, glancing at the living room and sipping his coffee.

I turned to go. My dress swished like a bell as I made my way to living room. There was a man standing with his back to me wearing a white T-shirt and a pair of black pants. There was little to no hair on the back of his head, and instant familiarity rushed over me.

With one movement of my new security, my heart stuttered and skipped a beat. My breath caught in my throat and I gasped. My eyes welled with happy tears and I put my hands to my face in joy.

"Lincoln!"

"Hey, Jess." He turned toward me.

My heart stopped as the man I'd presumed to be Lincoln, wasn't. My heart fell when I looked into the eyes of Sam Maxwell. "Max?"

"Hey you!" Sam was glad to see me, even if I was majorly disappointed. It wasn't that I wasn't glad Sam was here, but my whole mentality had been counting on that person being Lincoln. Damn!

Nevertheless, I took a deep breath and forced a smile. "Hi."

He looked me up and down with a returning smile. "Wow!" Sam said, astonished when he looked down at my very huge baby belly.

"Yeah, I am rather large." At least I was able to chuckle about my size.

Max approached me and placed his hands on my biceps. "I know I am not the person you hoped to see, but I am here for you."

I was so touched by his heartfelt words that I sniffled back a sob. He reached out to hug me and I fell into is arms. I nodded and close my eyes. Max knew the emotions I was feeling, and it embarrassed me.

"I'm sorry. I'm glad you're here. It's just...I thought at first you were Lincoln." I spoke into Max's chest and he rubbed my back.

"I know, I know. Mitchell is trying his best to get him here." Because of height, Max placed his chin on my head as he talked.

I pulled away and dabbed my eyes. I had so much going on emotionally that I was due for a breakdown. But I needed to hold myself together until I was alone. I prefer to break down in bed, or in the shower; no one else can see my weakness.

"I appreciate you coming. But um, I think I need to lay down." I gave Max another quick hug and turned toward the stairs.

"Jess," Max called, I turned back. "If it helps—" His eyes showed nothing, but sadness and it hurt my heart. He closed the gap between us. "If it helps, Lincoln is going crazy, and is doing everything he can to get to you. Especially now. I know how he feels, and I promised him to take care of you." Deep down, I could sense that Max was having regrets.

"Thank you, I really am glad you are here. I missed you. And our runs!" I wiped my eyes and started to turn away. I need to be by myself for a bit. Just seeing Sam Maxwell was hitting too close to home.

I walked up the stairs very slowly and went to my bedroom. Shutting the door behind me, I leaned on the back of it and cried. No idea how long I stood there against the door before my legs started to tremble and gravity started taking hold. At that sign, I moved over to my bed and sank into the pillows. It wasn't long before my pillow was wet with tears and I was slipping into unconsciousness. I just wanted to sleep and wake up with everything normal and happy again, not this hiding with boredom and depression every day. How was I going to bring a child into this world if I didn't want to be here myself...?

I was suddenly startled awake by a few raps on my door. "Jess, you up here?" It was Xander.

Max must have told him where I was. How much time had passed since I came upstairs? My head was foggy from my nap and I didn't intend on moving. Xander would just have to come in.

"Yeah, I'm here," I answered groggy.

Xander swung open the door and crept in. From the look in his eyes, he could see my bleakness. I did not move my body but only my eyes to look up at him.

"Max told me you came up here. I thought you would be glad to see him."

Slowly, I turned my head as he came closer to my bed. I was in no mood for company and solitude was calling my name. "Sorry. I needed to rest." Short and sweet.

"I can see that, but that isn't the problem." Xander wasn't buying it. "What is really going on? And don't give me that I'm tired bullshit."

That perked me up enough to pull myself together. "Bullshit? You think that is what I'm doing? I am pregnant and I am exhausted all the time. I want this kid out of me. I want my life back. And most of all, I want Lincoln." Once I started speaking, I word-vomited everything out. I was feeling very selfish right now, but fuck it, I didn't care.

"I know. But hiding all the time isn't healthy for either of you. We are doing what we can to keep you and your little alien safe." Xander paused and grinned. "Being in this situation isn't easy, but these are the cards we've been dealt, so we need to play them."

"I am not upset with any of you. This situation just sucks! I appreciate all you have done for me, but I just want to go home." There weren't enough words to explain my sorrow.

"Me, too." Xander placed his hand on mine. "My hope is, it will not be much longer. Once the baby is born, we can make more progress."

"In other words, use me as bait? It's me they want, and I am the only one who can get Aries operating."

It was true but being eight months pregnant I was a liability and the risk was too high to do anything other than wait it out.

"Unfortunately, that's true. But right now, we need to make sure you're safe." Xander smiled but it was so fake. They wanted to keep my child safe, but afterward I was expendable. Neither Mitchell nor

Lincoln had any connections to the Federation. They would care for the child. I realized I was just a surrogate, and my heart broke for the second time today.

For a few moments, there was silence between me and Xander. Both of us had much to think about but didn't want to say a word. I glanced out the window to see that night was approaching. I had slept for a few hours. At least they'd left me alone.

Xander finally broke the tension between us. "Tegan has returned with the other agent. I came up to see if you were up to waddling downstairs to see him."

"Another one?" Wow, Mitchell wasn't taking any chances. "Sam Maxwell is perfectly adequate. Why the extra?"

"Well, we need extra protection for you and Mitchell and Conrad—"

"*Conrad?*" I was shocked. Conrad didn't give a shit about anyone but himself. Asshole.

"Yes, Conrad was the one who ordered the extra protection. They have arrived if you want to go greet them."

I nodded and swung my legs around to the edge of the bed. I was a little winded. Xander saw my struggle and put his hand under my arm to assist. I was able to stand to my surprise and waddled out the door.

CHAPTER 30

THE HALLWAY WAS DARK AS THE SUN HAD SET AND NIGHT had fallen. I knew this house like the back of my hand, and I could find my way in complete dark. Xander went behind me as I walked toward the stairs. All I could see at the top of the stairs was Tegan with her short black hair. She turned back to me, talking to what sounded like Max. Stairs were becoming not so nice to me the bigger I got, so I had to take one at a time. Being huge isn't so cool after being so tiny for so long. And I longed to run again. Ugh!

A few steps down, I stopped abruptly, and everyone turned to look at me. My hands shot to cover my face as sobs came out of my mouth. The sight I saw was so overwhelming, there was no holding back. Trying not to tumble down the stairs, my pace quickened as my vision blurred.

The man whose arms I jumped into made my long, lonely struggle worth every moment.

Lincoln enveloped me into his embrace, and I cried like a small child. No one said a word as we had our moment together, long lost souls being united once again.

"Hey, I'm here. Shhh. I'm not going anywhere," Lincoln whispered into my ear as I tried to subdue my crying.

"I thought I'd never see you again!" I sobbed into his shoulder.

I looked up at him with soggy eyes. "I'm here," he said and kissed me. Not just a peck on the lips, but a real kiss of reunion. The moment seemed to go by in a blink of an eye, and I wasn't ready for it to stop. Something pushed us apart, and as we did, I couldn't help but let out a giggle through all my tears. He put me down, but I was not going to move away from him. I made sure I had some part of my body touching his.

"Holy shit, what are you carrying in there, a soccer player?" Lincoln asked.

So funny.

It suddenly dawned on me what had pulled us apart. Baby Matthews was doing somersaults. I place my hand on my belly and there was no doubt the baby was wide awake.

"Someone knows their dad!" So much joy filled my body, I felt as if I radiated the whole place with it. My depression had put me into a dark place and my world would have died if Lincoln hadn't reappeared.

"I would say so," Lincoln replied as everyone in the room let out a brief laugh.

I took his hand and placed it on my belly.

Once I came down from my high, I realized everyone in the room had been watching us. Tegan, Xander and Max were all witnesses as I cried my dark emotions away. My control was finally returning, and I wanted to hug each one of them for this moment. But I'd do that later. I wasn't letting this man out of my sight.

"Well," Xander interrupted. "Why don't you show Lincoln where he will be staying. I assume with you?" Xander looked at me with a smile. "We will be down here reviewing all the lovely new information Lincoln has brought to us. Courtesy of Mitchell Johnson."

I couldn't tell what Xander's tone had implied, but I didn't care. I had what I wanted.

Lincoln released me, snatched his duffle, and started for the stairs.

I went to follow but hesitated and turned back to the two people who had cared for me for all these long months. "Thank you both so much," I said with so much gratitude, and hugged them both tightly. They hugged me back just as tight.

"Go." Tegan pushed me gently as we pulled away. "He has missed you as much as you have him."

With a grin, I weebled and wobbled my way to him, and with a hand, he helped me upstairs.

AT THE TOP OF THE STAIRS, LINCOLN FOUND MY BED-room and led me inside.

I couldn't have been more nervous. My stomach was doing butterflies on top of the baby kicking. Great. If someone looked at me, they would think I had an alien in my body. Maybe I did. It was a Matthews child, and from the stories I heard, Mitchell and Lincoln were animals as children.

Inside Lincoln was looking around my room. I stood there examining his examination, and floods of sadness, happiness, joy, and depression hit me like a ton of bricks. I tried to hold back a sob, but it escaped.

Lincoln turned his attention back to me. Seeing his beloved face was so overwhelming, rivers of tears streamed down my cheeks and I clenched my eyes tight.

"Come here," I heard, and I took a few steps, collapsing into Lincoln. The instant I touched him, I cried. I sobbed and cried some more. His arms held me tight and I felt his heart pounding more the tighter he held. We just stood there, time stood still. This was exactly the release I needed. With all my frustrations and fears bottled up, I finally let the bottle explode.

Lincoln rubbed my back to make the anxiety float away, and my tears began to subside. He pulled away, cupped my face with his hands, and kissed me. Everything about that kiss...well, there were no words to describe the meaning of it.

"Oh, my God, please don't leave me, please," I cried when Lincoln stepped back from me.

With that, Lincoln locked lips with mine again and kissed me even deeper.

"I not leaving you again, I promise," he said looking into my eyes.

"I love you so much!" My voice quivered as I fell back into his embrace.

"And I love you more than you know." More back rubbing and comforting. Lincoln rested his chin on my head and waited patiently for me to come back to earth.

We both remained in that position for who knows how long, when we were once again interrupted.

"Holy shit," Lincoln said, pulling away and staring down at my stomach. The baby was making a ruckus. Lincoln placed his hand on my belly and got the same kicks I had been feeling for months.

"I think someone is a little jealous." I smiled. "I have been giving you attention, and someone doesn't particularly like it."

"I'd say not." Without prompting, Lincoln knelt down and was nose to nose with the creature growing within me. "Well, hello in there," he said into my stomach. "I know you are soon going to be absorbing all of your mom's attention, but she needs some loving too, and you are just going to have to share." He looked up at me with sparkles in his eyes. "You and I need to come to an understanding, little...?" His brows rose in question.

Knowing what his question was going to be, I already had an answer. "I never found out. It is just baby Matthews, until we can find out together."

With a nod, Lincoln turned back to my stomach. "Little Matthews. Mom and dad need time to reunite." At the word dad, the baby stopped all movement. It was if it knew that daddy meant business. Lincoln also felt the action cease and beamed up at me. Even though my tear ducts were practically dried out, I still managed a few tears at this precious moment.

Lincoln stood up, cupped my face once again, and kissed me.

Our lips pressed harder, tongues entangled, and I could feel my nerves coming alive with anticipation. My body had waited so long for this, I wasn't about to let him go.

Suddenly, Lincoln pulled away and rested his forehead to mine. Both our breathing and heartrates were racing as the seconds lingered.

"Please don't stop," I whispered.

"I don't want to but..." Lincoln gently kissed my forehead. "I really don't want our roommates to come up and see us getting it on with the door wide open."

We both giggled. It was true, the door was still wide open. Knowing everyone in the house, we would be the topic of conversation for quite some time. At this moment, I didn't really care if they saw me bare ass naked. Believe me, I don't have a hot body anymore. Lincoln on the other hand, still looked amazing. Amazing enough to eat!

"I won't leave you hanging forever," Lincoln said, looking into my eyes.

"Promise?"

"Oh, believe me, I promise. I had a hard-enough time holding back when I walked in the door and you jumped into my arms." Lincoln's use of the word hard was meant in more than one way. The bulge pressing against me was a clue.

Knowing Lincoln needed to tame his inner beast, I collapsed against his chest again, listening to his heartbeat.

"I saw your ultrasound picture on the mirror and noticed something."

"Yeah, what's that? That we make cute kids?" I smiled at the thought.

"That, and the name on it." Lincoln pulled me away from him. "Jessica Matthews." He looked deep into my eyes.

I stepped away and sat down on the edge of my bed, preparing myself for how he would react to my explanation. Lincoln just pivoted and looked at me puzzled.

"You can blame your brother for that one."

"Mitchell? Why?" He crossed his arms, curiosity pulling at him.

"As you know, Division has many identities for every person. Mitchell gave me my new ID cards when I left with Tegan and Xander." I hid my eyes. I thought Mitch would at least have told his brother. "He said you wouldn't mind, and that I was practically family already." I picked up my chin and gauged his reaction. For a moment his expression was still and empty.

Not the reaction I had anticipated.

Out of nowhere, Lincoln showed a hint of satisfaction.

"Please don't be upset," I added.

He knelt in front of me and placed his hands on my thighs. "It took me by surprise, yes, but it makes sense. When all this is over and we can live without all this protection, we can make if official. You are my world," Lincoln said and kissed my hand.

All I could do was nod in agreement. "That sounds wonderful!"

With that, Lincoln reached in, kissed me softly, and as the sound of footfalls came up the stairs, he pulled away.

CHAPTER 31

At the entrance to my room, Max stood looking very apprehensive. All his body language suggested uneasiness.

"Sorry to interrupt, but Jess, we have some questions for you about Aries and the Federation." Max directed his eyes down as he spoke.

I looked around Lincoln's head to answer Max. "Sure, what is it?"

"Well, actually, there is a lot we just don't understand." Max was a little more nervous and when he made eye contact with me, I could sense it.

"Yeah, not problem, I'll be right down."

Max was quick on his heels and almost bolted down the stairs. It was a surprise to see him move so hastily.

My eyebrows raised in curiosity. "I guess I am back to work." I smiled but that quickly faded when I looked back at Lincoln. He was tired of our months of our separation, and all he wanted was to stay with me. Regret at the mention of work appeared in his eyes for a moment and his body language change to disappointment. It saddened me to see this.

"I'm still going to hold you to all that official stuff," I said, trying to lighten the mood. He looked at me uncertainly, but I nodded in assurance and squeezed his hand.

"Okay," he answered and forced a smile.

"Now, I um..." I hesitated. "I kind of need help up." I may have giggled slightly, and so did Lincoln.

Instantly, he was standing up, my hands in his, and with little effort I was pulled to my feet. It was a struggle for me, but never fazed him one bit. My balance was a bit lopsided and I leaned more inward than I liked. Carrying around an extra 30 pounds didn't help. My forward movement stopped with Lincoln's help, and he was all too eager to steal a kiss from me. And ahh, didn't he taste good. Mmmm! Why did my job always ruin everything? We lingered, kissing, but finally let go. Boy, I could rip his clothes off right now and have my way with him. My inner girl was craving him, and I made damn sure he knew it.

"Later, later," he said, panting ever so slightly, and planted one on my head.

Once again, I nodded, grasped his hand, and we made our way downstairs.

Xander, Tegan, and Max were huddled around the table with many papers scattered around they were examining. At my approach, they made room for me. I scanned the table to see reports, photos, and scattered pages. Me being an organization freak, it was eating me alive seeing this disarray. It seemed like ants were crawling all over me as I scanned the mess. The baby even shuddered. I took a deep breath and focused on a photo in front of me.

It was a crime scene photo of a man. He had obviously been killed by a gunshot to the head. What got me was the position of his body and his face. The body had fallen perfectly, and I tilted the photo figuring out the puzzle. Another photo revealed what I was looking for.

It was of the man's face. At once, I knew the events that had led to his death. I lowered the photos and took a deep breath.

"What? Do you know this person?" Lincoln asked me from behind, not really getting a glimpse yet of who it was. The rest all cocked their heads, waiting for my response.

"Yes, and you should, as well," I answered, turning back to Lincoln. I handed him the two photos. To my surprise, he was still stumped.

"He looks familiar, but I can't place the face." Lincoln sounded aggravated.

"You should, because that is Mark Wallace, the guy your bother was seeing. And thief." I paused.

"Who is Mark Wallace?" Tegan asked.

"Mark Wallace or Marcus Walters worked for the Federation. He infiltrated Division to recover the Aries device and I imagine spying on me."

"But what does Mitchell have to do with this?" Xander asked. "He doesn't seem the type to pick a person like this. He is far too perceptive to be fooled."

"Marcus and the Federation are very clever and are able to forge credentials, anything to get him into any place, especially Division. Once in, Marcus must have sensed Mitchell attraction taking an interest in him. Of course, Mitchell is ranked high in Division and Marcus took advantage of that."

"So, Mitchell had no idea who this Marcus really was? They were dating?" Max asked.

"Mitchell has a way for picking the wrong guys, always has. Marcus is smart and probably did his homework. Mitchell doesn't flaunt his sexuality at work but it's not a secret either. Marcus used that to his advantage.

"Wait, what?" Max was taken back. "Mitchell is gay?"

That question took me by surprise. I just assumed everyone knew that. I mean, I knew from the first time I laid eyes on the man. But I guess it wasn't evident to everyone. "Yes, Mitchell is gay."

"Oh," Max was not expecting that. For as long as he has known us, this fact escaped him.

"Once the Emissary learned the Aries device was in the hands of the Division, he needed someone to infiltrate the organization. In comes Marcus, smart, charming. and that sparked Mitch. We all went to dinner, Mitchell introduced me, and Lincoln and Marcus figured out I was the traitor. I had only met Marcus once or twice when I was with the Federation but upon our dinner date, I sensed he was not who he said he was. It wasn't long after that the shooting started, and here we are today." I was hoping this would satisfy them all, but I guess I knew better.

"So, why does Marcus have a gunshot to the head? If he retrieved Aries for the Emissary, why is he dead?" Tegan knew a smidgen of the situation involving me, but nothing regarding Aries.

"Once Marcus returned Aries to the Emissary, they must have discovered that the device was...incomplete."

"Incomplete? But we recovered the whole device," Lincoln blurted out.

"Yes. But it is missing one thing." I moved around the table to get a better view of everything.

"What's that?" Lincoln inquired, and I was sure by his body language he had an idea what it might be. And he didn't like it one bit.

"Me," I said.

"How can you be the missing link?" Max asked. "I was assigned to you almost immediately upon your return."

"Aries is a very complex device and with just one line of the software tweaked, it will not open." I said. "I'm the only one who knows how to get past that."

"It was that easy? A complex device like Aries and it was that easy to tamper." Tegan asked.

"Yes, and no. You must understand that this was my assignment. While I was interning at the Federation, I also studied and analyzed every piece of information on Aries. All the ins and outs incase I succeeded. I did in fact obtain Aries and needed collateral for this reason. If the Emissary finds me, I have leverage."

"When did you have time to alter it? Someone has been with you, meaning me until you turned it over to Mitchell." Lincoln was puzzled.

"Right after we changed direction to Division. While you were driving."

"But I watched your phone smash on the side of the road."

"If you remember, I had another device. While you drove, I was able to plug Aries into my alternate device and change the necessary ingredients they might say."

Tegan finally asked the question I knew was coming. "So... What is Aries, exactly?

"Well, what do you think of when you hear the name Aries?" Time for a history lesson.

"Aries, isn't he the Greek god of war?" Max said.

"Yes, he was, and this device was code named Aries because of that. Meaning?" I stopped to see if anyone would pick up on it.

"Meaning, it contains information about war?" Tegan answered hesitantly.

"Yes and no. The device contains information for infinite power. Everything was compiled by multiple people. Many who sought to use its power as a weapon. It can annihilate any other power in the world. In the wrong hands, Aries could be as powerful as a God, and could destroy whatever is in its path.

"So, the Federation wants the device in order to become the most powerful entity in the world," Xander summarized.

"Yes. But on the flip side, if someone wanted to use the device for good..." I trailed off.

"That would put the Federation at a disadvantage," Tegan stated.

"Absolutely. The Federation coded the Aries device for its own advantage. If we looked at it from a peaceful perspective, our side would have called it Athena perhaps, the goddess of wisdom. It also contains many theories and information; ideas to end hunger and produce clean water. To make power useful for humans to survive as one. Not to be conquered. The device could be so resourceful in the correct hands."

"But the Emissary wants it for power," Lincoln said.

I nodded.

"Okay, that explains the power and resourcefulness of the Aries device, but why did you alter it? Why is Marcus dead?" Xander brought up key points, and they are not going to like my explanation.

"And...?" Max pushed with his body and mouth.

"It is only speculation," I said, "but I believe the reason Marcus is dead is because he brought the device back and it doesn't work." I got a "duh" look from everyone. "We know my sister Susan stole the device first and stashed it away until one of us was able to take it to Division. What no one knows the device was coded for multiple people. I had knowledge of that and made sure I was now the only person."

My body was getting tired of standing and I was beginning to hunch over the table.

Lincoln noticed my discomfort and came over behind me, rubbing my back. Xander immediately gave up his chair, and I plopped myself down with Lincoln's help. Even with my nap earlier in the day, I was starting to wear out, and I needed food.

And sex, but my coworkers didn't need to know that.

"And Susan is dead," Lincoln said.

I took a deep breath, exhaled, and continued. "Yes, my sister is dead. Her death was without cause." Thinking about her hurt my heart.

"So, what does this tell us?" Xander asked.

"I would surmise that the Emissary finally realized the Aries device is useless to him right now. There is staff that could decipher it but that takes time. He most likely killed Marcus because Marcus missed something. Whether the Emissary knows I am the key to open Aries, is unknown. From the brief conversation I had with him, I believe he might," I stated. "Therefore, I am now a target."

"You told us the Emissary believes you are carrying his child. What makes you think he knows anything else?" Tegan was catching on.

"The tone of his voice gave me a hint there was more than just a baby on his mind. He needs me. I became his right arm, and now..." I trailed off. The knowledge I possessed about the Federation was vast, and at a trial, could mean its demise. "He will stop at nothing to capture me. If I am with child or not."

With that, I was done. I looked down at my belly and wrapped my hands around my unborn child.

At my silence, Lincoln place his hand on my shoulder, and I reached up to hold it. I could feel his breath on my ear when he said, "It will be over my dead body before he hurts either of you." Then he kissed me on the top of my head.

I inhaled.

After a couple minutes of contemplative silence, the files were collected and placed back in order. I was encouraged not to move, and I didn't. All the information I had just spilled out, and everything I had kept to myself, was now catching up to me. All I wanted was to go hide in my room again, even though Lincoln was here. When you're in a rut, you tend to stay in a rut.

I sat in my seat at the head of the table, and as my new protection team cleared it and brought food in, it seem like time stood still. I have no idea how long it took, but before I knew it, pizza, chips, soda, and beer had been laid out. Yes, beer was a no-no, but Xander permitted Lincoln and Max to have one and only one.

Food was passed out and, in the background, was laughter. My mind and body were in a fog. Everything seemed so far away, even though they were right in front of me. It took Lincoln's touch to bring me back as he leaned down and kissed my neck. His warmth broke through my fogginess and I come back to the present.

"You all right?" Lincoln asked me as I cleared my head.

"Yeah, I'm okay." I flashed him a reassuring smile. "I am all of a sudden beat." I grasped his hand on my shoulder for comfort. God, I missed his touch and smell more than I ever dreamed I would. It was intoxicating.

"Can I have some pizza?" I asked, very subdued.

"No," Lincoln blurted out which took me by surprise.

I gave him a mock glare. I wanted some fucking pizza, and now was not the time to screw around with me. Later would be fine, but I was hungry. A beer would taste amazing, too, but the time for that would be a little longer.

"Pizza, please." Evil look. "Now!"

Lincoln's face was so expressive, full of happiness and joy. "All right, but only one piece. I don't know what Tegan and Xander have been feeding you, but you are looking rather skinny. Are you sure you are pregnant?"

I gawked at him. For the first time in ages I was speechless.

"Just kidding," Lincoln said quickly.

"You better be, buddy. I think you might have had a hand or other extremities involved with this, asshole!" My wiseass comment earned me a kiss and two slices of pizza.

CHAPTER 32

AFTER THE MEAL, MY BODY WAS BEYOND EXHAUSTION. With all the ups and downs of the day, I was ready to lie down and have Lincoln's arms wrapped around me. One look in his direction and he took the hint. He knew I wanted alone-time with him. I barely made it out of my chair, and Lincoln moved to assist. "Thanks" I said.

Regaining my balance, I was up right and almost winded. "Night, everyone!" I called out to the gang and waved them a good night. They all said good night in return, and I headed toward the stairs. Lincoln held back for a minute before following me. Maybe he needed ask a question. Tegan and Xander were so easy going that anything wouldn't bother them. I knew they were just glad to see me happy after of so many months of sorrow.

I hauled my body up the stairs and into my room. Within a minute, Lincoln was in the doorway. "Hey, everything all right?" he asked as I was finding clothes to change into.

I couldn't really care less what I wore, but it made me look busy. "Yeah, I am just a bit tired."

"I know there is more to it than just being tired." His comment perked me right up. His instinct had not faltered since our separation. Cop intuition.

Fiddling with my big, baggy shirt, I looked down and stopped. "No, you're right. That's not all." When I looked toward him, bit my lower lip. So many things were racing through my mind and body that I was overwhelmed. Granted, I was the type who usually handled stressful situations, but all my energy was zapped, and I was a big as a cow, so there wasn't much of a chance of that.

Lincoln came over to my side and grasped my upper arms. "What's going on? Really? Tegan filled me in on the last few months and how difficult it has been for you."

I looked up at him as a tear rolled down my cheek. "It has been rough to say the least. I have been stressed, overwhelmed and so scared." My body began to shake, and I was enveloped in Lincoln's arms.

"I know. Shhh, I know," he repeated, rubbing my back. All I did was cry into his chest. "I am not going to let anything happen to you, I promise." Lincoln kissed my head.

"They will find me. But I won't let anything happen to this baby," I said.

"I won't let it either. You are not going anywhere."

I tilted my head up and looked into his eyes. "The Emissary will come for me whether I am pregnant or not. I broke the primary rule and defected. He will make me pay for that."

Lincoln shifted his hands to cup my face. "I will not let that happen. You and our little alien are my life. I just got you both back, and I'm not about to let you go." He kissed me gently. I returned the kiss, but with a bit more force. His lips jumpstarted my libido, and the fear and pain vanished.

He pulled away from me as I was getting deeper into our kissing. "Are you sure this is okay?" So much hesitation in his voice.

"Lincoln, I am very pregnant, but I haven't seen you for over six months. If you do not fuck me right now, I will explode." There, take that. Blunt and direct. I needed to release, and right now.

I wanted to fuck.

Lincoln clamped onto my face, and instantly we were going at it like rabbits. Rapidly kissing, caressing each other. My hands moved up his back under his shirt, the way he liked to be touched, while his found the end of my dress and hauled it upward over my head. All that was left was my panties, bra and large belly. I lifted his shirt off and the feeling of skin on skin was so stimulating and so fucking hot.

We continued kissing, and I was slowly moved back to the bed. Lincoln guided me down and stood in front of me. I unbuckled his pants and dropped them, revealing his erection. God, how I missed this. I stroked him with tight hands; he began to moan, and his moans made me more excited. It didn't take long for him to unclasp my bra and cup my breasts with both hands. Holy fuck, I was so horny, I could detonate right then from his touch.

Slowly, he slid me back on the bed and I was able to lie down in slow motion. His smell, his touch, his everything, made time stop. For one brief moment, I saw hesitation in his eyes and a glance down to my stomach.

"It's okay. You are not going to hurt anything," I assured him, pulled him down on the bed and crawled on top of him.

I ran the tips of my fingers tenderly up and down his stomach and chest making the sensation more intense. Every nerve in our bodies were on high, and the moment I mounted him, I wanted to scream with unbelievable pleasure. Every touch was so invigorating and sensual that I was on cloud nine. Lincoln pulsed so gently and with every thrust into my body, I couldn't help but moan and cry out in pleasure.

My body craved a good fuck. Before we separated months ago, I would be on fire from his slightest touch or kiss, and we had sex a lot. But this time was so smooth and gentle, I can't explain how wonderful it felt.

Lincoln couldn't lie down on top of me, I was on the bed but he had all the right moves and I was beyond wet, all hot and bothered. My hands reached for his face and pulled him down for hard kissing. His eyes were glassy and there were so many emotional expressions in them, I couldn't read them all. I gave more moans and little cries from his delicate movements, and I moved right along with him.

We made love, and our movements together were perfectly synced. Slow and soft to deep and hard. God damn! I was not going to hold out much longer. My orgasm was beginning to build, and so was Lincoln's. My moans pushed him over the edge. Pulsing and thrusting, my insides were tightening, building and my climax was imminent. I cried out. I couldn't hold back any longer. There was no holding back, and as I peaked, Lincoln was there as well. His guttural shout amplified my sensations and prolonged the pleasure.

With our final cries, it was over. My breathing was so rapid, I thought my heart was going to beat out of my chest. My legs and body shook from the aftermath of my orgasm, and Lincoln's echoed mine. I tried to collect myself, but the only thing I could do was breath and try to calm my body down.

"Holy Fuck!" I murmured. Sweat streamed down my face. Between all the emotions of the day, and now this mind-blowing sex, I was a hot mess. Lincoln lay beside me and lifted me up to hold me close.

"I'm here." Lincoln whispered as he rubbed my back and, I was so blessed to be in the arms of the person I loved.

THIS IS A DREAM.

I lay in my bed, the baby playing soccer in my belly, and I stare out into the emptiness that is my room. Was yesterday all a dream?

Lincoln isn't really here, right? I didn't have mind-blowing sex last night either. It all just happened in my head. After all my years of analyzing other people, my brain was now making my fantasies into reality, and I wasn't sure what was real anymore. My longing for Lincoln had finally convinced my brain he was actually here.

I can officially say I may be going nuts.

I wasn't going to be able to stay in bed for the remainder of my pregnancy, or my life, because I needed to get up and pee really badly. Time was ticking, the race was on for the Federation to capture me...or for baby Matthews to arrive. My hope is baby first. The Emissary will not get the satisfaction of having both of us.

But it will be a close.

Waddling down the stairs, I swear I heard voices coming from the kitchen. I must be really losing my mind because I could swear, I heard Lincoln and Xander talking. Discussing something. My descent halted to eavesdrop on their conversation.

My God. He's really here! Lincoln is actually here. It wasn't a dream.

"She has had a rough time the last few months. I have tried my best, but your arrival proved she wouldn't have lasted much longer. Emotionally speaking," Xander said. I could barely hear him because of the distance between us. Once I got downstairs, I sneaked closer.

"It was a struggle for Mitchell to get me here. If I'd had to wait much longer, I would have found a way to get here. Conrad was briefed about the conversation she had with the Emissary and Mitchell rushed the order. Jess will only trust a few people, and he knew that." Lincoln paused.

Lincoln's words were very true. Since I escaped the Emissary and the Federation, I have been certain there are Federation operatives watching me. I overcame many of my fears during my sessions with Suzanna Kirkman, but there were still only a few I trusted. Mitchell has always looked out for me, and I trust him. But not Conrad.

"I wish I could have helped her more the all this time," Xander said. "It was difficult to hear her cry herself to sleep every night. I am glad you showed up when you did."

"She is a strong-willed person. I doubt she would have told you if there was something wrong, no matter what it was." Lincoln paused and I inched closer. "Mitchell bonded with her right away, and I fell in love with her the moment I saw her. But it took me a long time before I could read her. It has been harder this time without her than the last." Lincoln stopped and it broke my heart to hear him struggling.

The last time, we departed on bad terms and I still regret that move every day. I was forced into hiding this time, and every quiet moment, I wished for Lincoln to be with me.

"I was the same way with my wife. I fell for her at first sight. I agonized with you. I was so lost after my wife died," Xander sympathized and that broke my heart even more.

Silence from both men was the perfect time for me to make an entrance. I gingerly walked into the kitchen. Okay, there is nothing gingerly about my walk or waddle. I was as big as a house and I swished like a bell. Trying to make myself seem like I hadn't been eavesdropping, I walked by both men sitting at the table and straight to the coffee.

"Good morning," Lincoln called out to me, but I kept going toward the coffee.

I poured my first cup, cream and all, and inhaled the aroma. Ah, coffee! The aroma filled life back into me. Once I was able to immerse from my coffee trance, I was able to focus on the two men gazing back at me.

"Good morning," I answered Lincoln and inhaled my coffee again.

"Still enjoying your coffee!" Lincoln remarked with a smile at Xander.

"Well, it wasn't that way for some time. Jess wasn't able to drink or even smell coffee for a few months. It wasn't until recently I got to witness this coffee experience," Xander said with a chuckle.

I just ignored them.

"Jess without coffee, I imagine she was a bear." Lincoln was on a roll. "I think she is more in love with that cup of coffee than me."

I gaped at him. It took me by surprise, but then again, it may be truer than not. *Whoops*! Eek! Well, what can I say? I love my coffee.

"She wasn't this person with a smile and light to her eyes. This person is a happy person." Xander said, looking over at me.

I just sipped my coffee. "Oh, you guys were saying something...?" I said sarcastically, strutting closer to them.

Not a single word escaped from their mouths upon my approach. Lincoln swung his leg out and I sat down on him very gingerly. I would not be happy if I spilled my coffee. And Lincoln, well, I could squish him, but I thought better of it. I do love that smartass.

"Hey, you're going to squish me!" Lincoln, my wiseass man squawked as I sat across his legs.

My eyes widened and I gave him a love slap. Not too hard, but not weak either.

"Squish you huh?" Playfully, I gritted my teeth and adjusted myself.

"You can squish me anytime, babe!" Lincoln wrapped his arms around and squeezed.

"You better get used to people sitting on you, Daddy!"

The word Daddy caught him by surprise. Got him! He is such a smartass; it was now my turn.

He began to rub my belly. Biting his lower lip, he said, "Yes, I guess you are right."

I have to say, taking him off guard was kind of hot.

THE NEXT FEW DAYS WERE FAIRLY UNEVENTFUL. I HUNG out around the safe house and was only allowed to leave with one of my escorts, usually Lincoln. He wasn't letting me out of his sight during the days, and our nights, well, let's just say that I am happy to take naps during the day. He wasn't one for letting me sleep...or maybe vice ver-sa. Even with my big pregnant belly, the sex was as amazing as it always was. Our positions had to be tweaked some, but holy fuck, it was as Marvin the Martian says, "Earth-shattering kaboom!"

Max took me out for walks as well to give Lincoln a little reprieve. I certainly wasn't fast anymore, if anything I was snail speed. Max would poke jokes at me about my speed and now he would beat me.

"Yes, you can beat me. Only because I am carrying around a for-ty-pound bowling ball."

"So, if I strap an extra forty pounds on my belly, you're saying you'd still win?" Max was such a punk.

"Yes, I would. I have had many months to practice." I cupped my belly and looked back at him with a smirk.

"Yes, you have." Max was at a loss for words, and I sensed he was distressed about my situation. He wanted all of this to be over as much as I did.

A moment of silence fell between us as we walked down the side-walk. I wanted to speak my mind, but the right words were just not there. Max took a few steps ahead of me and I was struggling to keep up. When he realized I was behind him, he turned and halted, waiting for me.

"What's really going on, Max? There is something you are not telling me. And don't lie to me." I stopped in front of him. "I'll know."

"It's nothing. I wish you didn't have to be here in protective custo-dy, and we could have somewhat normal lives." He was holding back some frustration, and I wasn't going to let him get away with it.

"You don't think I want to be here, do you? I have been so alone the last six months. I want to go home. I want to feel safe and not scared all the time. I am having a baby and I just reunited with the love of my life. And to top it all off, the Emissary thinks the child is his. So, don't tell me it's nothing." I was losing my temper and I needed to calm down.

"I know, and I realize how hard it has been. It just shouldn't be this way." Max rolled his head around so I couldn't see his face.

"Believe me, I am beyond scared for everyone. If I could turn back time I would. But I can't." My top was ready to blow.

"I get that. I do." Max closed his eyes to take a moment.

"Okay, good. Now give your friend a hug." I smiled at him and opened my arms.

Max greeted me with a smile and wrapped his arms around me. His squeeze tightened my when my legs gave out and my head began to spin.

I crumbled into him like a ton of bricks.

CHAPTER 33

"HOLY SHIT, JESS! JESS! WAKE UP!" I COULD HEAR A VOICE but there was no recognition. My head was spinning so much that I felt as if my body was spiraling down a drain. Ever had one of those dreams where you felt as if you were falling forever? Well, that was me now.

I could feel arms around me, but I didn't want to open my eyes for fear I was really falling.

"Hey, I need some help! Jess has collapsed." Pause. "We are right around the corner."

There was another pause, and then I could hear the voice talking to me again. "Jessy hang on. Help is coming." I realized I was still with Max.

I was able to pop my eyes open but the world around me would not stop moving. Somehow, I had sunk to the ground and Max was holding me up. My head bobbled around and I saw two more figures coming my way.

Lincoln. *Thank God.*

He was stressing hard. Even through my dizziness, I could see his worry. I was being handed over to Lincoln by Max.

"Jessy?"

"Hey. I am feeling a little dizzy," I was able to say. As I leaned into Lincoln, I could feel his tremors. "I'm okay, I just need to go back to the house."

I'd lied. I wasn't feeling okay.

Lincoln lifted me into his strong arms and hurried back to the house. My body acted like a wet noodle as I was carried, and I could feel the shakes of his arms against the strain Lincoln was having by carrying me. Xander and Max went ahead of us and we were greeted with an open door and another worried soul, Tegan.

"Here, put her on the couch." Tegan was taking charge.

Lincoln brought me over gently laid me on the couch.

I could feel the cushions welcome me as he eased me down. My head still felt like a spinning top. My vision was clearing some, and I felt as though I was able to regain awareness. Something was wrong internally and I could feel it. I am usually stubborn about people hovering and babying me, but I would lose this battle about a trip to either the clinic or hospital.

"She needs to go to the hospital," Lincoln barked as he stood back from me.

Xander was pacing around the room running his hands through his hair. "Lincoln, just let me think for a minute. It isn't that simple."

"What do you mean? Jess needs to see a doctor. What if there is something wrong with the baby?" Lincoln was starting to panic.

I was able to speak softly. "He's right Lincoln, it isn't that simple."

The room went silent and all eyes turned to me. "The Federation is out there and they are looking for an opportunity to pounce. I am the prey they want." My voice was low but to the point.

Lincoln controlled his temper and came down to me. "You need to see a doctor. I just got you back, and I can't lose either of you." There was so much feeling in his words that they projected onto me. I could feel his pain and worry.

"I know, but we have to be smart." All of a sudden, my strength was fading and my soul felt as if it was draining away. Lincoln moved closer to me and put his hand on my face. I closed my eyes for a brief moment and moved my hand down to my stomach. Dribbling between my legs was what I thought was urine. Sorry, wrong, it was blood.

I opened my eyes and said, "On second thought, I need to go now. Whatever it takes, but I need to go." I didn't want to alarm anyone, but Lincoln could tell the urgency from my tone and his eyes proved it.

With a scoop of his arms, I was lifted and carried out the door. Everyone followed in Lincoln's wake.

There no sense of time, whether it took us ten minutes or an hour to reach the hospital, I had no recollection. Everything was so groggy. I knew what was going on and my surroundings, but time was not fathomable.

Lincoln stayed with me in the back of the SUV and Xander drove us to the nearest hospital. The clinic I had been attending for my prenatal checkup wouldn't have sufficient equipment for an emergency.

Lincoln carried me into the emergency room and Tegan followed behind while Xander moved the SUV out of the ambulance bay. Both Tegan and Xander needed to be with me to give our cover story , if necessary.

We approached the triage desk and Lincoln, still in go-mode, said, "Yes, hi. My wife is very pregnant and fainted. When she woke up, she was weak and not feeling well."

The nurse looked at both of us. I was still cradled in Lincoln's arms. How the hell was he still carrying me? I used to be very thin but now I was a cow. Lincoln is strong but for Christsakes, that only goes so far.

"What's your wife's name?" The nurse was patient with Lincoln even though he wasn't.

"Jessy Matthews."

"And how far along is she?" the nurse asked, jotting notes down.

This took Lincoln a second to ponder.

"She is about thirty-seven weeks, I think," Tegan stepped into comment. Thank God someone had a cool head. All the men were panicking. Leave it to Tegan to be a boss.

"Okay, let's get a gurney and move your wife into an exam room," the nurse directed as she came around from the desk to assist us.

I was placed on the gurney and everyone froze for an instant. "What's the holdup?" I squeaked out. Eyes went from me to Lincoln's arms and then back to me.

"Alrighty, then," the nurse muttered. "Let's get her into a room and page the OB on call STAT!" Hearing the urgency in her voice, I looked up to my very scared Lincoln to see his arm was covered in blood.

Fuck! This cannot be good. I'm bleeding. Fuck! Fuck! *Fuck!*

"What's going on?" I asked again as I was wheeled down a hallway and into an exam room.

"Mrs. Matthews seem to be bleeding, and we need to examine you for the safety of the baby and yourself. The on-call OB is on the way." The nurse was being very patient with me even though her expression was serious.

My brain was sucking in everything around me as I was being prepped for who knows what. Was I going to have the baby? Was I bleeding out and was going to die? I had no one clue.

Even though hearing the Mrs. Matthews part was nice, I needed to focus and listen.

Lincoln stayed by my side as nurses busied themselves preparing me for my exam. I had an IV inserted and they tried to remove my clothes, but with a belly as big as mine and I was being no help, they left them on. I must have had medication pumped into me because my brain seemed to focus a bit more, and I was able to comprehend what was really going on. My hazy eyesight was clearing as well. Lincoln didn't move but Tegan and Xander had to wait outside the room because they were not my parents. But they were scared for me.

Chucks were put under my butt, so I didn't bleed all over everything. I felt like a little kid again. If they put a diaper on me, that was it. I would leave, emergency or not. Everyone seemed to be discussing my situation amongst themselves but not with me. That was not so good in my book. But expressions can tell you a lot, and from what I could see, I was in serious trouble.

Time still had no meaning to me. I had no idea how long had passed since I left the house. It could have been hours or minutes.

But the moment the doctor walked into my room my heart literally stopped.

CHAPTER 34

NOTHING LIKE THE DOCTOR APPROACHING MY BEDSIDE to snap life back into my body and my brain's fog cleared. The OB on call was none other than Ross Edward. The same Dr. Ross Edward who had befriended me during my time with the Federation. Now he was standing in front of me. You think I was panicked before, guess again. Double trouble now.

"I'm Dr. Edward," he said approaching my gurney and held out his hand. Edward didn't skip a beat and glanced down at me with a warning. His eyes were soft with concern for me, but his body language meant business. Lincoln had no idea of the history we had between us but Xander and Tegan did. There were many Dr. Edward in the world, would they pick up on his name? I don't re-member if I ever described him to them. Would they see the terror in my eyes?

I had to hold back my emotions and shock over Dr. Edward. I got more tense the closer he got. Dr. Edward reached his arm over me and extended it to Lincoln as he introduced himself.

Lincoln returned the handshake.

"You must be Mrs. Matthews." Edward looked down at me with a smile. "We are going to get you fixed up."

With my eyes wide, I nodded yes to play along.

Edward looked over my chart and glanced down at me as he browsed through it. I didn't take my eyes off him. There was a lot going on that needed to be explained, and I knew with Edward here, it wasn't good.

"We need to get an ultrasound machine in here," Edward ordered the nurse, putting down the chart. He looked at me and said, "I need to examine you to find an explanation for your bleeding. I have ordered an ultrasound to rule out internal bleeding."

With his mention of internal bleeding, my eyes welled up with tears. This baby was the only thing that kept me going for the last six months without Lincoln.

Edward saw the look in my eyes and leaned down closer to me. "Hey, I am not going to let anything happen to this baby. You have my word on that." His eyes held proof that he meant what he said.

With fear in my heart and my trust in my Federation friend, I nodded in acceptance.

Minutes later, an ultrasound machine was wheeled into my room and Dr. Edward and a nurse were back in action. My dress was pulled up enough to reveal my belly, but the nurse draped a blanket over my lower extremities to give me some modesty. A warm blue jelly was squirted on to my belly and the machine head was placed on the gel. Edward had the monitor pointed away from me as he moved the instrument around, and at times he pushed.

I was so nervous my hands were shaking. Lincoln realized my distress and grasped my hand and kissed it.

"I'm not going anywhere," Lincoln said to me with so much emotion. Emotion from love or fear, it was hard to tell. All I could do was nod my head and squeeze his hand.

With a sound of wonder from Edward, both Lincoln and I shifted our attention to him.

Edward's eyes narrowed as he examined the screen. I knew that look, and it wasn't good.

"What? What's going on?" Lincoln's voice was full of panic.

Edward remained silent as he continued to move the probe around my belly and stare at the screen.

Lincoln was getting anxious and all I could do was...nothing. The feeling of being so helpless is the worst. I was stuck in this hospital, in the hands of a member of the Federation, and my baby could be in serious distress. If I could scream, I would have.

"Come on, tell us what is going on," Lincoln yelled. Hoping to calm him down some, I squeezed his hand.

Edward removed the probe and looked to the nurse. "Nurse prepare the OR for an immediate C-Section. This baby needs to come out now."

His words practically put me over the edge. My whole body began to shake, and I was crying uncontrollably.

"I'm not full term, it's too early!" Hysteria was overcoming me. What had I done? I did everything I was told to do, and I was still having the baby early. What if it's not healthy? What if my stress caused the early delivery? There were so many questions, and I blamed myself for all of it. There is no worse pain than guilt; it can do as much damage as a weapon in the wrong circumstances.

"Your wife needs to have an emergency C-section. We are taking her up to the OR immediately," Edward calmly tried to explain to Lincoln.

"But *why*?" Lincoln was adamant about getting an answer. Enough that he had a strong grip on my bed and wasn't going to let me go.

"She has a placental abruption and is bleeding internally. We need to deliver the baby and repair the damage before it's too late. This is serious, and I need to get her upstairs," Edward said sternly to Lincoln.

At that, Lincoln released my bed. The nurse and an aide were waiting to transport me. I think I was on the edge of shock from Edward's diagnosis. I needed to look at him to see if he was telling the truth or not. I know the Emissary sent him here for the baby, but I thought we were friends. He was the one who told me about the Emissary, and we had a friendly connection. I confided in him. Would he really put our lives in jeopardy?

I had no idea. My heart was telling me one thing, but my brain was undecided.

Another nurse hurried through the door and said, "The OR is ready for her."

My bed was released, and the rails were put up.

"Let's go," Edward ordered the medical team around us.

The wheels stopped when I grabbed one of Edward's hands. "Please, I need Lincoln with me. Please!" I begged through solemn tears.

Edward nodded. There was no hesitation, and from that I found a little reassurance. I looked at Lincoln and grabbed hold of his hand, not letting go as we rolled off.

I WAS RUSHED TO THE OR QUICKLY. MY BRAIN WAS STILL foggy but becoming more alert, my body was in complete terror. I was able to hold back my sobs as I was transported. It was only a matter of time before the flood gates opened. This was probably the most frightening thing I have ever experienced.

We went through the doors to the operating room and I was placed under a light, and the OR nurses took over my prep. Lincoln was still at my side.

"Sir, you are going to have to step outside while we get your wife prepped and you gowned up," a nurse said to Lincoln.

I still had hold of him when he turned to look at me. "I promise, I'm not going anywhere."

"I know." And that was all it took, the flood gates opened, and I was crying and scared shitless. "Please don't let anything happen to the baby," I pleaded to Lincoln.

He leaned down and kissed my forehead and then my lips. "I won't let anything happen to either one of you." I nodded and he put his forehead to mine. We shared a brief moment.

"Mr. Matthews, we really need to get you in a gown and finish prepping your wife for surgery," another nurse politely said as she put her hand on Lincoln's forearm.

"Yeah, okay."

"Once you're gowned, you'll be able to come back in." Her sweet voice made the situation a little less difficult.

But not by much. I was still on high alert to the people in my surroundings.

"I love you," Lincoln whispered to me and kissed my forehead. I looked into his eyes and saw the truth there. "I'll be right back. Don't go anywhere." Then he smiled.

"I don't think I have a choice," I joked through tears. His smiled faded and worried Lincoln came out. "I love you too!" My face was wet with tears.

I have been though many events in my life—terrifying, happy, sad, unbelievable, and many others, but this moment I was the most scared I'd ever been. Scared for the life of my child, my lover, and the destiny of my own life as it lay in the hands of Dr. Edward.

Would Edward remain loyal to me, or had he switched to the Emissary's side?

Lincoln kissed me once more before the nurse led him out of the room. I turned my gaze up toward the ceiling and stared into oblivion. Thoughts and emotions churned in my brain that were not recognizable. I was beginning to fade again as the busy staff worked around me preparing for the arrival of Baby Matthews.

Before I knew it, Edward was standing over me. He caught me by surprise.

"Please, Doctor." I paused to collect my emotions. "Please don't let the Emissary—" I swallowed. "You and I both know this child isn't his."

"Yes, I do. You know why I am here." Edward was talking very low, so the conversation was just between the two of us.

"I know you were ordered to bring in both of us, but I beg you please, let Lincoln have the baby. You and I both know the child will not be safe within the Federation." More tears streamed down my face.

"I am going to protect your child in any way I can. But you know they are coming for you, and a child is just a bonus." Edward was clearly trying to be neutral. In case there were other people working for the Emissary in the room. It was a scary thought.

"The Emissary doesn't need the child. He only needs me." I stopped, holding a sob back.

"I will not let anything happened to your child. You have my word on that."

I believed him. Even with his mask over his face, his eyes proved his sincerity.

"Thank you," I whispered.

"Jess, I have to get started so I have to put you out. There are too many unknown factors right now, and safety is the top priority for you and the baby."

"Lincoln?"

"Once we have you under anesthesia, we'll bring him in while the baby is delivered. Lincoln will be able to go with the child while we get your bleeding under control." Edward looked over to a nurse.

I was being restrained and a hair net was being draped over my head. Curtains were being hung in front of me to prevent me from seeing my abdomen.

"Okay," I said to Edward. I knew it was time for the surgery to start and I desperately wanted to see Lincoln.

"I promise I will not let anything happen to the baby. I will do everything I can for it," Edward reiterated.

I still was scared shitless, but I believed him. "Thank you!" I cried.

Edward nodded and stepped away.

I returned my gaze to the ceiling and there was nothing but bright lights. Tears streamed down my face and I tried to hold them back. The next thing I saw was a mask hovering over my face.

"I'm going to put this over your mouth and nose now. When you wake up, there will be someone waiting to meet you." This person had a sweet tone to her voice, but if she only knew my situation. How I may never see my child...or if I will ever wake up.

Whatever happened, my time had run out and my race against the Federation would soon conclude.

Win or Lose.

PART IV

CHAPTER 35

PAIN!

Darkness.

Solitude.

Pain.

That was all I could say right now. Was I dreaming or awake? Either way, my entire body was screaming in agony. I feel my abdomen has been sliced open and the throbbing is so intense, tears stream down my eyes. What the hell was going on? My body was crying out in distress and I'm suspended. Arms and legs are paralyzed, helpless. I have no self-awareness.

Ever had a dream where you have broken or injured something on your body and the pain is so real? Oh, I have. I was younger when I had a dream of spinning, my whole body was spiraling, and I ended up breaking my leg. I have not a clue how I broke it, but in my dream I had. The pain of the break was so vivid, I woke up with the worst pain in my leg. Apparently, I had a muscle cramp in my calf muscle during my slumber and it came through my dream as a broken leg. My brain was transferring the pain from my leg into dream form, to hopefully wake me. It was the weirdest sensation and I never forgot it.

Is that what this was, a dream? My pain, my misery, with my limbs immobile. I needed to open my eyes and discover if this was real or not real. Or was I in darkness and there was nothing for me to see? I was so confused. All I could register was my nerves firing along my abdomen. Did I dare try to wake up? There was only one way to be sure what was going one. I needed to open my eyes. Simple as that.

Fuck! Light! Bright light! Holy shit, I am practically blinded by the brightness of the room.

A room that was very foreign to me. I lay there on my bed motionless and surveyed the room with only my eyes. It wasn't a hospital room, but rather a bedroom. The walls had this old frilly wallpaper on it, like you would see in old houses where the paper was the only thing holding up the wall. My grandparents had rooms like this in their house, which I had only been to a couple of times. Susan and I visited and stayed the night in a room similar to this one before my mother left and my father became a hard ass.

With a turn of my head, I was able to see the room in its entirety. Definitely an old farmhouse room. My bed was that old wrought iron type of bed. There was a quilt on top of me and I seemed to be set up for a prolonged stay. Next to my bed was medical equipment.

Wait. What? Medical equipment. The realization hit me like a ton of bricks. I was not in a hospital. And as I glanced down at my covers, my belly seemed to be flatter. Last I knew, I was in a hospital having a baby. But now I was here with no crying baby, and no sign there ever was one here.

I tried moving my arms. *What the hell? I can't move my arms.* I look down and I find my arms have been restrained. I pulled at them in frustration as tears ran down my face. I was tied tight to the bed and I wasn't going anywhere.

I needed to feel my stomach, to make sure there was still a child in there. Or maybe I had just been dreaming of a pregnancy. But with that thought, pain returned to my lower abdomen. The pain was very real, piercing, and in a region where a C-section would have been performed.

I was not crazy; I had a child.

I needed to regain my composure and figure out my situation.

Okay, breathe! I am in a room, restrained, and have *no fucking idea* where I am. Or who has me. *Ahhh!*

I was so frustrated it was driving my bonkers. I pulled at my straps again with more force and grunts. But the more I pulled, the more intense my pain grew. Apparently, pain medication wasn't permitted wherever the hell I was.

I heard the door start to open and froze. *Fuck! Who the hell is it?* I lay still on the bed as my body came to full alert. I was able to prop myself up somewhat, but still lay flat. I wanted to see this asshole eye to eye and get the answers I needed.

More footfalls echoed. Another person was following behind the first.

The door swung open and two men came through the door. One was Dr. Ross Edward, and the other...

"Hello, Robert," I gritted out, as serious as I could manage.

Robert Emery, aka the Emissary, had graced me with his presence.

ROBERT EMERY, LEADER OF THE FEDERATION, THE ONE who I called my boss. The one who couldn't or wouldn't leave me alone. The one who put me in this position, brought up the rear as Dr. Edward came in. They both looked my way to see if I was alert or not. And by damn I was more than alert; I was seething. Ready for battle.

"Ah, my dear, you have finally woken from your slumber. Perhaps from the pain?" the Emissary taunted as he came around to the foot of my bed.

I never took my eyes off him.

Dr. Edward was tending to my IV and adjusting something, I have no idea what. "May I loosen her restraints enough to sit her up?" Edward asked the Emissary. "I will need to examine her incision for infection."

"By all means, prop her up. We need to have a conversation and it is more polite that way."

My straps were loosened, and Edward help me sit upright by placing pillows behind my back and sliding my body upward. The sliding and pulling was so excruciating I almost screamed, but I held back. Edward squeezed my hand and I gave him a death squeeze back. He knew I could not show weakness. The Emissary was watching every move we made, and I would not give him any satisfaction of vulnerability.

As I was propped up, the Emissary strode to a chair on the window side of my bed. Edward did not move from the other side. Good, I might need someone to restrain me from leaping after the bastard.

"Robert, what brings me the displeasure of your company?" I asked.

"Well, Jess, I am here to collect some information, and the whereabouts of my child. As you are aware, the child will be a very powerful person as it grows up. I will see that it knows all about its mother's betrayal of the Federation and how you left your child behind. Just as your mother did to you." The Emissary moved along the back of the chair before perching on it.

"I would never abandon my child and the child is not yours, Robert," I gritted out.

"Emissary. You will refer to me as Emissary." He suggested. "Oh, and I beg to differ, my dear. You see, if I recall correctly, I fucked you in my office right before you left on your little covert assignment. And I know I fucked you good and made sure I came inside you." He moved within inches of my head. "As I always did."

The thought was so nauseating, I turned away in revulsion.

The Emissary pulled back and continued, "I didn't know of your betrayal for some time. Frankly, I was taken aback when I was informed of your defection. You were my number two. Once I learned your whereabouts, your true identity, and the location of Aries, I put my best people to work."

"So, you sent Marcus after me?" I asked.

"Yes. And when I heard about your pregnancy, I knew the child was mine. I mean, who would want a whore like you after you had been with me? I mean, really." He snorted a little.

I repeated seriously, "The *child* is not *yours*."

"Like *hell* it isn't. The child is *mine* and I *will* take possession of it, and you will never see it again." The Emissary's temper was rising, and I knew I could be in trouble.

"*The child is not yours!*" I yelled.

Instantly, I was backhanded across the face by the Emissary.

I was still restrained. but really pissed off. My cheek hurt now, along with my abdomen.

The Emissary didn't look at me but directed his gaze to Edward, who was averting his eyes. "Where is my child?" the Emissary asked Dr. Edward.

"The child..." Edward turned toward both of us with a solemn tone. "There was a complication during the delivery." It appeared the news was unbearable to say. "I'm sorry. The child didn't make it."

"No! *Fuck no!*" the Emissary yelled and threw his hands up in frustration. If he had restraint, I didn't see any.

My eyes welled with tears. Short sobs escaped as I tried to keep my composure together in front of the Emissary. The Emissary was still seething with anger. Edward looked at me. "Jess, I did everything I could to save your child. I am so very sorry."

I looked deep into his eyes and face. For a moment, there was a hint of deceit and a leftward shift in his eyes. Edward was lying, and this was his way of telling me.

Thank God.

I forced out more tears and sobs to keep up my act. The Emissary didn't know the pact Dr. Edward and I had made.

"You promised you'd keep my baby safe!" I sobbed out; my face wet with tears.

He placed his hand on mine. "I promised you I'd protect him for you. I did everything I could."

"Him! The child was a boy!" the Emissary yelled. "I gave you *one task*—delivering the child to me and keeping her alive long enough for me to deal with. Now all I have is this bitch. I needed that child!" The Emissary didn't stop yelling.

"Yes, sir, you did. But there were complications, forcing me to make a choice. I was doing my job as a doctor. You wanted both, but I was only able save one—the one I believed had the best chance of survival." Edward was holding his ground and standing by his actions.

I jerked my head back and forth between the two men and stopped at Edward. His words were genuine, but there were little facial expressions that gave away his lie. Luckily, I could see that, and the Emissary could not.

Anger still boiling, the Emissary took a deep breath and calmed his tone. "When can I begin the extraction?"

Oh fuck! *Extraction*.

The bastard was going to torture me for information about Aries.

The shock of this drew my gaze back to Edward.

"She needs to heal before you will be able to try. I will not be responsible any damage while she is recovering." Edward was growing some balls.

"Then when the *fuck* will I get her? I need the information she possesses, and I need it now."

Yeah, I can see my future is going to be a very unpleasant one.

"Jessy will need at least a week for her incision to heal."

"Unacceptable." The Emissary began to pace in fury. "You have three days to get her up and ready. I will commence with the extraction whether she is healed or not." With this final declaration, the Emissary headed for the door. "Have her ready!" were his final words before he stormed out of the room and slammed it shut.

CHAPTER 36

I HAD ONLY THREE DAY BEFORE THE OFFICIAL EXTRACTION of information was to commence.

Great!

How was I going to get out of this one? I had multiple question for Dr. Ross Edward regarding the baby, Lincoln, and what actually happed the day of my delivery. I knew my room was most likely bugged in case I divulged any information, so I needed to choose my words with caution when I conversed with Edward.

Right now, I was alone and confined to my bed. I still had an IV in my arm, but it was not distributing any pain medication, and I knew why. The Emissary was going to do unenumerable things to my body and psyche, and narcotics would make his life more difficult and mine easier. Now we can't have that, can we? I was going to suffer for a great many things before joining my sister.

Edward occasionally came in briefly, with food or to examine my incision. No words were spoken between us. It wasn't until the end of day two that I caught his attention.

"I'm sorry for all this, Jess," he said.

"You and I both knew it was going to happen, that I would end up here," I said.

"Yes," he said with sad tone in his voice.

"Can I ask you about my delivery? Or would that be giving out too much information?"

Edward looked conflicted. He really wanted to tell me the truth about that day, but also knew his words could be used against him. His pause confirmed my suspicions. Luckily, he knew my talent.

"You said the baby was a boy? I asked, holding back some emotion.

"Yes." Eyes to the left. Edward was lying.

I have a baby girl!

"And how did he die?" I sniffled back a sob.

"You had heavy bleeding, and there was a point during surgery when the blood loss was too great. We had to deliver. I was forced to make a choice, but I made it too late. He had been deprived of oxygen too long."

I never took my eyes off him. Edward was biting down on his lower lip. Another tell sign of deceit. Both of his patients had made it through surgery.

"So, because you knew I was more important to the Federation, you chose me?"

A nod was all I got in response.

"So, in the end, I will suffer as much as my child did."

"The child didn't suffer. As to your future, I'm not sure what is to happen to you. All I know is I must make you healthy enough for questioning." Edward knew what was to become of me, but it wasn't his decision.

"I understand. But I'm not the one they are looking for," I said, knowing Susan was the one the Emissary needed but was dead by his own hand. He screwed that up.

"He doesn't care." Edward said, looking down at my restraints.

"I am sorry you have been put in this position. I only wish things could have been different."

"As do I." With those words, our conversation was over.

I rested my head back on my pillow and stared at the ceiling. I had a great many things to think about.

As my healing time drew closer to the end, I was able to walk around my room, use the bathroom and shower—thank God—and get some of my strength back. Lucky me, while I was doing all this, I had an armed guard watching my every move. It is so nice when you get to have someone watch you shower. Or poop. That was fun too. I hope he enjoyed the smell. You would have thought I'd have gotten a female guard. Oh no, he was probably the horniest male the Emissary could find and watching me must have been a delight. I was surely not at my prettiest. The bulge in his pants proved he really didn't care. But I'm sure the Emissary warned him not to touch, so I was safe for now.

I was provided food twice a day and it wasn't the most pleasant, but I knew I needed my strength. Dr. Edward came to visit me to check my progress. He would have liked to have more time, but we both knew that wouldn't be possible. The Emissary was going crazy waiting to get his hands on me. I will be in deep trouble when he does.

Day two passed without any problems. Edward sat with me and we had very casual conversation. Nothing that the Emissary could use against either of us, since I was being monitored heavily. What happened to the days of trust? Oh yeah, I burned that bridge when I defected. My guards switched out after about twelve hours give or take, and I paid no attention to them. They were just insects trying to bug me.

All I can say at this moment is I'm not restrained, and I'm not being tortured...yet! Lonely for my child and husband, yes, but I do have the satisfaction that they are both safe and away from the Emissary's reach. What is my daughter like? Does she have Lincoln's hair or mine?

Please tell me it's mine. Lincoln's hair is...well, not plentiful. I wish at least I'd gotten to hold her in my arms before I die.

The end of day three came and went, and anxiety was rising. There had been no sign of the Emissary and I was becoming concerned for what was to come. Sleep evaded me all day, and the closer to the end of the day, the more ran through my brain. What was I in for? What would he do to me?

They need me to unlock Aries and will not kill me until I comply. I must hold my emotions together and focus my brain on holding out any possible information. The Federation cannot have the Aries device, or I should say, the Emissary cannot have it. The possibilities for power are endless, but it was meant to do good in the right hands. The Emissary is far from good.

Darkness was enveloping my room and I had been left alone. Dr. Edward had not been in this evening, and my guard, whom I named Tito, was not eyeing me like fresh meat. Instead, he had eyes of sadness. Maybe because he knew my fate...or because he didn't get a piece of ass.

Anyway, I decided to sit in a chair close to the window with a blanket and try to rest. Who knew when I would get to sleep again once my ordeal began? The blanket warmed me, and I began to drift off to sleep.

CHAPTER 37

"Ahhhhh!"

Screams escaped me as muscular hands and arms forcefully wrestled me awake. I was being dragged out of my slumber and upright. The room was dark and the disruption was making my brain unfocused and confused. As my captors pulled me out of the room, I couldn't get hold of my footing and my feet dragged behind my body.

I was dragged out the door and down a hallway and a set of stairs. I began to resist and the grasp of the men dragging me increased, bruising my arms.

"Where are you taking me?" I yelled as we made our way through the old farmhouse. I surveyed my surroundings even though it was dark.

My God. I knew this place.

"Shut it!" one of my guards yelled back at me without missing a step.

We entered a large room like a living room. I struggled to get hold of my footing and fought back. I jerked against the guards and they pulled harder. I was no match against two muscular men to my post-baby body. Nine months ago, I would have stood a chance, but not now. My body had no power to it.

I was dragged to the middle of the room. My arms could easily have broken from the force they used. One light was turned on, and I knew what this room was. It was the room where I'd experience one of my torture sessions—the drowning incident. My sister had stood behind me and watched as I was shoved into a tub of water and struggled for air.

Trauma filled my body the closer we got. We halted, and one metal chair was placed in the center with a light shining on it. This wouldn't be good.

I resisted even more, but failed miserably against them, and they hurled me into the chair. My brain was telling me to sit still and wait, but my body fought to get up. Well, bad idea. I was forced back into my seat. My healing period was over.

My nemesis came into the light. Seeing his face and body paralyzed me.

With a deep breath, I bravely said, "Hello, Robert." Using his real name pissed him off but I tried to show all the confidence I had. This person was not going to break me. *Do what you must but I will not break.*

Smack! I was cold cocked across the face. My head snapped to the left and blood oozed from my mouth.

Fucker!

Focus, spit out the blood and focus. And that's what I did. I gave him the most hateful stare I could muster.

"Nice to see you again, Robert," I said.

Another fist hit my cheek. This time my head whipped to the right. Blood came out of my mouth and my nose. He must really dislike his name.

"I want it!" he demanded, rubbing his knuckles.

It took me a minute to refocus. I am a tough cookie, but I was a little out of practice. I mean, for Christ sakes I'd just had a baby. My whole fucking body had been altered for the child that I have never seen. I was not going to give in.

Fuck you, Robert Emery.

"Want what?" I asked with hatred as I brought my gaze back to him.

"I want Aries!" he calmly said, backing up about a yard.

My arms might be restrained by the guards, but my feet were not...

"You should have thought of that before you killed my sister." So much loathing came out in my words. I wasn't going to give in.

"Your sister, huh?" he asked.

"Yes, my sister. She had Aries before I did, and she encrypted it," I explained, still seething.

Leaning slightly forward, I spit, then sat back with my chest puffed. I wasn't going to put up with his threats.

"Your sister was a traitor and was disposed of. As you will be, after I get what I need from you." The Emissary inched himself closer to me. Slowly, he bent over and came so close to my face I thought he was going to touch noses with me.

"I can't help you," I said. "You don't think I tried to open Aries myself?"

"I believe your sister told you how to open it before I captured her."

"Well, you thought wrong. There was no discussion on how to open Aries, and you killed the one person who could possible help you!" I was losing my patience with the Emissary, even though I was in the hot seat. Yes, I knew what to do, but I wasn't going give up my only card in this game.

"You do know." The Emissary pulled back from me and stood up. He turned his back to me and walked out of the lighted area. "Jessy, I became very fond of you, and it pains me to see you in this situation." He turned and I could just make out his face behind the light. Evil coming out of darkness. "Let's just say I believe your statement regarding your sister, and that you have no knowledge how to unlock Aries. Then what do I do with you?" Another step closer to the light and more shadows crept across his face.

"You really only have two logical courses of action," I answered.

"Enlighten me."

"One: You could be a respectable human being and let me go. I will suffer enough pain trying to cope with the loss of my child. Or two: You will eventually accept I have no useful knowledge and will kill me."

I needed to see his facial expressions, to see what was really going through his mind. But he stood just far enough away so I could not see him. I believed he was doing this deliberately. To mind-fuck me.

"You are a very smart woman and I commend your honesty. You did just lose a child, and that will damage a person. But you and I both know that I won't let you go. You have information I need, and we can't have you giving it to the wrong people."

"Who are the wrong people? Many say you are the wrong person." I stated, trying not to strain to look at him.

"I was thinking more of your bosses at the Division. They wouldn't have the faintest idea what to do with information like this. I do, therefore I am the only choice for Aries," the Emissary answered.

"The Division, huh? Well, do you see any my Division co-workers here right now? No. Do you see what value I have to them? None, obviously. I am here with you, and I am fucked either way this goes. So why don't you just get it over with?"

Yup, I was going down the wrong road.

The Emissary's tone changed. "You have no idea how much damage you have done to the Federation. You have no idea what has happened because of your defection and the theft of Aries. Damage after damage. All caused by you and your bitch sister."

"You have already disposed of Susan, why wait for me? I'm here, get it over with." I flipped my hands up in a "fine, whatever" gesture.

"No, you will have your time." The Emissary stepped back into the light and I could see his eyes. "I'm going to make you wish you died like your sister."

I looked deep into his eyes and there was no playing around. He was going to make me suffer, and in many heinous ways. There were no words.

"Good, I see your scared. Now that I have your full attention, we will continue this conversation later." His voice was calm now, but it could change in a matter of milliseconds. He looked up to his men and gave a quick nod. "Please take Jessy to her new accommodations." His eyes came back to me. "I hope they are to your liking."

The Emissary stepped closer to me with his hands behind his back, hiding something. Before I could register his action, volts of electricity surged through my body from the taser the Emissary thrust at me. I lasted only seconds, then I passed out.

CHAPTER 38

WHY AM I SO DAMN COLD? MY WHOLE BODY IS SHIVER-*ing. It is so dark. Every ounce of my body is stiff and sore. My vision is dark. Why?*

Moments of confusion went by until my brain began to process what had happened. My internal checklist you might say.

I had been captured, yes;

I am being held, yes;

I was and will be tortured for information, yes.

Okay, step by step I can get this.

I was captured by the Emissary and the Federation.

I just had a baby, and the Emissary was gracious enough to let me heal for a few days. Ah, how thoughtful. After my time was up, I was confronted by Robert Emery, aka the Emissary.

The bastard interrogated me for information that I will not reveal. *Once I do, I'm dead. Just like Susan.*

Okay, yes, all of that sounded right. Now I needed to figure out where I am and why I couldn't see anything. Blink, blink. *There is nothing to see. There must be something wrong.*

I gathered up my strength to move, even though it hurt like hell, and tried to determine where I was. My hands planted down behind my back. The floor was cold and dirty, like a dirt floor, and it had some moisture to it. This was helpful.

I got myself up and probed around my prison.

My feet got their balance and with my hands I search around the room for clues that could reveal where I was. With small steps I do encounter something. A wall of what? Cold, dampness and more dirt. Check. I shuffle to the other side. After a few feet, the same thing. More cold, damp dirt. Inching myself back, I can feel my eyes adjusting to the dark hole, when I realize there's strip of light emanating from the floor. I reach out and feel something other than dirt. Wood. Feeling, touching my way around the wood, I deciphered what it is. A door. I am in what I can only conclude to be a root cellar of some sort.

Great.

I'll get to mold in here. Lovely.

Time has no meaning when you are being held captive. I have no idea how long I have been in this hole or what day it is. Luckily, my body has acclimated to the lower temperature and I've stopped shivering. Now, if I could only get some food. My stomach is beyond empty and I sure it's for a reason. I remember my last encounter with the Emissary and my jolt into unconsciousness. My muscles and nerves certainly remember. Every inch of me remembers. So, I have no clue what to do but sit here or step about my cell and wait. There is no point in yelling out the door. It is solid and heavy.

Tick tock. If I had a clock that was all I would hear. Instead, to keep myself from overthinking everything, I counted. I counted steps around my cell, I counted how many hands my walls are high. I counted everything. And when I wasn't, Lincoln filled my mind. God, I wanted his arms around me. His warmth and embrace would give me the confidence to get through this alive, or at least die with dignity and power. Power the one thing Emissary could not take from me.

Not knowing anything, I thought I heard movement outside the door. I had nothing to defend myself with, so I parked my ass back down in my dirt corner and waited. Since it was dark, my other senses had taken over. I felt my body tense up as the locks on the door began to release. Bolts were pulled back, and clicks echoed as the wooden door swung open. I was blinded by intense light and hid my eyes.

"Food and water for you," I heard from the delivery man. The voice sounded familiar. It was soft. By squinting, I could make out the figure.

"Thanks," I answered, adjusting very gradually to the light to see Dr. Edward.

"Are you okay? Are you hurt?" he asked with concern.

"I'm okay." No information to anyone. I had to keep quiet.

"Are you sure? You just went through a trauma and now are imprisoned. You can tell me," Edward insisted. I still couldn't make out his face but knew it was him.

"No, I can't." I responded, reaching out for the food and water. "Thank you for the food." Taking the bottle and sandwich out of his hand, I turned back to my cell and took a deep breath.

"Jess, I'm—" He paused, frustrated. "I'm trying to help."

I turned back and tried very hard to hold my tongue. If looks could kill, I'm sure Edward would have a hard time staying alive right now. My arms dropped to my sides from either fatigue or annoyance.

"Ross, how can you help me? Huh?" I demanded. "I am locked in this dirt cell, waiting for the Emissary to kill me. There is nothing you can do about it. Nothing, nada."

"I want to help you, whether that means talking to you when I'm here or just sitting with you in silence. If I could get you out, I would. We both know that isn't possible." Edward was sincere, but troubled. The trembling in his voice was obvious.

"Does the Emissary know you are here?" I asked.

"Yes, I offered to bring you food and explained that he had to at least feed you if he was to continue."

"Oh, how generous. I'm sure he didn't like that." I knew what the Emissary's reaction probably was when Edward demanded this common act of decency.

"No, he didn't, but I insisted that if he was to continue with the extraction than he needed to gain some ground with you. We both know how stubborn you are, and giving food was a good place to start. You need strength and energy."

I was at a loss for words. Edward was helping me and going against the Emissary. That wasn't an easy job.

"How do I know whether the food is poisoned or not? I wouldn't put it past the Emissary to poison me slowly."

"I can assure you the food isn't poisoned. I made the sandwich myself and the bottle of water is still sealed."

"Seals can be tampered with." I insisted.

"Yes, but I did not. I'm a healer and we're not killers. At least I am not." His tone changed. "I'm here to help you."

"I understand and have no choice but to believe you. I know it wasn't easy to convince him to treat his prisoner like a human being. Thank you for the food and water."

"You got that right and you're welcome. Is there anything else I can do for you?" I could tell our conversation was making Edward uneasy.

Yes, I thought. I needed to get word to Lincoln. Tell him I love him, take care of our baby girl and keep her safe. I had so many things I wanted to say, but I had to remain quiet.

"No," was all I could say to Edward.

With a nod of his head, the door began to shut. I was once again in darkness, except for the tiny light strip on the floor.

More time passed, how long I haven't the faintest idea. It could have been hours or days. By the sound of my stomach and my parched mouth, it had maybe been a day since Edward brought me food. Possibly hours, but it seemed like an eternity. I kept counting, but it still made the mind games and paranoia continue. How long was the Emissary going to keep me in here before another round of interrogation? I estimated not much longer.

The sandwich Edward gave me was a protein packed one. He must have known what I was going to need to keep going. It looked like dog food, but I knew what was in it. You can make beans and humus look nasty, but in truth, it is full of some of the best protein your body can take in. He was one my side. I had to eat and drink very slowly not to make myself sick, and to make it last.

More time passed.

And more time.

And more.

I was now feeling the effects of starvation and dehydration. My body slumped to the ground and I didn't move from there. I felt as if I could hear every little thing, but most likely I was going crazy.

Clicks echoed in my cell again and the door swung open. I was able to look up and two shadows were outlined in the door. *This can't be good.*

"Get up!" I was ordered, but in my weakened condition that wasn't going to happen. So, I just sat there. "I said *get up!*" he yelled at me again.

"Make me!" I choked out.

I was hoisted to my feet and hauled out of my cell, my toes dragging behind my legs.

I tried to focus on my surroundings but going from complete darkness to bright lights was painful, and nothing looked right. Shadows, lines and objects were blurry. We went upstairs, and I was still being dragged until we reached to top. A door swung open and I was able to make out the smallest thing. The old wooden floor of the farmhouse. We were still there, in the middle of nowhere. There was little hope for me.

Out in the middle of the large room, I could make out the chair they had left for me. Let the games begin. This time the chair was much heavier looking. The first thing I thought of was one of those chairs you'd see in a movie. They type they used for electrocution in prisons. It was a solid wooden chair and there were belts on the arm rests and legs.

I really hoped that wasn't how I'd go.

When the reality of that chair hit me, my body tensed up and I struggled against my guards. But my degrading body was no match for the two men. I was pulled forward with so much force, I'm sure they left bruises on my arms. They hurled me into the chair and began strapping me down. I wasn't giving up. I kicked one of them in the nuts and wiggled every inch of my body. I still was no match, and a backhand across the face stopped my resistance. It stung enough for them to catch me and belt me down.

There was no point fighting. I would use up all my energy to break free from something I wouldn't break free from.

"Stay there, bitch!" one of my guards yelled, standing back. Then he spit in my direction. Asshole. If looks could kill, I'd have killed that one in a heartbeat.

"Fuck off!" I yelled.

"Enough!" A voice came from behind me. That voice could only belong to the Emissary.

I could hear footsteps coming around behind me and then finally into view. Yup, there was the smug-looking Emissary looking powerful as he sauntered in and stood in front of me. All I could do was tilt my head up in disgust.

"Well, my dear, I see the last couple of days haven't made any improvements to your attitude. That will change soon enough," the Emissary said, skirting around me. He began looking me over like meat, tilting his head from one side to another. Checking out all my features. He grabbed my chin hard and held it up as he spoke. "I see the lack of food has damaged your beauty. That is a shame, but you were looking a little pudgy."

"It not like having a child is easy on your body," I said. "But how would you know that? You're just a feeble old man!" I put much emphasis of the last three words, dragging every syllable out.

Smack! Another backhand to my face opened my nose and I started bleeding. Before I could bring my head back, he punched me in the abdomen, making me lurch forward. The blow took the wind right out of my lungs, causing me to cough. That wasn't what I'd expected.

"Pull her back up. I want to look her in the eye while we are talking."

The guards did as they were instructed, and I was hoisted back upright, now with blood dripping down the creases of my mouth and the corners of my lips. I'd be lucky if the Emissary didn't crack a rib.

"I have nothing to say to you. You might as well kill me now instead of wasting your time." I felt so much loathing, I couldn't hold back.

"Oh, but I think you will. I want the key to unlock Aries and I know it will only be a matter of time before your sing like a bird." The Emissary was back in my face and I was not liking it.

"I already told you, I don't have the capability to open Aries." I was furious, and let out a cough with more blood. I tried to spit it in the Emissary's face, but I missed. Boy, that would have been a lovely gift.

"Liar! I know you know how to open it," the Emissary stepped back and bellowed at me.

"Susan was the only one who could open it. And you just happened to dispose of her. Maybe you should have thought of that before you slit her throat," I hollered back.

"Bullshit! You were twins and nothing was left unsaid between the two of you. I want Aries, and you are going to give it to me."

I lowered my voice. "I can't give you something I don't have."

"I don't believe you. We have tried to unlock the device with no success, and you *will* help us." The devious tone from the Emissary crept in the air.

"I'm telling you, there is nothing I can do. Susan was clever and would make it impossible for anyone, including myself, to open it. What do you not understand about this statement? *I am not Susan!*"

I received another punch to the abdomen, and it keeled me over once again. The Emissary was making this personal. Susan was once his right-hand person, and she pushed me forward right into his lap. Idiot. Little did he know that we were not who we said we were. The Emissary claimed to be a smart man, but he was just a lot of talk. I could tell how frustrated he was with me and his inability to open Aries. Body language can say so much. And he was an open book.

Before I could pick my head back up, the Emissary turned and walked over to a table he had set up with equipment and a computer. When I regained my composure, he was fidgeting with objects I couldn't quite make out. But when he turned back around, his eyes were full of hatred. In his hand, were a pair of brass knuckles.

This wasn't going to be pretty.

"Tell me what I want to know, or I will start using these. It has been some time since I used my knuckles, but I seem to recall they can break bones rather easily." He moved closer, rubbing his hands.

"There is nothing to tell. Haven't you done enough damage to me already?" That question made him stop.

"Damage? Have I done you damage? Enlighten me. I would love to hear what damage I have done to you." He got a chuckle out of my question. But not a good chuckle.

"You remember the first time you *raped* me? Or tried to drown me? Killed my sister and made me watch? Or all the other heinous things you did to keep your power?"

Silence.

"You are so caught up in your conquest for power that you will do anything to keep it. All the mind fucking games you play. They will fuck a person up, and you are a prime example of that. You are just as fucked up if not more than the rest of us."

With that, I was walloped across the face and now had a broken nose and possibly a cheek bone.

Blood gushed from my nose and tears welled in my eyes. That certainly hurt. I would receive no medical attention so my nose would never be the same.

The Emissary stood back and watched my reaction to the punishment and smiled. He was enjoying roughing me up and I couldn't give him any satisfaction. His eyes were full of rage and excitement. I'm sure if he was alone right now, he would be ten shades of hard.

"I own you, Jess. I have since the day Susan brought you into this company. I made you, and I will destroy you. If I want to beat you, I will." He came closer to me, almost eye level. Blood was caking my face and the tears coming from the corners of my eyes made the blood glisten.

"If I want to fuck you, I will," the Emissary continued. "You are mine, and when I decide to kill you, I will. Now—" He paused, standing upright. "Tell me what I need to know to open Aries and I'll consider making your death less painful than Susan's."

I inhaled deeply, holding back so much anger. "Susan. You need her to unlock Aries." I gritted my teeth to hide my pain.

I may need to give him something. Something that he will not be able to get.

"*Susan is dead! Give me what I want!*" he screamed in my face.

"You need *Susan*! "I screamed back. And with that, I was punched in the stomach again. It bent me over and I coughed violently with blood spilling out of my mouth. If I'd had food in my stomach, I'm sure that would have come out too. "She is the only one. You need her fingerprints, and seeing as you killed her, I'm sure they have long decomposed by now. So, you're *shit out of luck*!"

The Emissary processed my admission. Confusion came over his face...and the realization that he really wasn't going to be able to open it. That piece of information, I'd had to give up, but I still held the cards.

"Fingerprints. Susan coded Aries with her fingerprints?" That wasn't true. If the Emissary believed it, I wasn't going to deter him.

I gave an acknowledging nod.

"My smart little Susan. I'll give her credit for that one." He almost smiled but didn't. The Emissary look up to one of my guards, giving him the order. "Griffin find everything we had that belonged to Susan. There is bound to be something with her fingerprints on it."

"Yes, sir, but it is unlikely we have anything left," Griffin answered with a crack in his voice.

"What the *hell* are you talking about?" The Emissary was not a happy camper, and I wasn't the cause now.

"Your orders were to destroy any connections to Susan after her disposal."

"Are you *fucking kidding me*? There is nothing left of her but her piece of shit sister?"

Oh boy, I'm doomed.

"No, sir!" Griffin answered, but I could tell by his voice his confidence was lacking.

"Look again, Griffin! Look *again dammit*! There has to be something left." The Emissary turned back to the table. He was pissed.

"Yes, sir. And what would you like us to do with the Jessy, I mean our prisoner?"

Oh, shit, Griffin used my name. That meant there was connection and I was an actual person, not some average piece of trash. I had meaning and purpose to some of these men, and that perked my brain into action.

The Emissary was quiet for seconds, only looking over his table and fiddling with some of the objects. I stared in his direction and then jerked my head back toward Griffin. His eyes showed concern, and I was hoping they were in my favor. We made eye contact and that was all I needed. Griffin could be turned very easily to my side. So, the Emissary wouldn't get suspicious, I redirected my focus, and he turned around holding a syringe in his hand.

I tried not to show any reaction to the syringe, but this was not going to be good. I did not speak but tensed my body, holding every muscle tight.

"Jess today is your lucky day," the Emissary said, plunging the syringe and tapping it for air bubbles. A clear liquid filled the syringe and squirted from the tip.

"Lucky me," I muttered. My eyes never diverted from the syringe.

"Yes. Lucky for you, we have a new product that you get to try out. There are going to be times that physical methods of interrogation are not going to be allowed. So, we have developed a serum to help, and you get to be our official tester." He took slow steps toward me as he explained.

"As I said, lucky me." In the shadows, I saw another figure. By the shape, it could be my friendly doctor.

"Now, as this drug is experimental, I need Dr. Edward to monitor you while it's administered. I am not ready to kill you just yet." The Emissary looked at Edward and the good doctor approached with a medical bag.

"Dr. Edward is going to note how this will work, hoping we administer the right amount. I promise you this is going to hurt tremendously, and you are going to wish you were dead, but not yet. The dose, I hope, will not kill you."

Edward came closer, dropped his bag, and unzipped it. I could see that he was not terribly excited for this course of action by his heavy breathing and slight lift to his shoulders. I knew where Edward stood and what side he would choose if a choice was given. There was an AED defibrillator device in his bag, and he took out the monitor pads to place on my chest. If I had a heart attack, he could revive me and magically bring me back to life for more torture.

Yay! Thumbs up. Go me.

Edward placed the pads on my chest and my eyes met his. Through the tears and blood, my silent message was clear. "Please don't do this."

"I'm sorry," he said in a low tone, pulling my shirt back down. Then he looked back to the Emissary. "They are in place, sir. You may proceed." Edward stepped back and my level of terror rose as the Emissary drew closer.

"Thank you, Doctor." The Emissary gave the doctor a nod.

"Sir, before you administer the serum, I would advise starting off with a small dose. Jessy isn't very big, and we don't know the correct dosage yet. I would hate for you to kill her on our first go around." Edward said with concern. He needed the Emissary to know that he could kill me but hide what his actual motives were.

"Understood. Now get. Out. Of. My. Way!" The Emissary was in full control. There was no one who would stand in his way. Or dare to.

There was no point in struggling, I was in the hands of a monster. With my hair all askew, the Emissary with his rough hands moved it aside, revealing my vulnerable neck. He jammed the needle into the point where the shoulder and neck connect and plunged the syringe. All I could do was hold on for dear life for what awaited me.

"So, Miss Connors, Bowman, or whatever your name is, I have just injected you with a nerve agent that will amplify and cause pain in all of your nerve endings. It will be unbearable, and you will scream. I hope this will be the only time we use it, and I get what I need." The Emissary tilted his head at me and tried to sound sweet but failed. The Emissary doesn't have sweet in him.

In an instant, I began to sweat and wince as my pain level escalated. Slowly, my body felt as if it were on fire and every inch was ablaze. I was being cooked from the inside out without flames. There was nothing I could do. I tried to hold back the screams, but as the sensation travel throughout my body, I couldn't hold back anymore. I screamed as loud as I could. For how long, I will never know.

CHAPTER 39

I FELT LIKE I WAS WAKING UP FROM A BAD DREAM...ONLY it wasn't a dream. My mouth was bone dry from screaming for hours. I wish what I had been through was only a dream, because if it were, I be waking up next to Lincoln and he would hold and comfort me.

He wasn't here, and the last twelve hours had not been a dream.

After the Emissary injected me with the vial of pain, I screamed and screamed and screamed until I had no voice left, no life left in my body. The fire that burned inside me was so intense, you would have never known it wasn't happening around you. Feeling like a cooked marshmallow and silently pleading it would end was the worst. I never begged for it to stop because that would make the Emissary more pleased with himself. The more I screamed in agony, the happier he got.

Dr. Edward was there until the end. When the serum wore out and my pain levels returned to somewhat normal, I was escorted, dragged was more like it back to my hole in the ground. Immediately I collapsed on the cold dirt floor. It was a relief from feeling you are on fire to the depths of my cold cell. The door was locked, I cried and passed out. A dream I'd hoped, but there had been no dream, only the truth and dare of the Emissary. My truth to his dare. And I would die before I give up my truth.

I have the card he needed, and he doesn't even know. A wild goose chase will keep in busy for a brief time.

Time. Hours must have passed, or even days before anyone came close to my cell. But finally, someone did come. Dr. Edward came delivering food and to examine me. My body hadn't moved from the time I'd laid down on the cold floor until now.

I saw his shadow through the bright light, then he walked in and sat down beside me on the floor. I thought of moving, but every time I tried, I failed. My body was frozen and trying to recover from my torture session.

"Jessy, I need to check you out." He placed my sandwich in front of me and set his bag down.

My body was failing, but I was to be kept alive. All I could do was shift my eyes to look at him. "Why?" I asked weakly and tears dripped from the corners of my eyes. "To make sure I am still breathing for the next round. I assure you I am."

"Yes. I had orders to patch you up, but I didn't." He took a deep breath and I could sense he was trying to find the right words. "I never wanted to see you hurt. Let alone for him to use that serum on you." The sincerity in his voice was evident. I was not his enemy.

"I know, but you didn't stop it either," I said in disgust.

"Yes, I know." He lowered his head with shame.

Seconds passed. Minutes, possibly hours, before either of us said anything. I lay motionless, and he sat there staring into oblivion. I needed to drink water, but my body was so stiff, I didn't want to move.

"Ross," I called.

He turned to look at me. "Yes?"

"I want to go home." With my heartfelt plea, I struggled to sit up. Now that the light had filled my cell, I could see its walls, floor, and the things Edward had brought with him.

"I know," was all he said.

"But that will not happen." I propped myself up and Edward handed me a bottle of water. My parched mouth and throat ached as I sipped.

"Slowly," Edward advised, never taking his eyes off me.

I did as I was told and lowered the bottle. "Have you ever sat somewhere and just started writing?" I asked, looking at him.

"No, not really. I never had much extra time for anything other than my studies."

"I do...or I did. When I was younger, I would write about anything—a dream I'd had or places I had been. As I got older, it would flow from my hand and I'd develop character and a real story line." I was trying to make my thoughts clear.

"Tell me about them." Edward opened his medical kit and took out some equipment.

"I had this one character named Lincoln and he became my focal point, the main topic of my stories," I began as Edward examined my eyes with his otoscope. And then my ears.

"Lincoln, huh?"

"I like history, and that was a president I admired. So, Lincoln it was."

Edward sat back for a second and changed out instruments. Stethoscope was next. "Lincoln was a good one." He listened to my heart.

I took deep breath on command but continued. "He would go to many places and explore. I had this one story where he found an old farmhouse and things had happened there. Haunting things. People had been murdered in the house and people were being visited by the dead." I paused, hoping my tale would perk some interest in Edward, but be just chatter to the others listening. Nonsense. "I kind of miss my days of dreams."

"Sounds very disturbing to me, almost psychotic," Edward answered.

"Yes, it does. Maybe I'd be another Stephen King. Focused on my writing and not the career path I took. Authors usually don't end up in these kinds of situations." That was it, I was done talking. I rested my body and shut my eyes.

With my silence, Edward continued his exam. He placed his fingers around my nose and cheek bones. "Jessy, you have a broken nose, and a possible fracture in your cheek bone. Without an x-ray, I won't be able to determine how much damage."

I just nodded and a tear leaked out of my closed eyes. The pressure of his fingers was painful on my face. The injuries weren't making me upset, but the mental damage I had endured and will continue to endure cut deeper than a knife.

Edward moved down to my abdomen and began pressing into my stomach and ribs. I winced at every press he made. This hurt more than the face. "Ouch!" I blurted out.

But he continued to press. I gritted my teeth the more he pushed.

"I'm sorry, but you have some broken ribs, and possibly a bruised spleen and pancreas," he explained.

Great. I was a hot mess. "Lovely. To go along with my broken nose." Still laying back, I opened my watery eyes and looked over at him. "Add it to the list."

Edward concluded his exam and sat back. I didn't move. I hurt and was exhausted.

"Jess," Edward said to me after a long silence.

I turned my head slightly to look at him, but whatever he said wasn't going to change my outcome.

"You need to be strong now and rest up. Eat and drink slowly. I usually would wrap my patient's ribs but, in your case, I am prohibited."

"I guess the Emissary believes I might hang myself with the tape. Smart man, I just might have." I was losing my will to stay awake.

"Well, I will give him my report and with luck, you'll have a few days to recover." Edward gave me a faint smile, but I didn't return one. I just blinked my tears away and rolled my head to my left side.

"I hope you find Lincoln. He is quite a character," I said as Dr. Edward got up and proceeded to leave.

He turned back to look at me. "Maybe I will someday. It seems like an interesting read, my friend." With that he turned away and the door was shut.

I was locked back into darkness.

CHAPTER 40

DARKNESS ENVELOPED ME FOR WHO KNOWS HOW LONG. I had one other meal besides the sandwich Dr. Edward brought me. Lucky for me, it was the same meal. I didn't move much, and I was able to drift in and out of sleep. Every ounce of energy I had was used for my body to heal as much as it could. It was only a matter of time before the Emissary was going to bring me back for more torture sessions in the room of pain. If my thoughts didn't travel so much, I might have been able to center my thoughts. When I drifted, I had to shake my head and focus my brain by singing or counting.

Otherwise, I would see people or hear things that weren't there.

One time I heard a baby crying and cried myself. My instinct was to find the child, but I was restrained. Other times I saw Lincoln and tried to get to him, only to find it was just a wall. My mind was fading away as fast as my body. Whatever the Emissary had next for me I wasn't going to fight but most likely give up. Lincoln and Mitch would raise our baby girl and make her into a strong woman. She would know her mother died to save this country from possible war. How much her mother loved her even though she'd never met her. I think that's what killed me the most. I had never even seen my baby girl.

Another meal came and went, and I continued with my sanity games. I imagined that every meal meant another day. My guards were at least decent enough to blindfold me and take me to a bathroom. They were becoming the only things to keep my sanity alive. But my finish line was coming quickly. I was losing the race.My count was at five meals, and then meal six came. Around my water bottle, I could feel a difference in the label. It seemed to be thicker and doubled up some way. Curious. That sprang my brain and body into an awakened state, scooting closer to the light coming from the bottom of the door. I leaned closer to it and found a piece of something squeezed beneath the label. With shaking fingers, I pulled out what appeared to be toilet paper. It was thin but it had some discoloring it. Almost like words.

Blinking numerous times, I was able to decipher what it said.

LM found.

Adrenaline coursed through my veins and I was warm and tingly. What did it mean?

Had Lincoln been appraised of my situation? Were they looking for me? Was there hope for me? Holy shit! The thoughts going through my brain were like a whirlwind. I was so excited that I forgot the pain I was in from my broken ribs.

I needed to use caution the next time I saw Edward. He was my only source of communication to the outside world, and I needed that. I had to think of key words and phrases that would be meaningful to him but not create suspicion. The toilet paper was a brilliant idea. If I were searched, I could eat the paper and it would be gone before they got the door unlocked. Kudos to you Edward!

I read the note repeatedly, lying in the dirt for the light. Man, could there really be some hope for me? My best hope was Lincoln figuring out my location before they killed me.

Knowing Edward, he won't give out our location. He was being monitored nonstop just as I was. But if he was smart, key phrases could give my location away. God damn, I hoped he... I don't even dare say what I hoped.

My thoughts began to drift as I was disturbed by a loud *bang* outside the door. It startled me, making me jump. Immediately, I crinkled up the piece of toilet paper and stuffed it in my mouth. The paper began to dissolve with what little saliva I had. My mouth became parched from my disappearing note, but it was a good thing it was gone, because the cell door opened.

The light from the outer room once again blinded me, and I used my roughed-up hands to shield the brightness. Without a moment's notice, I was hauled to my feet and dragged out the door. With my arms being pinned by my guards, the light was cutting into my eyes like needles. Also, because of my possible broken ribs, I couldn't keep from crying out. My strong side was fading fast, and the amount of pain I was continuing to endure was going to kill me. Which was what the Emissary had planned all along.

Once again, I was dragged into the room of pain and sat back down in my chair. Buckled back into the restraints, I sat back not making a sound, only breathing deep. My eyes surveyed the room to see what form of torture I would have the pleasure of today. There was a towel and what looked to be a hose and bucket. My eyes were still adjusting so I couldn't be positive.

"Well, nice of you to grace us with your presence." The cold voice of the Emissary filled the air.

"You know where I am. Right where you left me," I answered with arrogance to my tone.

"True, but I do enjoy our visits. Have you pondered our last conversation? How I might be able to open Aries?"

"I know you are not a stupid man. And I have already explained to you, I *cannot help you!*" Did this man listen to anything? Or did he have selective hearing like most men? "You might as well kill me now and get it over with. I know *nothing!*"

"Bullshit!" he screamed. "You were my number two person. I find it hard to believe you didn't find out anything. You're far too clever for that." The Emissary strutted toward me with a towel coiled around his hand.

The pieces were falling into place for what he was going to do to me. The hose and a towel. My brain sprang to alert with the realization. Ever drown, or had the sensation of drowning? Well, I have, at the hand of his truly, the Asshole Emissary. I was tested by getting my head shoved into a tub of water and felt the water trickle into my lungs. By the looks of this gear, I may get to experience that sensation again.

Waterboarding.

The torture where the unlucky victim is laid back into prone position and has either a towel or plastic is placed over the person's face and water is poured over it. The feeling of suffocation and drowning happen simultaneously and there is nothing the victim can do but wait and hopefully make it through.

My eyes grew about three sizes when I understood my fate today. I had to calm my breathing and inhale deep breaths. This was going to be fucking crazy. *I hope I will meet my end soon, for I don't know how I'm going to last much longer. I can't give up my last card, so death will be my last stand.*

"Yes, I am clever, but don't you think by now I would have cracked? What have I got to lose now? Huh?" I was getting worked up. "You already killed my child, why not finish the rest? I have nothing to give you." There was no need for any more outbursts or confrontation.

"You may be correct. But this isn't just about Aries." He was so confident it was so distasteful. He moved toward me with a swagger to his step and fiddled with the towel in his hand.

"What are you talking about? Aries is everything to you." I was a little confused.

"I realized this wasn't about Aries, but your defection from our family." He stopped in front of me.

I was at a loss for words. "Our *family*?"

"Yes, our family. You were welcomed into the Federation with open arms, worked your way up to command level, and once you had an ounce of power, you felt your loyalty was better served elsewhere. You betrayed us, your family." The words conveyed complete astonishment. Like, how dare you? Nobody does that to us. I wave my finger at you.

"Oh yeah. I was very welcome. Sure. My first experiences were drowning or being raped. Yeah, that is being welcomed with open arms. Please, spare me the speech." I may have been restrained but I wasn't giving him satisfaction. It wouldn't matter what I said. He was trying to get me to soften so I'd talk.

"You have no idea how good you had it. If you'd ever talked to your sister, she would have told you, her welcome party was far worse than yours," the Emissary said right in front of my face. "I won't go into detail, but let's just say, for Susan death was welcomed." He stood up and backed off.

His words sank in and I understood a little more of my sister's actions. My twin was tougher than me, and she was protecting me from the all the other heinous actions the Emissary could have done. No wonder she wasn't going to give in to him. That would only prove his power over her. She was one tough bitch.

"Susan was one tough cookie and I am proud to say she was my other half," I blurted out.

Suddenly I was tipped backward. The movement made me gasp as the feeling of falling scurried through my veins. In a prone position, a damp wet towel was placed over my face. My breathing escalated from the speed of these actions. There was no way for me to calm myself before the water was poured over my face.

The cold wet trickle ran down the back of my throat and nose burned my lungs as the water enveloped the air. I began to wrestle against the water and towel over my face, but it just made the torture worse. There was nothing I could do but fight against suffocation and hope I could hold out.

Flailing, arching my shoulders with the hopes of disrupting the torture long enough for air to make its way in was a losing proposition. The more I moved, more cold liquid seeped into my lungs. I was dying slowly by drowning, as the burning began to cascade down my entire body. I jerked my body but there was no end to the water.

As my body began to lose strength and power, I was hoisted back up and the towel dropped to the floor. In a panic, I sputtered and coughed as air began to fill my lungs with refreshing oxygen. Hours seemed to pass as I regained my life force, but in actuality it was probably only seconds or maybe minutes. Whatever the fuck it was, it was forever. I shook with cold as the icy water permeated my frail body and I regained my composure. My breathing was still not completely under control, but I tried. Drowning face down would be horrible, but with that experience of facing upward, I would rather die face down.

I will never be able to look at water again in the same way.

Our eyes locked as the Emissary looked deep into my eyes. I was so full of hatred I could have lunged at that man with every ounce I had. I would have happily murdered the man. He could see my face as I hung forward in my chair, still grasping for air, drenched.

"Are we ready to cooperate?" he asked me calmly.

"*Fuck off!*" I screamed.

His look of disbelief was so frustrating. I wanted to growl and scream at him.

"As I suspected." He looked at the guards over my head. "Take our prisoner back to her cell." His gaze came back to me. "I would love to watch you slowly die in front of me, but I think I'll let you lie in your filth and let hypothermia set in. Next time we chat, you'll be singing like a canary." His snake eyes pierced into me as the cold began to seep into my body and I began to shake.

"So be it!" I spat into his face.

The action took the Emissary off guard, and with every action comes a reaction. Well, mine came with a backhand to the face. The force of his swing knocked my chair to the floor.

I hit the floor with a hard thud and blood dripped from my mouth. I glared up at him. I was beyond pissed off, but helpless. There would be no rescue, and it was only a matter of time before my possible broken ribs broke punctured my lungs. Then my lungs will collapse, and I will not be able to breath.

When I make my move, it better be worth the effort, because it will most likely be my last.

So many things zipped through my brain as my guards hoisted me back up to a sitting position and released my restraints. I was lifted up by my armpits and was escorted back to my lovely home, drenched and cold. The shakes began to overcome my body and I was having a hard time walking down the stairs. The guards began to drag me when my body gave up. The hallway to my cell was endless, and I thought I was going down a tunnel. Or was it just tunnel vision? Finally, I see the end. The door was opened, and I was shoved inside. The door was slammed, locked, and darkness once again took over.

Soon, I needed a game plan. One that would most likely result in my death due to my injuries. But right now, I could do nothing. I was so fucking cold. Hands crisscrossed into my armpits, I huddled down as low and as tight as I could, to preserve my body heat. There was nothing. I had nothing right now. There was nothing in my brain but cold, and the cold began to overtake my consciousness.

Rustled awake from my chilly slumber, my cell door creaked open, unveiling bright lights and a shadow that blocked my view. I had no idea how long I had slept, but I was frozen, and the shakes still ached my body. With the bright light in my eyes, I raised my shaking arm up to block the view. The mystery shadow stepped into my cell, placed food and water down, retreated, and closed the door.

Though my frosty body was hesitant to move, I forced myself toward the food. The light from the bottom of the door was just enough to make out the silhouette of a cup of something and a sandwich. Yeah! Thumbs up for me. *Fuck this life.* The closer my fingers got I could feel warmth coming from the cup. Adrenaline raced through me. Yes! I could feel warmth in my fingers. The cup was holding warm liquid. Trying to control my shakes, I grasped the cup, a mug, and slowly drank.

The warm soup trickled down my throat and it was as if new hope was being placed into my soul. I must slow down, but it tasted and felt so good. One, two, three small sips, and my hands slowed to normal without shaking. I wrapped the cup with my hands and inhaled deeply. The aroma of the chicken broth filled my lungs, and bright light formed from darkness. As the minutes passed, I was able to release one of my hands and grab the sandwich. Plain and simple today, grilled cheese to complement my soup.

As I nibbled the sandwich, something caught my eye. There was discoloration on the napkin. Curious, I leaned closer to the floor to decipher what I was seeing. Was it my imagination? Or was there actually something there? I squinted and there appeared to be words on the napkin. Although they were smudged, so I wasn't able to figure out my clue.

Shit!

I felt grease on my fingers and rubbed them, trying to get it off. I could rub it onto my tattered clothing, but I noticed for an instant they were discolored.

Wait.

"Grease is colored!" I said to myself, and immediately flipped my sandwich over and inched it closer to the light. *Holy fuck!*

Hold on.

"Hold on" was spelled out on my sandwich, with edible marker or pen. I needed to eat and my supporters on the outside would not risk my safety with poison. At least, I hoped not. The words "hold on" repeated over and over in my head and froze my actions. What the hell did it mean? Hold out long? Help is coming. Well, whoever was trying to help me better hurry the fuck up. I was not going to last much longer, mentally or physically.

The wheels were turning now, and I sat up against a wall and continued to eat my sandwich and sip my soup.

Game on.

CHAPTER 41

I HAVE A PLAN. WELL, I THINK I DO.

I have had many, many hours, days to ponder and to scheme, and I think I can execute my plan. A plan that would most likely result in my death, but at this point death was welcome. Why should I sit in a dirt cell and rot away like some root, hoping someone, someday would find my decomposed corpse? Not really my style. I am a doer, not a sit-back-and-wait-er. I had been doing that, and it was now time to get off my ass and get the hell out of there. I was fucking done with this situation.

Done. End of Story.

So, my plan was very straightforward, but I hoped it would get me out of my cell long enough for the Emissary to catch me. And hopefully, kill me. Fingers crossed I would get that lucky. The days and months of sitting and sleeping on dirt are over. If he was going to terminate me, it would've happened by now. I am nothing to him but a good fuck, and he can't work up the balls to get rid of me. So, I'll help the process along.

Now, I wait. Wait for one of my guards to open the door, and then I'll make my move.

Between dozing off and on, my captors have not returned for some time. I am due for food, a pee break and my next round of torture. Hello? Do they know my schedule? Probably not.

"Please! Let me out!" I stood up, yelling and banging on the door. If there was no action, I'd make action. With my fists, I continued to pound on the door and yelled some more. "Come on *assholes*! Let me *out!*" More pounding. I couldn't give up. Not yet. Someone would hear me and open the door. "*Fuckers! Let me out!*"

I banged on my side of the door a few more times, until I heard the lock shift. Some idiot heard my screams and was unlocking my door. *Sucker!* Preparing myself, I stepped back as far as I could go so, I could ram the person, allowing my freedom. Speed and force would be my only way out. My body was weak, but adrenaline coursed through my veins, pumping all my nerves up.

One more click and a shift, and it was go-time. The large bulky door opened so slowly it was as if time had gone into slow-mo. This was my only chance. The door was pushed open, and I moved. As daylight blinded me, I ran as fast as I could in a running start. The guard who'd uncaged me didn't know what hit him. He landed on the floor. I was blinded, but there was no way I was going to stop. My eyes would adjust soon.

Down the hallway, I remember there was a staircase not far from the end. I would need to sprint up it and keep going. Shaking the bright light from my eyes and trying to make them focus, I kept running. I wasn't fast, but nothing was going to hold me back. My legs pumped...but my momentum was drawn backward. My head was yanked back by the hair, and I bellowed out a scream. This was not what I was expecting.

"What the *fuck* are you doing?" my captor yelled into my ear. "*Shit*, Jess, they are coming for you."

Damn, I knew that voice. It rang in my ears and I knew it must be Hunter Griffin. He was always a supporter of mine. He just played both sides.

"Let me go!" I squealed, trying to get away. The more I moved, the more hair I could feel ripping out of my head. With the backs of my elbows, I tried to jab them into Griffin's stomach.

He deflected them easily. "Shut up!" he commanded, grasping hard to my hair. "You don't listen, do you?"

"Let me *go!*" I ordered sternly.

Griffin wheeled me around, releasing my hair but not releasing me. Instead he held onto my biceps and arms so tightly it would bruise. "I told you they are coming for you. You need to go back," he said in a lower tone, but still very abrasive. He pulled my body into a dark area so we wouldn't be as noticeable.

Good news for me, it would help my eyes adjust.

"Griffin, the Emissary is not coming for me or to set me free. He will let me rot in my dirt cell before he kills me," I said, struggling to free myself. "At least this way, either my death will be quick, or I will escape...or die trying."

Griffin eased his grasp on me. Finally. "It's not the Emissary," he said with wide eyes.

It took a moment for me to understand what he was implying. Was Division close to finding me?

"You need to go back before—" Griffin's eyes shifted up the stairwell.

My head snapped around at the sound of slow clapping that came from up above. Heavy footfalls stomped down the wooden stairs as the claps continued.

The Emissary's evil devilish grin beamed. "Well, well, well." His arrogance was revolting. "I knew it was only a matter of time before someone helped you out, Jessy." The Emissary halted about three stairs from the bottom so he could tower over us.

I turned around to face him head-on and showed absolutely no fear, only confidence.

"Ah, that's the girl I know. No fear. That's my girl!" He was so smug I wanted nothing more than to punch him right in the face. Couple black eyes would do nicely.

"I am *not* your girl!" I said. My words were solid, but my insides were shaking.

"Oh, my dear. I beg to differ. You may say you're not, but I created you. You merely lost your way until now. I was waiting to see just how long you would sit in your hole in the ground before you made a move. Honestly, it took much longer than I imagined. Now, here we are. You have finally returned."

"*Bull shit!* You were not waiting for my move. You were waiting to see who would betray you. See who was loyal to me and not you. Well, I have news for you, I broke out all by myself with no help from your pathetic guards." I was furious and wasn't going to stop. "You act like this was your plan all along, but I saw the surprise in your face when you saw me. Knowing I did it all on my own. Your plan to let me rot failed. Remember I was your number two. I have my own loyalist."

His expression went from a happy smug to an instant fiery pissed-off look. His eyes turned blood red with fury, and I knew I had struck a nerve.

"Enough! I know you had help. Little notes being passed to you, and small talk between you and fellow employees. It was only a matter of time before one allowed you to escape." The Emissary slowly stepped closer to me, coming off his perch.

Behind me was Hunter Griffin, and with one of his hands he gave me a nudge of reassurance.

"I'm sorry to say, but it wasn't one of *my* men that let me out. It was *yours*." I added to my previous statement. "I was able to barge through the open door when one of your men came for me. I ran down the hallway and would have made it out if I hadn't been stopped by Griffin. Life doesn't matter to me anymore. I will die either way."

The Emissary was now eye to eye to me. "You may have gotten out, but I know someone assisted you." His voice got very low and deep.

"Prove it!" I shot back. My entire body was coursing with adrenaline. My only concern was to keep my cool and not show how weak I really was.

Quickly, the Emissary whipped around and grabbed a handful of my nasty and messy hair. The action took me by surprise, and I winced as locks of my hair were yanked out as he grasped it.

"I don't have to prove anything. You want to die? Fine, I'll make it happen. Even more painful and agonizing than your sister's execution. You will feel every ounce of pain and watch as your life drips away."

He was so cruel. Plain and simple.

"So be it." He tightened his grip, but I jerked my chin upward. "As long as you don't have Aries, my death won't be in vain."

Instantly, my head was yanked backward. "You *bitch!*" he screamed into my ear, pushing my body forcefully forward but still clenching tightly to my hair.

Of course, with my body accelerating forward and my head not, my legs gave out from under me. I fell to the floor, my head was still in the grasp of the Emissary. Many strands of hair were ripped from my head as I tried to regain my footing. I tried my best not to scream at the pain, but a few escaped.

"*Fuck you!*" I yelled through sweat and tears.

"Fuck you, huh?" he causally said as he pulled me back into proximity to his body. "I might just do that," he whispered into my ear and ran his tongue up my cheek.

I wanted to vomit. My whole face crinkled up in disgust and I tried my best to pull away.

"What's the matter, my dear?" the Emissary whispered into my ear. Words were lost for me.

The Emissary moved one of his hands into his jacket pocket to retrieve something. With a jolt, pressure was shoved into the small of my back. He pulled me closer and I could feel something puncture my skin. Sharp pain erupted in my back, and my eyes grew big with the realization. Griffin noticed the change and took a step closer. But this was my battle, and I needed to handle it without anyone else getting injured.

"I'm going to gut you like a fish!" The Emissary's voice was cold but held a hint of pleasure. He would enjoy that a little too much.

Could this be my fate? Very well could be. The Emissary didn't usually joke about forms of execution, and when there is a knife involved, he gets a little too knife happy. I will be lucky if my body will be recognizable afterward. If my fate was to be gutted like a fish, it would be ten times worse. All I could think about was the fate of my family, and oddly, I wondered what a gutted human looked like. Was he going to start from the front and let my intestines hang out, then move on while I hold my own innards? Or from behind and not face me? Showing his power...and his weakness to kill without looking into the eyes of his victim. The Emissary could be a strong man as much as a coward.

"Please send my regards to your sister Susan when you see her. I do miss having her around." He put more pressure with the knife into my back.

"You can tell her yourself!"

The Emissary yanked my hair back again, exposing my neck.

"You really are a piece of work, aren't you?" he whispered.

"Does that surprise you?" *That's right keep him talking.* This conversation of ours seemed to take an eternity, but, it was only a matter of minutes. My time was running out.

"No." The word echoed as the Emissary plunged his knife deep into my lower back.

Pain seared though my body, and I could feel my adrenaline sky-rocket. Every nerve was on high alert, and I cringed and gasped. The knife was pushed deeper, and with a flick of his wrist, my wound was twisted open and even more damage was inflicted. My body cried out in pain and the Emissary released my hair, shoving me into a nearby support beam.

My head slammed into it with enough force to knock me backward and onto the ground, face down.

My vision and hearing were becoming blurry, but there were muffled sounds all around me. The death wound in my back leaked blood at a rapid rate. My life force would soon leave this world.

There was something surrounding me that sounded like multiple yells and footfalls. With what little strength I could muster, I opened my eyes to see lots of feet...and felt the blood seep out of me into a pool under my stomach. Something stopped in my vison. It was blurry, but I could make out a pair of boots.

"We have her! She needs medical attention!" A loud voice yelled in proximity, even though it was muted and muffled. All I could feel was weight on my back, and sleep was overcoming me. Or was that death?

Either way I would welcome it. My time had lapsed.

CHAPTER 42

MORE SOUNDS.

More voices.

Everything was muffled, as if blocked by a sheet or towel. I could feel myself in a trance state, unable to fully awaken. It was as if I was floating on a cloud.

Was this death or some kind of afterlife? Maybe it was purgatory, where the voices torture you, as you can hear them but can't make out what they say.

It is what it is.

But if I'm dead, where is Susan? So many questions. And then everything was silent.

Then the voices were back. I'd thought I wasn't crazy, but now I think I maybe I was on my way. I hear them, I feel like I am dreaming, but I can't wake up.

Ugh! This is frustrating. Why can't I figure this out? I am smart and can figure out what is happening by deductive reasoning. Yes, that was the way. *Slow down and think about what is out there. All I see is darkness but hear a beep and words. What the hell are they saying?*

I have no idea how long I have been here, in my crazy mind and this new world. I must be in hell because the nut house must have been full. I was not a religious person, but hell to me was meant to be a hot, miserable place. Logically, hell was a place of no pleasure, only punishment.

This must be my personal hell. All of psychology couldn't explain what my brain or spirit was telling me. There was no body, just the soul. I needed to let go of it so I could take my eternal nap. The voices and beeps needed to stop.

Oh my God! What the hell was that?

"Please, come back. Don't leave me now!"

Words, I can comprehend words. Someone was asking me to come back. But I was dead, there was no coming back. My wounds caused major life-ending damage to my body, but I fully made out what was being said. The words were so horribly sad. Sounded like sobs as they came to me.

"Jess, please!" Pleading words. More words, coherent words.

I am not going crazy!

What the hell should I do? My vision is dark but doesn't seem as dark. How can it be? Then the words became muffled once again. Darkness overtook me.

PRESSURE, THERE SEEMED TO BE PRESSURE SOMEWHERE down my body. It felt like it could be around my hands or elbows, maybe? Possible. Like a rock was put on top of my hand to weigh me down. I can't move it. Was this my body dying? Was I dying, and the feeling of dead weight the beginning of decay? Boy, my brain would drive someone crazy with all my theorizing and analysis. It surely didn't help me right now...and right now was all I had.

Not only did my arms feel heavy or restrained, the voices were back. There were multiple voices this time, and one was deep-sounding and not happy. Nothing was clear, but the tones were a dead—no pun intended—giveaway that things were not going very well. Other voices were calm and cool, but the deep one was upset. God damn it, why is everything so—

Ah! I can't hear anything!

This is so frustrating. Come on, brain. Work!

More loud sounds, this time they echoed...and then silence.

"He's just scared. Scared he's going to lose you, Jess." There was a pause. "He isn't alone. I don't know what we will do without you. Please! Jess, wake up."

I knew that voice, those words, that tone. I understood every essence of those words. It was my best friend, Mitchell, pleading to me to wake up. But I'm dead, not sleeping. There was no way to wake the dead. He must be sitting by my grave and I am a spirit.

Yup, that was it. I was nothing but a spirit.

Then, more force fell upon my arm or hand. This time it was harder and... almost soothing. With every ounce of strength, I tried to move it. It didn't seem to be working.

Move, dammit. Move!

Sobs. I could hear sobs from Mitchell. He was crying, weeping over me. I must try again to move.

"Holy *shit*! Jess, Jess! If you're in there, please open your eyes." Mitchell pleaded.

There was a squeeze. I felt a squeeze, and I tried to return the squeeze as best I could. My darkness began to get brighter, almost light, when I felt the flittering of my eyelids opening. The first thing to come into my vision was a very hazy, wet-faced Mitchell.

Everything was so bright that I needed to keep blinking to get my eyes to adjust. Eventually, they focused, and my best friend's face cleared.

I was *not dead yet*!

"Jess, thank God, Jess. You are awake. Can you hear me?" Mitchell began to ramble.

All I could do was look at him with cloudy eyes. The knowledge that I was not dead, only sleeping was overwhelming. Floods of emotion roared over me. What do I say? Can I say anything? I can see him and understand him, but can I speak?

I mouthed the first thing that came to me. "Lincoln."

"What?" Mitchell looked at me inquisitively.

With more effort, I tried to squeak out the word. "Lincoln. Baby."

"He's here. He is out talking to the doctor. He hasn't left your side since we found you." Mitch wiped a tear off his cheek. And of course, seeing him tearing up made me emotional. I think some men are way more girly then some women. My best friend was certainly one of them, and I'd missed every moment of it.

"Baby," I repeated.

"She's safe and wonderful."

"Where?"

"I need go get him." Mitchell tried to release my hand, but I held it firmly for a second. He looked down and knew I didn't want him to leave. "Jess, I'll go get Lincoln. I promise and I'll be right back. Lincoln should be the one to tell you about your daughter." I nodded and release my death grip and he leaned in to kiss my forehead, then he turned and left my room.

I tilted my head to peer around my hospital room. Monitors and an IV were next to my bed beeping away. The room was dull looking but it wasn't the dirt cell. Which I am very thankful for. I'm just thankful I'm alive. There were big, bright windows and a couch and chair on one side, and the other was loaded with medical equipment. There were many devices, including oxygen among the equipment. I must have been in bad shape to require this much. My head was moving very slowly but my eyes absorbed every detail of my surroundings.

The door began to open, and Mitchell appeared first. I was able to rotate my head to look at the door when another face appeared.

"Lincoln!" I called out with little to no voice. With my sight clearing up, I called out again, "Lincoln." This time the word was audible, and the flood gates opened as Lincoln came over to my side.

Sobs, and more sobs were all I could muster as Lincoln collected me into his arms and held me to his body. I have never wanted his comfort as much as I did at this moment. Safe in his arms and out of harm's way. There was never another time in my life I was so thankful to be weak and let someone be strong for me. Lincoln was always the one who could banish any troubles.

"Oh my God, thank you. Thank you!" Lincoln sobbed quietly, holding my head against his chest.

My cries were not so quiet. Wailing was more like it. I don't know how long I cried into Lincoln's chest, but it didn't matter. He was here, and anyone around us would either understand or not. The ones that didn't, well they could suck it.

Finally, my eyes had dried out and my sobs lessened, and Lincoln pulled me away to see my face. His eyes were so incredible. How I missed very fleck of color in them. How long I had been in the Federation's grasp? I imagine it was quite a while.

"I thought I'd lost you." Lincoln looked down deep into my eyes and I could see tears were overtaking him.

"I thought I had died, and then I kept hearing sounds. Voices telling me not to leave. I had no idea if I was alive or dead," I said, slow and drawn out, full of emotion.

"Do you remember what happened?" A voice from behind Lincoln asked as a very emotional Mitchell came closer.

Lincoln wasn't letting go of me, but he did release me enough so I could look at Mitchell. I wiped away my tears and the snot dripping from my nose.

My throat was so dry, I sounded hoarse as I spoke. "I remember the Emissary stabbing me, collapsing to the floor, and then being surrounded by blood. I was bleeding out. There were boots all around me as I lay on the floor, but I imagined they were my brain grasping for hope." I was rather proud I could remember all that.

Mitchell was trying to compose himself but was having a harder time than I was. He was always so much more emotional then Lincoln or me. "That sounds accurate," was all Mitchell said.

That was it. No other detail, nothing. I needed to know what had happened to me. How long was I held captive? Where was my child?

"Where is the baby? Can I see the baby? Is she alright?"

The doctor interrupted and said, "Mr. Matthews, I need to examine Ms. Connors now that she is conscious."

Lincoln looked down into my eyes, leaned down, and laid a big fat kiss on me. It was incredible. I still had many questions.

He got up and I tried to pull myself into a sitting position. There was something not quite right. I knew I had no strength in my arms, but I should be able to at least slide myself into an upright position.

There was no feeling from my waist down. I felt nothing but dead weight.

Fear and panic filled my entire body. What I could feel of it.

"I can't feel my legs! Why can't I feel my legs?" Hysteria overtook me.

I looked from the doctor to Mitchell, and then to Lincoln. Not one face gave me an answer I was looking for. Why? Another shiver of terror and fear coursed through me, and I could hear the heart monitor beep increase.

Lincoln came back over and held my hand, trying to ease my panic.

"Ms. Connors, I really need you to calm down so I can examine you," the doctor said as Lincoln sat on the edge of my bed.

Breathe, Jess. You need to breathe. Answers are what you need. Not confusion.

"Okay, okay." I was breathing deeply and could feel the anxiety decrease.

"Good," the doctor said, and came closer to listen to my heart and lungs.

My blood pressure was taken and then my blankets were taken off my feet and legs. Lincoln still sat on the edge of my bed and held my hand. I squeezed so tightly for fear of what I was going to hear.

With my feet exposed, the neural examine began. A sharp pen-looking device was pushed into my toes, then feet, and then moved up my legs.

"Can you feel any of this?" the doctor asked, still pricking my legs.

"No, nothing!" There was no way I was taking my eyes of this doctor. He clearly knew what the prognosis was but wasn't going to confirm it until I was awake.

"How about now?" he asked, pricking my knees and up into my quads.

All I could do was shake my head. Nothing. Frustration filled my body and I had to lie back on to my pillow and throw my hands over my face. More tears leaked out and I didn't care.

The doctor continued with his pricking, and suddenly I sprang up. "Wait, I can feel that! I felt that!" This was exciting. I wasn't sure where he had touched me, but it was a good sign, right?

He pricked that spot again and I was so excited, I smiled through my tears. It wasn't until I saw where he had touched me that I went cold again.

Lincoln and Mitchell both look horrified, and that freaked me out even more. Both hung their heads.

The spot where I felt sensation was above my waist. There was no feeling from my waist down.

CHAPTER 43

"You are paralyzed from the waist down, I'm afraid. The wound you sustained severed parts of your spinal column and surrounding nerves." He paused. "We were hoping when the swelling went down the damage would be minimal, but it seems to be as we feared. I'm very sorry." The doctor gave his speech, and that was it.

"Is there anything else we can do?" Lincoln asked, keeping his temper in check.

The doctor had said his piece and was attempting to make his exit when Lincoln's question stopped him.

He turned with his tablet in hand, breathed deep, and looked back toward us. "Right now, the only thing we can do is wait."

Not the news we were hoping for. I breathed in deeply, Lincoln gazed into the floor, and Mitchell gave out a crying squeak.

Lincoln was very upset. He met eyes with the doctor and conveyed his disappointment. "Wait? We have to wait. How long are we supposed to wait?"

"I don't have that answer. I'm sorry." With that, the doctor shot me an apologetic look "I wish there was more I could tell you. We will keep monitoring your progress and hope with time there will be some recovery." He said and exited the room.

There was nothing else to say or do but wait. That was my only option, and I must accept it. This must be what the Emissary wanted, not to kill me but make me suffer. To cripple me. I was no longer a threat after the infiltration of the farmhouse, but just in case, he'd made me this way. There was no possible way I'd be able to find him in a wheelchair.

Silence filled the room between Lincoln's fury and pacing, and Mitchell quiet sobs. What could I do? I had so many emotions going through my mind, and my support people are breaking or shutting down.

Wait, this is my life and my body. I should be the one in outrage. Me! This was about me, and now I must live with my new paralysis. No running or walking...

Suddenly, my breathing became irregular and I was hyperventilating and crying.

Both men turned to me in panic.

Lincoln sat on the edge of my bed and began to rub my arm and forehead, trying to calm me. "Hey, it's going to be all right. We will figure it out. I promise."

My eyes filled with tears as I looked over to Lincoln. I could see in his eyes, he wanted to be strong for me. But it wasn't his life completely turned upside down. I glanced over at Mitchell, and he was in the same situation. It was almost like they pitied me, but also feeling sorry for themselves.

"What the hell am I going to do?" I was losing my shit. Literally, I just woke up, and now I am paralyzed. I had every right to lose my shit.

"Hey, look at me!"

I wasn't looking at either of them. I was so fucking mad and sad that I couldn't pull my eyes up off my useless legs.

"*Look at me!*" Lincoln sternly said, lifting my chin and turning it toward him. I could see him through my watery eyes, and his face showed so much strength. It made my helplessness even worse.

"We will get through this. I promise." There was no lying in his eyes as he reiterated his words. "I'm not going anywhere." He placed his forehead on mine.

All I wanted to do was scream, run or punch something. It took me some time before I was able to collect myself after hearing the terrible news. There were still so many questions I needed to have answered, and I was not in a patient mood. Lincoln never left my side through all my tears or panic. Mitchell eventually had to leave the room. He was becoming almost as frantic as I was, so Lincoln bluntly told him he needed to vacate the room. Mitchell's emotional status wasn't helping the situation. As much as I needed them both, Lincoln was correct with this course of action.

Once my panic attack wound down, my body was so exhausted that sleep started to take over. Lincoln slid my dead legs over and curled up in my hospital bed with me. He let me rest my head on his chest, planted a kiss on it, and rubbed my hair. It was soothing, and it wasn't long before I drifted off to sleep.

I HAVE NO IDEA HOW LONG I HAD BEEN ASLEEP, BUT I WAS awakened by the rumbling in my stomach. Being familiar with that feeling from my captivity, I was trying to ignore it as I was used to doing, but Lincoln also heard it.

"Man, what do you have in there?" he asked with astonishment.

Okay. It was loud.

"Nothing, apparently," I answered and looked up at him. He hadn't moved during my nap, and I was so grateful. Being alone in darkness for any amount of time was troubling. His presence was most comforting.

"What would you like to eat?" Lincoln asked, slowly moving my body off his so he could get up.

"I really don't know. I haven't had any options lately, so I'm unsure." My brain started working in overtime with pictures of food pop into it. So many things I wanted, but knowing that my stomach shrank, I wasn't going to be able to enjoy much.

"You know I'll bring anything you want here. Anything!" He was dead serious. I looked at him through sleepy eyes and smiled.

Another moment of thinking, and then, "Soup!" was the first thing I blurted out. "Some hot chicken and rice soup, and a piece of bread with butter." Oh man, was my mouth watering with that idea. Hot food wasn't something I usually went for, but boy it sounded like the best thing in the world right now. And my child. That's what I really wanted at this moment, but food was a necessity.

"I'm on it." Lincoln hauled out his phone and began texting to God knew who. I would get my soup. My eyes never left him as he scrolled and typed on his phone. The sight of him brought a happy tear to my eye.

"It's on its way!" Lincoln said, looking over at me. Then he saw my tears. "Hey, no tears. You are safe now." Lincoln pulled me to his body again and I wrapped my arms around him.

"I'm okay. I'm just so happy to be with you." I wiped a tear from my cheek. "I never thought I would see you again. I had accepted that. I accepted that I would never meet our daughter. I'm sorry if I'm a little more emotional than usual."

Lincoln pulled me away and kneeled, looking deep into my teary eyes. "Believe me, it scared me to think we would never find you. If we did, what would we find; a corpse. Our daughter would grow up without a mother. But Mitchell and I were never giving up. It was only by chance we found you." He picked up my hand and kissed it.

"Wait, what?" That perked me up. "What do you mean, by chance?" My body was hungering for information now.

Lincoln got up, pulled the chair in the corner over to my bed, and sat on the edge of it.

"We were left breadcrumbs, clues where to find you."

"Crumbs...like, breadcrumbs?" I was baffled.

"Yes, little clues to help us figure out where you were. But maybe we should wait until after you eat. All this information might overload you."

"No, please. My head is buzzing. Just give me something. The baby, information, anything." I was almost to the point of begging.

"I know you. If I tell you one thing, you're going to want all of it. Food is on the way." Lincoln knew me so well, but I was itching for information.

"Please!" I gave him my best puppy dog eyes.

"God damn it, you know I can't resist those eyes."

I knew I had won, and a smile of victory emerged. "I know. Now I want to hear everything."

"Ah, not everything just yet." Lincoln caught my hint and I got shut down.

"Shit."

"Nice try. But I will let you in on something," Lincoln said playfully.

This was going to be just what the doctor ordered. The mystery of my rescue.

"What's that?" I asked.

"I have known you way too long to fall for that." He smiled and sat back into the chair. "You'll just have to wait."

CHAPTER 44

LINCOLN, OH LINCOLN. HE LOVED TOYING WITH ME. He made me wait until Mitchell arrived with my requested food, and never gave me a hint of information. Asshole. I love the man with my whole heart, but he can be a dickhead when I really want something. Making me wait.

I have been waiting forever for this. I had been captive for God knew how long, in a coma, and now awake. I wanted answers. I was totally entitled to them. And Lincoln just watched me as I was pouting like a little child.

"It's killing you, isn't it?" Lincoln asked with the biggest smirk on his face. He knew damn well I was going crazy.

"Duh! Yes, it is." My high school attitude was coming out.

"Well, once you have had something to eat, we will tell you." Lincoln was a bit more serious, and I made a scrunched face at him.

Waiting impatiently, I crossed my arms and laid back on my pillows. I did not like the unknown. It pissed me off at times. Argh!

A knock came from outside my room. Lincoln rose to open the door and there stood Mitchell and my soup.

295

"About damn time!" I said with a little more attitude than I probably should have. He was my boss and my best friend.

Pausing inside my door, Lincoln closed it behind him, and Mitchell said, "Who peed in your cornflakes? I am just the delivery boy."

"Jess is being a wee bit impatient at the moment." Lincoln said, moving around to face him. "I told her I would explain how the events of her rescue unfolded, but not until she ate some real food. Then possibly a visit with a certain someone."

Boy, that was a look. A nice look to his brother, and a stern look toward me.

"Ah, that explains it. She doesn't like not knowing or waiting." Mitchell glanced my way.

"Has anyone told you that you both can be assholes?" I muttered.

"Yes!" They responded together.

"Well, have no fear, your questions will soon be answered." Mitchell paused for affect. "After you eat." Mitchell was trying to be the funny man. Not working so well. While Lincoln was slightly chuckling, I was not so much.

"Just give me the damn soup," I barked. Mitchell did as he was told and brought the paper bag over to me. Lincoln was behind him with the table. He slid the table into place over the bed, and Mitchell laid out the soup and unwrapped the bread.

Holy. The aromas escaping from the packages were heavenly. My nose was in overload from all the good smells. I have been eating plain, nasty food for weeks, my only source of food even though Dr. Edward made sure it was loaded with protein. This food looked like a gourmet meal. I was used to eating crap.

"Did you see that?" Mitchell blurted out, looking at me. I focused back on him.

"What?" Lincoln asked.

"You didn't see that look. It was almost a coffee-gasm look." Mitchell, Mr. Funny man, got a snide look from me.

Lincoln of course was going to ride that one, but one look from me and he shut his mouth and smiled.

"The only thing I want to hear from the two of you right now is how you got me out." Right to the point. "And where is my child? What happened to her?"

"Eat!" was the only word I got out of Lincoln's mouth.

He got another dirty look.

Fine, I gave up. Taking the plastic spoon out of the paper bag, I commenced sipping on the soup. Fabulous! The soup was incredible. It could be Campbell's Chicken Soup for all I knew, and it would still taste amazing. And the bread, ah! Delicious! A few bites into my meal and I could feel myself getting full. My stomach had shrunk in the last few weeks. The boys had adjusted themselves around my bedside. Lincoln sat on the edge, down by my useless feet, and Mitchell sat in the chair Lincoln had been sitting in.

"All right, I have eaten. I want answers now," I demanded.

Both brothers looked at me, to each other, and back at me. I wasn't playing around.

"That's all you're going to eat?" Mitchell looked at my food in shock at the tiny amount I had consumed.

"Yeah, for now. I don't eat much these days. Now, please, give me something. I need it," I pleaded.

"Fine." Lincoln stood up, removing my portable table and food. My hand sprang into action and grabbed the buttered bread before it was wheeled off.

"Valuable cargo. I need to make sure nothing happens to it."

Oh shit, did I just say that out loud? I am hoarding my food. In captivity, I was never sure when I would eat again, so I saved pieces for later. I even held it close to my body so no one would take it.

The looks I was getting from the brothers were concerning.

"Hey, we are not going to take your food," Lincoln assured.

"New habit, I guess." I was feeling embarrassed for my action.

Mitchell gave me a reassuring smile to help, but it almost made me cower. Looks were just as damaging as words, and both Mitchell and Lincoln were trying to instill confidence back into me. All I can say is bring on the therapy. Again.

Lincoln sat back down on the edge of my bed and no one spoke until I made the first move. "So, what are the juicy details?" I tried to make a joke, but it wasn't funny.

"As you remember, you had been admitted to the hospital and rushed into surgery." Lincoln began. "I waited for you and the baby to come out of surgery, but only one of you came out. The baby. I was instructed to go with her until you were moved. I did."

"Wait? She's ok?" I stopped him as my eyes welled up with tears again.

Lincoln clasped my hands and squeezed them. "Yes, she is amazing." The moment was getting to both of us. I glanced toward Mitchell and back to Lincoln, taking deep breaths.

"She is beautiful!" Mitch piped up, with a smile from ear to ear.

I forced a smile and nodded. He'd said is, not was. My baby girl is beautiful and with Lincoln. The Emissary never got wind of her or went looking. Thank God.

Lincoln squeezed my hand again and continued. "Hours went by, and there was no word on your condition, so I went searching. When someone finally gave me information, you had been transported out of the hospital without authorization. The three of us raced around looking for evidence of who or where you had been taken. Tegan and Xander were just as panic as I was, but there was nothing. Xander contacted Mitch, knowing your prediction was correct and the Federation had taken you. Tegan and I stayed with the baby while a Division team was assembled. We didn't want to risk her if the Federation came looking."

Lincoln began to struggle as he recalled the events.

"I was told the baby had died while the Emissary was in the room with me," I said. "Dr Edward was the one who delivered the baby, and I made him swear to protect it from the Emissary. When he told me my baby boy had died, my soul was crushed, and I wanted to die along with him. Later, I was able to decipher by Ross' expressions that our child hadn't died. And in fact, was a girl." My words were slurred as I explained my side of the story.

Mitchell said, "Dr. Edward kept his word regarding your daughter, but the fact still remained that you had been taken and we had no idea where. The Federation is slick and had plans in motion before Division even blinked."

My eyes went back and forth between Mitchell and Lincoln. Lincoln never released my hand and I was grateful for that.

"Days, went by and we still had nothing regarding your whereabouts and panic was setting in." Lincoln stopped. Reliving the memory was clearly not something he wanted to do.

"It wasn't until sometime later, a couple week, we received an anonymous tip." Mitch took over with a deep breath. "All we got was a note. The note told us to read your stories."

"I told one of my stories synopses to Dr. Edward," I explained. "It was about Lincoln. He was my main character. In code of course, so the Emissary wouldn't believe I was giving away information. I was trying to keep everyone safe."

"Mitch told me about the note," Lincoln said. "We turned every inch of the loft and safe house upside down until we found your notebooks. Between Tegan, Xander, Mitch and me, we read through every page you had written about the Federation and its facilities. That was the information we need to start our search for you." Lincoln stopped and looked down at me.

My eyes never left his. "What about the baby? When can I see her?" I asked.

"Soon. She is safe in Tegan's care." Mitch stopped.

I was very anxious to meet my daughter and for all the information. Deep down, I felt as if the information would wait. I really wanted to meet her. See her smile, eyes, little toes.

A moment of silence made the room tense, so Mitch continued. "Unfortunately, Conrad halted our investigation as soon as he heard that Lincoln was assisting. Between the four of us, we were able to convince him that Lincoln was a valuable asset in our search for you." Mitch was obviously still upset at Conrad for this.

"Conrad was going to let me die, wasn't he?" My voice cracked at the realization. I was dispensable. "Who convince him? I know neither one of you would be able to persuade him." Conrad was the biggest dick there was, and I knew how he operated. There was no love lost for me.

"Actually, it was Max. He was the one who convinced Conrad to let us to continue our search for you. You are a vital member in our unit, is what Max told Conrad, and apparently it worked. I'm sure there was more said. Conrad also gave Lincoln access to our investigation, under my supervision." Mitch explained.

My gaze fluttered from his to Lincoln's, grateful for Max and all he did.

"Max is a good man." My voice was low with extreme thankfulness for him, but there was still a bubble in my throat.

"Believe me, I thanked him profusely," Lincoln said with another squeeze of my hand.

Another a moment of silence after Lincoln's comment. I drew a huge sigh inward and my chest hurt. Hurt from all this new information, from my recent events, everything. Mitch was almost in tears again.

He wiped moisture off his cheek and said, "Once Lincoln was cleared, we continued our search. Maps were brought out to locate the places you had described in your notes. Some we were able to search, but they turned out to be nothing."

Mitch stopped and Lincoln picked up. "More time had gone by and we were no closer to finding you than we were when we received our anonymous tip. Xander and Tegan were helpful in more way than one. Desperation to find you was driving me insane, but I also had an infant to care for. And..." Lincoln paused and gave a slight sob. Hearing him sob made my waterworks flow harder. It was breaking my heart to hear him in so much agony. He was able to collect himself and began again. "Every time I looked at her, I couldn't help but cry, feeling how lost I was without you, and she reminded me of you with every look."

As the whimpers escaped, I was able to ask, "What's her name?"

Lincoln looked into my eyes. "Rayna. I remembered what you had said about the baby we lost, and what you would have named him. So, Rayna became my ray of sunshine when you were gone. When I felt hope was gone, I would look at her and see you. How was I going to explained to her about her mom when we had no idea? That's when we knew, Mitchell and I, we were not giving up until you were found, no matter what."

Oh my God, how did I get so lucky to find someone like Lincoln? My heart melted at every word he was saying.

"Rayna. It's perfect," was all I was able to get out.

A knock came on the door, which took me off guard. I wiped my face to try and look human. If it was a physician, she would ask the boys to leave, and I couldn't have that. Mitchell was able to compose himself enough to go see who it was. He didn't open the door enough so I could see who my visitor was, but it must have been important. He left. He slipped out the door without a word or glance back at Lincoln and me.

Confusion swept through me. Why would he leave without saying anything to us? I looked up at Lincoln, and he met my eyes with the same thought.

A few seconds later, I was able to speak. "I was so scared you wouldn't find me. The more time that passed and sessions with the Emissary, the less I believed I would be found." I was feeling a little ashamed for the emotions I had felt during my captivity.

"I never gave up. I never gave up the first time you left, and I wouldn't when I knew the Emissary took you." Lincoln's words were heartfelt, and I felt so much emotion hearing them.

Mitchell interrupted our moment when he poked his head back into my room. "Linc, you got a second?"

"Yeah," he said, got up, composed himself and stepped out.

I was once again alone.

CHAPTER 45

DEEP BREATH, BREATHE, DEEP BREATH. I AM NOT ALONE. I *am not alone*, was all I could say to myself. But the silence was beginning to overwhelm me. Trying to focus my thoughts and my mind, I closed my eyes and tried breathing slowly. The moment I closed my eyes, all I could see was darkness and I was back in my dirt cell. Tears ran down my face as the memories flashed through my body. Panic began to overtake me, but with all my might, I tried to slow my breathing and remind myself I was safe.

"I am safe, I am safe," I whispered to myself.

Lincoln had been gone for what seemed like forever, but the door creaked open and he was back. I let out a huge breath as the anxiety eased just from seeing his face.

My face must have shown fear because he rushed over to me and held me. "Hey, you're okay."

I couldn't hold back my fears any longer and I leaned into him, shaking.

"You're safe. I promise."

I just nodded and held on tighter to him.

I was able to breathe easier, then Lincoln pulled me back. He was so sweet, brushing my hair off my face and wiping away a tear with this thumb. He gazed at me and leaned in to kiss me. If I had any feeling in my lower extremities, I would be so fucking horny right now.

"There is someone here to see you, if and only if you are up for it," Lincoln said, pulling away from me.

"I just don't want to be alone. And if they don't mind my appearance." I tried to make a joke. I was certainly not looking my best. Between the amount of weight I had lost and I imagined I had dark circles around eyes that made me look like a zombie. I was exhausted. I knew I looked like hell and all I wanted was a shower and sleep. And not in that order.

"You are always beautiful." Lincoln kissed me on the forehead. "I don't think they will mind." He smiled at me. He was so sure, but everyone judges. Everyone. But I nodded in agreement.

Lincoln got back up and popped his head out the door. I took my eyes off the door as it swung open. I wasn't ready for whoever my visitor was. Out of the corner of my eye, I saw Mitchell come back in, and behind him was Xander and Tegan. My mentors.

Lincoln had his back to me as I looked at my visitors. So many emotions came over me as I saw them—thankful, happy, scared, were only a few.

"Hey, Jess." Tegan said with sad, happy eyes.

I just smiled and wiped other tears away. What I was really waiting for was for Lincoln to turn around and come back and sit with me. I looked over at Tegan and Xander.

"How are you holding up?" Xander asked, coming over to the side of my bed. He wasn't afraid to come closer.

All I could do was shrug my shoulders. "Ok, I guess." I replied. "I have had better weeks."

"We are so glad you are safe now." Xander was never a person who was a loss for words, but right now, he was.

Lincoln still had his back to me. What the hell? What was he and Mitch talking about? I could only hear a few words, but it was enough to annoy me. "Turn the fuck around and talk to me," I wanted to scream. But I didn't.

Mitch must have sensed I was looking at them. He looked at me and back at Lincoln. Lincoln nodded at him, and finally turned to me.

"There is someone who wants to meet you," Lincoln said turning around with something in his arms.

Holy shit. I couldn't breathe. I tried to catch my breath when I realized what Lincoln was bringing to me. Looking around at everyone for reassurance and they all nodded at me.

"Oh my God!" I gasped.

Lincoln had in his arms an infant of about six weeks old. My baby girl. He brought her over and laid her down in my lap.

There was no restraining my feelings now. Shock, excitement, fear, all came out. "This is Rayna. She would like to meet her mom," Lincoln said with a smile that enveloped his face.

My baby girl held her head up and, knowing who I was, looked all around the room to the people she knew.

"Hi Rayna," I said. "I am your mom." I was so overwhelmed. She looked at me with recognition of my voice and gazed at me. I glanced up at Lincoln. Our daughter did the same and fussed some when she saw her dad. I tried my best to comfort her.

"Hey, you're okay." Lincoln said to her.

She might be, but was I?

"Hello Rayna." My voice brought her back to me. "It's nice to meet you. You have no idea how long I have waited to meet you. I hope you know."

I had to stop as I began to get emotional again. *Pull yourself together. You got this.* I took a deep breath as Rayna look at me like I was nuts.

"You don't know how lucky you are to have so many people who care about you," I told her. That was it, I couldn't say anymore. With those words, Rayna did the one thing I wasn't expecting and put me in overload. But a good overload.

She laid her head on my chest.

After a long week in the hospital, with doctors' exams, psych evaluations, and poking and prodding, there was nothing new to report about my paralysis—I was confined to a wheelchair and would need to adapt to life without legs. For a runner and an athletic person, that was harder for me to swallow than anything. If my father were still alive, he would consider me useless, and what was the point of life if you had no use? But he was a dickhead was just pissed he had girls. Oh yeah, he was a sexist pig too.

Even with my ups and downs, Lincoln never left my side while I was still in the hospital. He was holding my hand, giving me hugs, and lying in bed with me. If I needed a change of scenery, he would pick me up and wheel me around the hospital. We even got Rayna to ride in my lap, and she did nothing but look at all the lights. It was a step for her and me. Getting to know each other, I realized there was so much more life left, even though I was in a chair.

My neurologist believed that maybe over time my body might regenerate and heal itself. New advancements were being discovered every day, and I shouldn't give up hope. Deep down, I knew that to be true, but I was a person who analyzed a situation and tried to understand it. Right now, I was in a wheelchair and must accept that was my fate. Something new might come along, and it may be an option for me, but right now this was all I had.

You are probably wondering what the rest of the story was with my rescue. I thought the same thing, since it took them two more days to tell me. Lincoln wasn't about to put more stress on me with all the activity I was having, and now my little Rayna of Sunshine was coming around more. Dorky I know, but she is my strength. He has been so good to me, and Rayna was now recognizing me and my touch. Her spirit lifted mine every time I saw her, and the smile and light from Lincoln was unbelievably uplifting. So, many times, I would catch Mitch tearing up over all of us. He was the emotional one, after all.

Anyway, I am getting off topic. I was told Lincoln, Mitch, and a team of Division personnel read through my notes, looking for clues as to where I might be. Anonymous tips were also being delivered to them, containing clues of my whereabouts. A couple of people were assisting the search team from inside the Federation. From further discussion, I learned that Dr. Edward and Hunter Griffin were the contacts on the inside, and been my support. I knew of Edward, but Griffin had always been tricky to figure out. Sometimes I couldn't tell who he was loyal to, but this information certainly told me it wasn't the Emissary.

Finally, all the pieces of the puzzle came together, and I was eventually discovered in one of the Federation's safe houses—or kill houses—in the middle of nowhere. Convenient for the Emissary, but not convenient enough. Plans were put into place and I was to be rescued. What wasn't in the plans was my own escape plan and me trying to escape from my dirt home. I mean, if they had informed me of their plan, maybe I would have stayed put. Then I wouldn't be in the predicament I am in. But I had just wanted to be dead or alive and couldn't— wouldn't—wait any longer.

The Division team invaded the house and soon took charge of the situation, but not without incident. I, of course, was the target, but I was on the brink of death when they discovered me. Before me, they'd found another causality. The Emissary had discovered our informant within the Federation and tortured him. The body of Dr. Ross Edward was upstairs when they busted into the house. My first friend and been tortured and stabbed multiple time before the Emissary finished him off. He cut him so badly, it was almost impossible to identify him from his face. When I heard that, my heart sank. Edward was my only saving grace in that place, and when I first came to the Federation. Now he was gone. He'd died for me.

Too many people had died for me. How do I cope with that?

Once I was discovered on the floor of the basement, Hunter Griffin stayed close to my side and identified himself to Mitchell and the team. The Emissary was quickly taken into custody and has been locked up ever since in a maximum-security facility. He won't see the light of day for the rest of his miserable life. So much evidence against him had been accumulated, there was no chance. I would rather see him be tortured as he did to so many others, but that's not going to happen. I'm sure people in prison will handle him just nicely.

Lincoln, being part of the rescue team, was the one to carry me upstairs to the paramedics. He shouldn't have even been near the scene, but there was no stopping him and Mitchell didn't even try. Since then, Lincoln hasn't left my side. Well, maybe to shower and pump himself full of coffee, but knowing the brothers, one of them was always with me.

So, here I am at this point of my life, with all the pain, guilt and fears ahead of me. Lucky for me I have Lincoln, and support from so many others. And of course, my precious baby girl. It was going to take some time for my body and mind to heal, but I knew I'd get there someday.

CHAPTER 46

A MONTH WENT BY SINCE MY RELEASE FROM THE HOSPI-
tal. We ventured back to the east coast and tried to get back into normal life. Confined to a wheelchair, I found everyday tasks frustrating
and difficult. Tegan was a Godsend. She was there just about every day,
helping me cope and adjust, helping with Rayna. I was still recovering,
and there were some things my body would just not allow me to do.
As much as I wanted to do everything, I had to wave the white flag and
give up, asking for help. It wasn't easy for me, and Lincoln chuckled
slightly when I got so frustrated. It put me in a piss poor mood, but I
could not have done anything without him.

Lincoln could and would have turned the world upside down for
his two girls. He carried me up the stairs for bed and back down in the
morning. Sweet. I know that's fine and dandy for now, but what happens when we get older? Ah, he just waved it off and said we'd figure
that out when it came time. Men. Why couldn't they see the practicali-
ty in things? Always the difficult way. Anyway, we were adjusting.

One afternoon I was rolling myself out of Rayna's room, which used
to be the spare junk room, when there was a knock at the door. Lincoln

was in the kitchen and went to answer it. I was coming into sight when I saw Lincoln shut the door holding a large manila envelope.

"I just put for Rayna down for her nap. What's that?" I asked, wheeling myself over to him. I looked at him inquisitively.

He didn't take his eyes off the envelope, shutting the door behind him.

"Hmm." He was startled by my question but looked at me. "Someone just dropped this off for you. They said you would be interested in it." Lincoln handed me the envelope and leaned back against the counter.

I was unsure what it might be and hesitated to open it. There was no writing on the envelope anywhere, and I got the prickles on the back of my neck.

Oh well, better rip the band-aid off and open the thing. What was the worst that could happen? Yeah, it could kill me. But after what I had been through, I doubted it.

So, I turned it over and ripped it open. Inside was a small stack of papers bound together by a paper clip. This made me a little curious but cautious. You can never be too cautious. I was able to scan the first page very easily, and it intrigued me. So, I flipped to the next page and kept going. What I read took my breath away, the more in depth I got.

Lincoln noticed my reactions and shifted his stance. "What? What does it say?"

I took a second to collect my thoughts and organize them before speaking. "It is background information about Robert Emery, aka the Emissary. The first page had a copy of the newspaper article about his arrest and charges. The next page described the charges in more detail...but they are not just recent charges, but also much older ones."

I kept scanning the documents.

"What made you stop breathing?" Lincoln asked.

A tear trickled down the side of my cheek as I said, "They have evidence of other murders the Emissary committed in the past, including

Susan's. There are many more, but hers was one of the most brutal." I muffled sob for a second then said, "She is finally going to get justice."

A moment of silence filled the room as we both remembered Susan. My sister, friend, and confidant. I missed her every day, and now the Emissary would pay for her murder.

"Yes, she will," Lincoln agreed.

I put the papers into my lap and Lincoln came over to hug me. In his arms, I nodded my head. Justice for Susan would happen at last.

While Rayna slept, I was able to read through the packet of information regarding the Emissary. He was a very disturbed individual. I couldn't believe how his path went so wrong after college. From the descriptions, there seem to be no sign of aggressive tendencies until later in life. He was married, and after the death of his wife from a horrible form of cancer, he just changed. He was angry at the world for her death and wanted everyone to pay the price. So, the Federation was formed, and with supporters of his cause and hatred, it grew extremely fast.

Robert Emery became one of the most feared men in the nation and was well known around the world. Not so lucky for anyone in law enforcement, there had been no evidence of his wrongdoing before now, so no one could touch him. Years passed before little things started to pop up. Division and other authorities became aware and began to investigate him. Money or goods would work their way in and out of the United States and there was no paper trail. Emery was smart and knew what he was doing. I realized that when I went to work for the Federation. Not long after joining, I regretted my choice. Susan had gone too deep, and if she'd left—

Well, it didn't matter. All that matters, she sacrificed herself for what was right.

As for Robert Emery, the Emissary was in solitary confinement awaiting trial.

I have a crying baby to take care of, and I knew I was going to be okay.

EPILOGUE

THE ARIES DEVICE WAS SAFE AND SOUND WITH DIVISION. Yes, with high-ranking officials of the Division, not the newbies. It took some serious convincing and interrogation before I would unlock the device. I was the only one who could unlock the device and release the data into our world. A world of hopeful peace and aid to the people around world.

Aries is now a part of my past and I must move on. There are days the past haunts me and I can't move past it. Lincoln and my family—Rayna, Mitchell, Tegan, Xander and many others—have stuck by my side. Not to mention the counselors and doctors who got me through this dark struggle. I even have been able to go to my new desk job at the Division and get adjusted to my surroundings.

Conrad, my asshole boss, has taken my situation better than I thought he would. I have been given tasks to keep myself from going utterly crazy and to retrain my brain for work again. It has been a nice change to be able to contribute. Not that I haven't liked being at home but being confined changes the game a little bit and I am finding it very difficult to sit still.

One good thing I can say is my upper body strength has improved. Before, I was all legs and no arms. Well, that actually sounds very depressing since I went from an athlete to disabled.

Enough, stop being like that Jess. Life is good.

Being able to move around freely helps my mentality. For the last two years—wow two years. Damn has it been that long? Well, anyway, I have been under pretty close watch. Just think, I can go outside without a bodyguard. Yay! Go me! But going to the office, I must have someone drive me and meet me at the entrance. Hey, most of the time it's one of my friends or Lincoln. Lincoln has become pretty cozy at the office. I truly think he misses the involvement. I told him to go back to work, but there is always some excuse why he can't. What about the baby? Or what if you need something? Blah, blah, blah. It will come to a point where he will drive me up a wall and I am going to go nuts with him around.

Well, that's my life now. Going from very active and always on the edge to meh, boring. Lincoln and I did have an interesting conversation about getting married. Getting married was the one thing I have giggled about lately. Lincoln asked, "What's so funny?"

My response was, "After all the shit we have endured over the years, that is still on your mind?" All I could do was chuckle.

After Lincoln's subtle hints, and not to so subtle hints, I finally gave in. We were married on the beach where we reconnected. Despite my hesitation over my paralysis, our day could not have been more beautiful. With the help of our friends and family, everything was as perfect as it could be. Mitchell stood with Lincoln, and Tegan, Xander, and Rayna with me. There was not a cloud in the sky. At home, I stared constantly at our wedding photo—Lincoln scooping me up and me gazing at his face. It always took my breath away.

A few weeks after we were married, I was able to go back to work on a regular basis.

Praise the Gods! I was going stir crazy. Unluckily for me, I had to work up to a full day. I left Rayna with my trusted friend Ms. Tegan, as we call her now. I had a hard time with the distance from my baby. But over time and many open cases to study, I was up to a full eight-hour day. My tiny office was enlarged for my wheelchair, and my desk has never looked so full. It was Mitch's way of saying Welcome Back.

I was pretty rusty at my profiling, but soon got back into my old methods. I even got a cramps in my hands from so much writing and typing.

One of my earlier afternoons, Lincoln surprised me and asked me if I'd like an afternoon sweet. As most everyone knew, I had a horrible sweet tooth and ninety-nine percent of the time never say no to something sweet. So, I finished up my last few notes and called it a day, but I made sure I said goodbye to Mitchell, and maybe rubbed it in his face a little that we were off to the bakery for some warm fresh cookies. My favorite. In return, Mitch gave me a not so friendly glare and waved me away.

"Love you too," I responded, blowing him a kiss. With that, I wheeled myself beside Lincoln and we were off down the hall to the elevator. With a *ping*, the doors opened, and down we went.

"So, what are you thinking for sweets?" Lincoln asked, knowing the obvious answer.

"Cookies, duh!" Pause. "Warm, fresh and gooey!" My face erupted in a smile.

"Nope, they are all out." Lincoln was dead serious.

Jerking my head to look at him with my most serious look, I said, "What? They are not out!" My eyes never diverted from Lincoln and it didn't take long for him to break.

Break into a smile that is.

"Asshole!" Not cool. "Did you really think I was going to believe you?"

"No, but it was worth a shot to see that look." Lincoln leaned down to me. "It was worth the effort." He kissed me on the head and stood back up.

"Ah, for that you owe me two!" There was no joking about sweets.

"Fine," he responded and grabbed my hand.

A few more seconds passed, and the elevator reached the main floor, and the doors parted. Lincoln released my hand and I began to wheel myself out. We were about halfway to the revolving doors when I stopped dead in my tracks. Outside the entrance, a dozen or more of what looked like reporters were milling around, phones, cameras, microphones in hand, ready for a poor victim to come out.

Lincoln quickly halted with me and was also taken aback by the paparazzi. "What do you want to do?"

"I don't know. Something doesn't feel right." My tone was uneasy and quiet.

Lincoln and I exchanged looks, and that was all it took. My name was being yelled by almost all the people hovering around the exit.

"It her, Jessy Connors," they yelled. Some called out to me, while others raised their voices to be heard.

"Holy shit!" Lincoln blurted out. "What the hell do they want with you? Haven't they bothered you enough?"

Apprehension flooded my body. I was not sure of any action. I knew they were not permitted into the building without a pass, but I was not the fastest agent anymore. There was no just taking another exit. This was my only way out.

Immediately, Lincoln sprang into action and was on the phone. "Mitchell, get your ass down here. There are reporters bee hiving the doors. No, Jess is who they want. Fine." Lincoln hung up the phone pissed. "Mitchell is on his way." Lincoln was not just my husband at the moment but my protector.

"What do they want with me?" I asked, rather frazzled. I'm a go-getter and I wouldn't be held back by fear.

"I don't know," Lincoln answered, still uneasy.

A few moments passed, Mitchell's elevator pinged, and out he came in full force. He wasn't happy either. Both brothers definitely had the same pissed off look. Lincoln met up with Mitch and they conversed. I, however, was done waiting.

So, my wheels began to turn, and I headed for the doors.

"Shit, Jess. Where do you think you're going?" Mitch was fast and stopped me before I got to the doors.

"I need to know what is so important that they need me for." My words cut right through Mitchell and he gave Lincoln a glance.

Both brothers knew not to reason with me when I have made up my mind. They knew what I was going to do, with or without them.

Mitchell nodded in agreement as did Lincoln. "Okay, but we will be right next to you." Lincoln placed his hand on my shoulder. I gave him a reassuring nod. Mitchell led the way and Lincoln wheeled me out.

"Miss Connors, over here!"

Reporters enveloped me as I came through the doors. Again, they were yelling and badgering me for attention. It was extremely overwhelming, as if the animals were hungry and I was the meat.

"Excuse me!" Mitchell raised his voice above them all. "What is the meaning of this?"

Once again, more calling of my name. And it wasn't my married name. Many people bombarded me with questions but there was one that caught my attention.

"How does it feel, knowing you're in command of the Federation?"

"*What?*" I asked with disbelief. What the hell?

With my voice raised, everyone quieted down. This was something they wanted to hear.

I looked over to the woman who'd asked the question that brought me to life. "What do you mean?" I asked, looking directly at her.